MURDER BY DEWEY DECIMAL

A *Measurements of Murder Mystery*™ Novel

By Stephen B. Bagley

Measurements of Murder Mystery is a trademark of 51313 Productions.

Visit Stephen B. Bagley's Web site at *www.51313.blogspot.com*.

Purchase *Measurements of Murder*™ products at *www.cafepress.com/harborstreet*

Founded in 2002, Lulu is the world's fastest-growing print-on-demand marketplace for digital do-it-yourselfers. Please see *www.lulu.com* for more information.

ISBN 978-1-4303-2642-7

Printed in the United States of America
10 9 8 7 6 5 4 3 2 1

Dedicated to the following for their support over the years:

Kent Bass, Gail Claunts, and Eric Collier

And to these loyal readers of 51313 Harbor Street
who encourage me endlessly
and must now shoulder part of the blame:
Frenzied Feline, Michelle, Trixie, Gloria Williams,
Jean Schara, Crystal, Jon Smythe, Nightrider,
Rain, Peggy Graham, and Marie Montelongo

And to Holly Lisle and Forward Motion
for reviving the dream

And to my siblings and family
who remain my first audience

And finally to you who purchased this book:
I and my creditors thank you.

CHAPTER ONE

Later, Bernard would remember he had looked around for more blood – not that he knew how much blood there should be. It had just seemed to him that there should have been more. He would also remember how small Agatha Ryton-Storer looked in death; although her considerable poundage remained the same, without the vicious fire of her life, she seemed shrunken, tiny, even feeble. Later, he would remember those things. But, at that moment, he stood frozen by shock, unable to think, his eyes tracing the thick red line that marked her open throat.

Her death had crossed Bernard M. Worthington's mind before. He often fantasized about it. Earlier that morning, as he drove to work, he had indulged in one of his favorites – the old crone boiling in a pot of oil surrounded by screaming natives who were preparing to sacrifice her to the deep, dark god of libraries. He smiled at the image as he turned the car onto Main, driving past the still-closed shops and businesses that lined the street.

He was so lost in his thoughts that he barely remembered to turn his head away as he passed Hyatt Realty & Accounting. Seeing the name of her father's office always reminded him of Sherry and the wreck she had made of his life. Of course, he admitted, trying to remember to not look also made him think of her.

He sighed and concentrated on the drive to the Ryton Memorial Library, his mind fogged by another sleepless night. He didn't know why he was going to work early. The library wouldn't open until nine, but he needed to go somewhere. And this early in the morning, he would have the library to himself for a couple of hours before Hagatha (he liked to add the 'H') arrived.

He never looked forward to her arrival, but this morning, he dreaded it. Every Tuesday, Agatha held her weekly library meeting where she would rave about the wrongs that Bernard and the library aides had committed to her domain. Bernard rated the meetings on his list of Favorite Things To Do right below having a root canal without an anesthetic. And he expected to be flayed alive in today's meeting because he was responsible for allowing Jay Jones, the library janitor, in her office yesterday while she was gone on her usual two-hour lunch.

Her scream of rage had echoed throughout the library and brought Bernard running down the stairs. When he reached her office, he halted at the door. Her tantrum was already in full tirade. Jones stood in the middle of the room, a vacuum cleaner by his side.

"How dare you come in here!" she snarled, stabbing a finger at the hapless Jones. "This office is private, do you hear me, private!"

"I was going to clean –" Jones began, his face beginning to flush with anger.

"You are to clean my office only on the second Monday of each month," she cut in. "That is the way we've done it for years. And

2

this is not the second Monday! This is the first Monday! Or did you forget how to count?"

"Mrs. Ryton-Storer, I told him to do it," Bernard said, stepping into her office and immediately regretting it as she turned on him.

"Who do you think you are?" she shouted. "I'm the Head Librarian here! This staff answers to me and me only! Who do you think you are? Answer me!" Wisps of gray hair escaped from her tight habitual bun as she shook with rage.

"Jay is going to take his vacation next week," Bernard said, his stomach knotting up. "He asked me about cleaning your office while you were gone for lunch, and I told him to take care of it now."

"You have no right to make any decisions," she snarled. "Just because he will be gone means nothing!"

"I'm sorry –"

"Shut up! SHUT UP! Get out! Both of you get out!"

Bernard and Jones got. She slammed the door behind them.

The two men looked at each other.

"Well, that was pleasant," Bernard said. "I'm sorry I got you into it."

"Wasn't your fault," Jones grunted, picking up his vacuum. "She's always in a tizzy about something. Been that way the whole time I've worked here, and I've been here nearly twenty years. She's not going to change." He started to walk away. "But she can't live forever." He grinned. "No, sir, she can't live forever, and no one will care when she goes. I might even dance on her grave." He headed for the storage closet, chuckling.

Agatha sulked in her office and refused to talk to anyone for the rest of the day. Bernard was certain, however, she would have plenty to say at the meeting.

He was dropping her headfirst in a vat of acid when he noticed her car was already in the parking lot. Agatha never arrived before ten, and it was only eight. He frowned, considered going back home for a while, but decided that he might as well go on in since he was already there. And the library – even with Agatha in residence – was better than the emptiness of his apartment.

Bernard had attempted to like Agatha, but it was a doomed effort from the beginning. Agatha Ryton-Storer had held the library in her claws for the past thirty years, and she was not impressed by Bernard's master's degree. "It's nothing but a piece of paper," she had said. "Experience is what counts."

Unfortunately, for all her thirty years of experience, she was a terrible librarian. Bernard had discovered so many misshelved books that he wondered if she and the aides even knew how to count, much less understand the Dewey Decimal system. Half the books in the library weren't even in the card catalog. The Library Board had recognized she was slipping when she started refusing to allow people to check out books. As she put it, "How do you expect this library to have any books at all if we let anyone who wanders in off the streets to take them at will!"

The Board had politely suggested retirement; she had impolitely told them to eat dirt and die. They would have fired her, but they couldn't. When Eliah Ryton, her grandfather, donated the Ryton mansion to the city to be used as the library and gave a generous endowment for the care of the same, he made one condition: any of his direct descendants must be given the Head Librarian's job for as long as the descendant wanted it. Agatha Ryton-Storer had wanted the job for the last thirty years.

Fresh out of college with a master's in library science, Bernard seemed perfect to modernize the Ryton Library. The Library Board told him that Agatha would resent him, but she would slowly be won over. They told him that his title would be Assistant Librarian, but he would have the real authority. They lied.

"You'll change this library over my dead body," Agatha said, shaking her finger under Bernard's nose. This was in the first five minutes of their introduction. Bernard thought the relationship couldn't get worse, which he later decided was proof he was not a prophet. Any idea he wanted to try was treated as if he'd suggested they all strip naked and dance down Main Street singing "The Star Spangled Banner." He complained to the Board members who, collectively, sighed, shook their respective heads, and changed the subject. Sherry had told him to wait Agatha out. He stopped that thought immediately. Thinking of Sherry could only make this already dreary morning worse.

Bernard closed his car door and walked down the sidewalk to the side entrance. After six months, he spared the library only a short glance. At first, its architectural style – which could only be classified as Colonial Gothic – had sent his mind spinning into conjectures about Eliah Ryton and whatever had possessed the old man to add a tower and a turreted roof to a huge house already well on its way to ugly. He did notice that the shrubs along the street still needed to be trimmed. He made a mental note to tell Jay about it again. He hated to nag the janitor, but it seemed to be only way to get any work out of the man. If I keep bringing it up, Bernard thought, he'll trim them eventually. That or run a mop through my body. Either way, I win.

A piece of paper fluttering in the breeze caught his eye. He picked it up. It was a shipping invoice for new books. I'd better make sure this gets filed or Hagatha will hit the roof, he thought. He opened the door. He found it odd that the lights were off. Agatha was not one to stumble around in the dark, and she certainly didn't care about conserving energy.

He flipped the light switches, and the overhead fluorescent bulbs flickered on and illuminated the rows and rows of books. He turned left, slowly walking up a narrow aisle to the front of the library, taking time to savor the quiet. Despite Agatha, the library had a fair number of patrons, and during open hours, it echoed with sound: pages turning, people whispering, footsteps as people walked across the marble floors, the occasional book falling followed invariably by the giggles of teenagers. These sounds would return when the library opened at nine. A few minutes before that time, Millie Sader, the librarian day aide, would rush up and unlock the doors, and the Ryton Memorial Library would be open to the public.

He furtively glanced at the door to Agatha's office. It was shut. Good, he thought. If luck is with me, I'll be lost in the shelves before she thinks to look for me. Agatha's ample size was maintained by her love for sweets of all sorts and her hate of work and anything remotely resembling it. She would rather lie in wait than hunt him down.

Quietly he took a cart filled with books that needed to be shelved and wheeled it toward the elevator. Once it had carried him to the second floor where the nonfiction was kept, he sighed in relief. Another confrontation avoided for a few hours.

As he shelved books and spot-read the shelves, he began to weigh the job offers he was considering. Any of them would be better than staying in Ryton where he ran into Sherry at least three times a week. He grimaced and tried to think of something else, but he failed this time. Sometimes he had to scratch at the wound.

It unrolled for him again as it had so often the past few weeks. Meeting Sherry Hyatt in college and falling in love. The way her hair caught the light. The walks by Theta Pond. Her sharp wit and force of will. The way she walked. The soft hairs at the base of her neck that felt cool when he ran his lips across her neck. Her calmness when he asked her to marry him. His delight when she said yes. All the laughter they shared. And all the pain that followed.

She was the reason Bernard was in Ryton. With his degree, Bernard could have gone almost anywhere and set his own salary, but Sherry convinced him to come to her hometown to live. Ryton would be good place to raise their children, she said. Her father had pull in the town and convinced the Library Board to hire him. So here he was, in a rotten job, and Sherry, while still in Ryton, was not with him. In fact, she had made it plain that she would never be with Bernard again.

"You don't have it anymore," Sherry had said.

"What does that mean? Have what?" he asked.

"It's just not there. You've lost it." Sherry turned away. Then she said the words that nearly shattered him and haunted him now. "We're done. I don't love you anymore. Don't you understand? I don't love you."

Bernard gave himself a mental shake. It did not help to replay the fights that followed over the next few days. It had been two months. Sherry was not coming back. He would leave Ryton and find a life somewhere else. He tried to push the cart forward, but it caught on something. He looked down. The cart's wheels were lodged against an ankle. His eyes traveled up the dark-hosed leg, to the polyester plaid skirt, to the crumpled sweater, and to the dark line of blood that marked the slit throat of the quite-dead Agatha Ryton-Storer.

So later he would remember the lack of blood and how small she seemed, and he would also decide that he handled the situation well. He walked to the front of the library, called the police, hung up, met Millie at the door, and told her that Mrs. Ryton-Storer had suffered an accident and was dead and that the library should remain closed until the police arrived. Millie was agog with curiosity, but he firmly told her to wait outside. He went into the restroom, splashed cold water on his ashen face and shaking hands, and threw up until the police arrived.

*

Lisa Trent closed her eyes and opened them again. And repeated the procedure. It did no good. The naked man in the bed remained Leonard Brewer. She groaned. She had actually been drunk enough last night to sleep with Leonard. Or had she? Steeling her courage, she glanced down. Thank God, her jeans were on. And buttoned, too. Too bad her bra was missing.

Carefully, she eased out of bed, hampered only slightly by the jackhammer that was cutting through her brain. Leonard groaned, but didn't wake up. Where was her bra? She looked around. It was lying on a chair, next to a pair of tiger-striped men's bikini briefs. Lisa had actually been drunk enough to go to bed with a man who wore tiger-striped briefs. Bikini briefs. She felt sick.

She dressed as quickly and quietly as she could and made her wobbly way to his front door. What were the odds, she wondered, of Leonard being too drunk to remember she had gone home with him? Not good. And he would brag about it to the rest of the boys in the backshop. Then she remembered that he couldn't and why she had gone to Rochelle's Bar and Grill with him and the boys last night; she had wanted to forget her life was ruined.

The *Ryton Journal & News* was closed, finished, done. The publisher told them yesterday that he couldn't afford to keep the paper open any longer. The local economy was in a slump, and the paper was in debt up to its figurative neck. As news reporter/headline writer/paste-up person, Lisa was out of a job. Out of the best job she had ever had. Other jobs had paid her more money, but this one had been special in what it had given her.

She heard Leonard groan, and she quickly stepped outside. She couldn't face his leering face this morning. She looked around for her car. Leonard had been so late to pick her up that she had driven to his apartment last night to see if he had remembered their date. She was glad now that she had done so. Probably the only smart thing I did last night, she thought.

She vaguely remembered parking her car near the street so she walked around the building, finally spotting her beat-up Topaz hidden by a truck parked next to it. I would have to park all the way over there, she thought, wincing at the sun.

She got into her car, but she didn't start it. She couldn't decide where to go. Home, she guessed. It felt so strange to not go to work. In the four years she had worked for the Journal, she had been absent only one day and that was because she had to attend a funeral. She closed her eyes, resting her head on the steering wheel. The sun was too bright, but its warmth was welcome. She felt cold, tired, and beaten.

Beaten by the loss of a job. She shook her head slightly, remembering how she had felt when she joined the Journal. She had believed her chance had finally come, that she could finally overcome her poor past. Not that she was ashamed of her mother or, for that matter, even her father despite what people said about him. Sometimes late at night, when she was tired, she would indulge in a fantasy where they would pick up a Journal and see her byline and read her stories. Her mother would have been especially proud. She had always bragged about her daughter's grades as she poured coffee and took orders at Al's Truck Stop.

Lisa had made good grades in school, hoping for a scholarship to a college. She received one, but it wasn't much. She would have still attempted to go, but cancer seized her mother. She stayed in Ryton, working at the truck stop, driving her mother back and forth to the hospital for the year it took Abigail Trent to die. Then her dear, sweet, befuddled father finished drinking his life away. She buried him six months later.

For a year, she wandered through her life, going to work, coming home, having a few messy flings with truck drivers, drinking too much, and crying alone. One rainy day in May as she hurried down

Main Street, a notice in the window of the Journal caught her eye. 'Office Help Wanted,' it read. In the hard rain, she stopped. Something broke free inside her, and the hard knot of grief was pushed aside. She went through the door, determined to have that job.

Two years later, after she had pushed and nagged her way into reporting, John Towers, the editor, said he had only hired her because no one else applied for the job, but it was one of his all-time best decisions. She worked hard to become an excellent reporter, and she enjoyed how the locals responded to her. People who before thought it was beneath them to notice her now smiled and said hi.

"You've won their respect," Towers said. "But don't get the big head. You're a small-town reporter on a small-town rag. You're not ready for *The New York Times* yet."

Now she never would be. Thinking of her prospects, she was tempted to climb back into bed with Leonard. He would be a little better than being alone, which had been the only reason she had agreed to go out with him last night.

Remembering those tiger stripes, she dug her keys out of her jeans and started the car. Perhaps some coffee would help. She decided to go by the truck stop. If worse came to worse, she knew she could always get rehired there. And it might come to that. She simply didn't know how to get another reporting job. How could she compete with people who had college degrees in journalism? Towers had always said that experience counted more than college, but what real experience did she have? Writing obituaries and covering agricultural news hardly qualified her for the big city newspapers. She supposed she could maybe get a job with some other small town paper and start all over again. But where in the world would she get the money to move? She had a savings account, but it barely had enough to cover her bills for a month.

She drove down Main, heading for the truck stop. Sunk as she was in her thoughts, she still noticed the police cars, their lights flashing, heading the other way. First, one car, then two others. For a moment she resisted the impulse to follow them, but she decided that it wouldn't hurt to find out what was causing the activity. The cars turned in at the library entrance. She slowly drove past, taking in all the police cars – at least four, which was half of Ryton's force – and the County Coroner's van.

Something big has happened, she thought, her pulse quickening. Maybe big enough to impress an editor at another newspaper. Like that editor at *The Oklahoma City Dispatch*. What is his name? Cameron Veit. If I call him with a big enough story, who knows? It could be a beginning.

She turned around and drove up the library driveway.

*

Most people who knew Ryton Police Chief Charles Donaldson knew he had an ulcer. When one of his officers was being a particular pain, he would look the offender in the eye and say, "You're aggravating my ulcer. I wouldn't do that if I was you." Officers who aggravated the chief's ulcer usually ended up patrolling Rochelle's Bar and Grill on a Saturday night and could count on at least one knuckle-busting and body-bruising fight. Citizens who aggravated his ulcer usually ended up in jail. Most people also thought his ulcer had been caused by sixteen years as Ryton's police chief. They were wrong. His ulcer was caused by peaches. Or more correctly, the lack of them. Five years ago, the chief purchased an orchard, a "peach of a deal" as the real estate agent had put it. His wife didn't see it that way.

"A waste of money," Maggie had said, pacing around their kitchen. She turned and faced the chief. "You should have taken our retirement money and burned it. At least that way, we would have got some heat from it!"

"You wait. That orchard will give us a good living when I retire," he told his wife.

Maggie looked coldly at him, and, for the first time in their many long years of marriage, turned and walked out. The kitchen door closed decisively behind her. The chief should have realized the door was an omen, but he was relieved – and puzzled – because it hadn't been as bad as he thought it was going to be. She'll come around when those peaches start bringing in money, he thought.

That might have been true if the orchard had cooperated. The first year, the weather warmed early, then froze again, killing the peach buds. The second year was a repeat of the first with a drought thrown in to keep things interesting. The third year, the weather was perfect for both the peaches and bugs. Lots of bugs. Biblical levels of bugs. The county agent said the orchard should have been sprayed early. The chief sprayed late, but to keep the bugs to some controllable level, he had to spray so much that he finally decided that it was cheaper to let the bugs have the crop that year and spray early next year. The fourth year, nothing happened. But few of the trees budded. Too much stress, the county agent said. The comment was about the trees, but the chief was under a strain, too. This year, everything looked good. The chief kept waiting for another disaster to happen, and the suspense was keeping his ulcer aggravated.

And one of the most annoying things about it was that Maggie refused to comment on the orchard. She wouldn't talk about it, neither good nor bad. No 'I told you so's'. No 'You should have known better's'. For five years, not a word about it passed her lips. It didn't exist for her.

"The orchard looked good today," the chief would say.

"Debbie – you know, Edith Worney's granddaughter – has the chicken pox," Maggie would say. "I do hope none of the rest of the kids get it. Although it's probably best they get it now when they're young. Darlene Ogg got it real bad when she was twenty-five."

"I think we're going to have a good crop."

"Darlene had a horrible time with it," Maggie would continue. "You could hardly see her face for the sores."

And if Maggie didn't bring up Darlene, it was Alison Henderson's cats or P.C. McGetty's drinking. If the chief kept pursuing the subject, she left the room. He had done everything he could think of, but she remained silent about the orchard. The chief had made Maggie mad before – after all, they'd been married for nearly forty years – but she had never done this before. Usually, after giving him a good scolding, she would forgive him. He would have never thought he could want a tongue-lashing, but he had discovered it was preferable to silence.

He'd been at the orchard when this call came through. Murders didn't happen often in Ryton, The last one had been about six months ago and resulted from a domestic squabble. The wife turned herself in.

Hardly any investigation was needed. In his experience, the chief had found murders were usually easy to solve. If you questioned the husband, wife, boyfriend, mistress, or business partner, you found the murderer. People killed other people for passion or profit. Bernard, for instance, might gain by Agatha's death since he would probably become the Head Librarian. People had been killed for less.

Yet, as the chief sat behind a desk in Bernard's office, watching Bernard answer questions, he was thinking he had never seen a more unlikely murder suspect. Something in the way Bernard held himself and the shocked look in his eyes told the chief that murder was not in Bernard's working vocabulary.

"So what did you do after you found the body?" Lieutenant Ron Sims asked Bernard.

"I went up front and called the police and told Millie – Millie Sader, she's the day aide – that Mrs. Ryton-Storer had been in an accident and that we shouldn't open the library until the police came, and then ... then I was sick." Bernard looked pale.

"Did you see or hear anything suspicious?" Sims asked.

"No." Bernard shook his head. "There was no one around."

"Why didn't you leave the library and wait outside?" the chief asked.

"Should I have?" Bernard asked. "Because I might have disturbed the evidence?"

"Well, there's that, too," the chief said. "But what if the murderer had been inside still?"

"I never thought of that," Bernard said slowly. "Do you think he was?"

The chief shrugged. "Maybe. If so, he's gone now. Did you notice anything missing? Does the library keep any money in the building?"

"We have about twenty dollars that we keep for change if someone needs to pay a fine. I don't know if it's missing. I didn't look around so I don't know if anything's gone, but the library doesn't have much besides books, a couple of typewriters, and a photocopier."

"I've read where rare books are worth lots of money," the chief said.

"Yes, but we don't have any that I know of."

"Computers? Fax machines? TVs?"

Bernard shook his head. "Mrs. Ryton-Storer didn't allow them."

The chief thought for a moment. "Maybe someone was mad at her. Had she fought with anyone that you know of in the past couple of days?"

"Well, practically everyone who came in here," Bernard said. "She wasn't very friendly, you know, but I don't think she made anyone mad enough to kill her."

"What did she fight with them about?"

"Mostly about the books. If they kept them too long or if she thought they were in worse shape than when they were checked out. Sometimes she would inspect the books before she'd let them be checked in, and if they were damaged, she'd try to make the person pay for them. She really made a lot of people mad. To be fair, she had a point. A lot of books are destroyed or stolen here. It's quite a problem."

"Did she fight with the staff?" the chief asked.

"Well, yes." Bernard seemed reluctant to continue.

"Did she scrap with anyone in particular?" The chief leaned back, but he watched Bernard closely.

"Yesterday, Jay Jones, the janitor, got on her wrong side. Her office is supposed to be cleaned only on the second Monday of the month. Jay's going on vacation next week so I told him to clean it yesterday." Bernard grimaced. "She wasn't pleased with him or me, and she let us know about it. But he blew it off, and so did I. If you let everything she did annoy you, you wouldn't last long here."

"Did you like her?" the chief asked.

"I ... No, she resented me being here," Bernard said. "I was going to leave in a month or so. I have some job offers I'm looking into."

"Who all has keys to this place?" the chief asked.

"I do. Millie does. Jay has a set. And I think that's it." Bernard frowned. "In fact, a couple of months ago, the county assessor wanted to get in here after hours, and they had to call Mrs. Ryton-Storer because City Hall didn't have a set. She was extremely careful about security."

"Were the doors unlocked this morning?" the chief asked.

"No. I remember unlocking the side one to let myself in and the front one to talk to Millie. The other two doors are fire exits, and if they were open, the alarms would be going off."

"Have you ever been arrested before?"

"No, never."

"I keep thinking I've heard your name before."

"I've never even had a parking ticket here."

The chief studied him for a moment and then turned to Sims. "Take Mr. Worthington around the library and see if anything's missing or not where it should be."

Sims left the room with Bernard in tow. Deputy James Harris stuck his head in the office and asked, "Do you want to talk to the Sader girl now?"

"What's her story?" the chief asked.

"Basically she doesn't have one. Worthington didn't let her in when she came to work because of the victim's 'accident.' She went to the drugstore and picked up some stuff and came back here."

"In that case, no. Just send her on home and tell her we may need to talk to her later. What about Jay Jones? Is he out there?" the chief asked.

Harris shook his head.

"Tell Worthington that I want to see Jones as soon as he gets here." Harris left. The chief sighed and decided to see if the coroner had anything for him. He stepped out into the library and looked around the lobby. He had visited the library once about four years ago and probably only a couple of times in the years before that, and he needed to set the layout in his mind again.

A huge check-out desk dominated the small lobby, squatting squarely in the middle of the room. To the right of the front doors were Agatha's office, which was the tower room, then Bernard's much smaller office, and finally the lounge. To the left were the two restrooms, a workroom, and the elevator. About twenty feet behind the checkout desk, wide marble stairs rose gradually, leading to the second floor. A large storage closet was underneath the stairs. Going around the stairs would lead into the fiction area, which was filled with rows of shelves. Down the center of the room were reading carrels.

The chief strode across the black and white marble floor and up the stairs and paused at the top. The layout of the second floor where the nonfiction was kept was similar to the fiction area but smaller lengthwise, beginning where the elevator opened, allowing a two-story ceiling for the lobby below. It had no carrels, although there was room for them. The body had been found on the right side of the room, a few feet from a wall display case that featured Civil War items. The chief remembered the display from his visit four years ago when he was trying to find some books on raising fruit trees. He also remembered that Agatha hadn't been much help in locating any – not that she had put out much effort to do so.

The chief walked over to where County Coroner Josh Dimes was preparing the body for shipping. As he watched Dimes, he began to get angry. The chief had never cared much for the old broad, having listened to her complaints about the money the police department received when it should be going to her precious library, but no old lady, no matter how sour she was, deserved to have her throat slit open like a butchered pig.

Harris approached the chief. "Worthington says Jones was supposed to come in at nine. He hasn't heard from him."

"Take Hayden with you and see if you can locate Jones," the chief said. "Ask Worthington for the address." Harris turned to leave. "And be careful, just in case Jones is our killer." Harris nodded and went down the stairs.

Dimes finished and directed a couple of deputies to carry the body out. He took off his rubber gloves, dropped them into a small plastic baggie, and dropped the baggie into a case that contained his tools. The chief stepped forward.

"Well?" he asked.

"Won't know anything for sure until I get it back to the morgue," Dimes said. "You know that. I can't think of how many times you've asked me for information before I've even had a chance to find anything out."

"And I can't think how many times you've said that and then given me what I wanted," the chief said. "So give me what you've got so far, Josh."

Their ritual completed, Dimes looked around and said, "Well, first thing, she wasn't killed here." He gestured at the floor. "Not enough blood. Of course, you've probably already figured that." At the chief's nod, he continued. "I'd guess she died around seven or eight this morning. I think the murder weapon is probably one of those hunting knives that are serrated near the hilt because the cut is a bit ragged on the left side and some skin is missing. I couldn't find any signs of bruising or any other wounds so unless something turns up in the autopsy, that's what killed her." Dimes paused. "That's about it."

"Was she ..." The chief hesitated.

"Raped?" Dimes frowned. "Don't think so. No signs, but I'll know for sure later. Do you have reason to think she was?"

"No, but in this day and age, you can never tell what kind of sick bastards are running around."

"True enough," Dimes said. "Any suspects?"

"Not really. The assistant librarian found her. He's the best so far, but I don't think he did it. No stomach for it. He's been puking for the past hour."

"I know Bernard. Met him at church," Dimes said. "Seems nice enough, although I've always wondered what a young man was doing as a librarian."

"I've been told librarians with a degree can make a pretty good living," the chief said.

"So what's he doing here?" Dimes asked. "The city couldn't be paying him much."

"It doesn't pay him. When Ryton gave this place to the city, he also left most of his money in a trust for the library. The City Council is also the Library Board, and they administer it. He probably makes more than both of us combined."

Sims had walked up while the chief was talking and was waiting patiently. The chief motioned at him.

"We've finished searching the place," Sims said. "All except the victim's office. It's locked, and Bernard doesn't have a key. Otherwise, no signs of anything that shouldn't be here. No signs of a forced entry. We found nothing."

"Were her keys on her body?" the chief asked Dimes.

"No," Dimes answered. "In fact, she wasn't carrying anything except some tissues."

The chief motioned to one of the other deputies. "Edwards, get a locksmith here and open that door."

"Yes, sir." Edwards left.

"You'd better stick around a bit," the chief told Dimes. The coroner nodded. The chief and Sims walked downstairs to the front desk.

"Anything missing?" the chief asked.

"Not as far as Bimmer could tell," Sims replied.

"Bimmer?"

"Yeah, that's what we call Bernard because his initials are like the car ... B.M.W. And Bimmer's the car's nickname."

The chief grunted. He had figured it was something dumb.

"He's pretty shook up," Sims continued. "I sent him outside for some air."

"You know him very well?"

"I guess so," Sims said. "He used to play softball with me on the First Baptist team until he split up with Sherry Hyatt. I haven't seen him much lately, but he seems like a good guy. Do you think he did it? I wondered why Sherry dumped him. Maybe she sensed –"

"I don't think anything yet except that someone killed an old lady and we have to find out who it was," the chief said pointedly. "Get some men and look around the neighborhood. See if anyone saw or heard anything." The chief didn't hold much hope of finding any witnesses, though. If Agatha had been killed in the library and at the time that Dimes thought, the businesses surrounding the library would have been closed. Still, they could get lucky.

"Yes, sir," Sims said.

"And tell Worthington to stay close. I'll want him here when we open her office."

"Okay. Chief, City Records finally found a phone number for her next of kin," Sims said, handing the chief a piece of paper. "It's the only relative she listed on her health forms. It's her brother-in-law."

The chief read the name. Richard Storer. It was an Oklahoma City phone number. "Well, I guess I'd better call him. Tell Worthington I'm going to use his office." He let the number ring several times, but no one answered. He hung up, reminding himself to try later. The chief sighed. He could already feel his ulcer churning. No suspects worth having. No clues. A big fat nothing. The City Council was going to love this.

*

Leonard Brewer was pleased with himself despite the beginning of a pounding hangover headache. As the hot water of his shower streamed down his broad, hairy back, he grinned. He'd finally got Lisa. Although his memory of the night was pretty fuzzy – most of what happened after he fixed the flat tire was a blank – he knew she came home with him because her purse was in the living room. And in his experience, any woman who went to bed with him once was easier to get the second time. Teddy, another one of the Journal's pressmen, said the first time lessened Leonard's revulsion factor.

Leonard chuckled, thinking about Teddy's shock when the paper folded. Bet it's going to be hard to keep his brats in food now, Leonard gloated. Leonard wasn't particularly worried about the job loss. He figured to draw unemployment for a while. Maybe he could convince Lisa to move in to share bills. It'd be nice to have a woman around. With his and her unemployment, they could have some good times. At least until he got tired of her.

And a man could get sick of Lisa pretty quick, he thought, remembering how she had treated him in the past. Uppity, that's what she is. Always acting like she's so much better than the rest of us when everybody in the county knows what her old man was. And her mother was just a waitress that everyone knows got tips for being real friendly after hours. Still, Lisa does have nice –

The doorbell rang. Leonard swore and decided to ignore it. He didn't have anyone that he particularly wanted to see this morning. It was probably a salesman or some religious nut. He reached down for the bar of soap. The doorbell rang again. He soaped his arms and chest, jumping when the bell sounded again. Then again. And again.

Swearing savagely with all his considerable skill and extensive profane vocabulary, he stepped out of the tub, slipping on the wet floor and only saving himself from a nasty fall by catching the side of the sink, which certainly didn't improve his mood. He grabbed his towel. Whoever is leaning on that bell is going to be real sorry when I get through with him, he thought angrily. As he knotted the towel around his waist, the bell rang again.

"I'm coming," he yelled, stalking in the living room. "Ring that bell again and I'll rip off your head and spit in your neck!" He hit his shin on the coffee table and sent a couple choice words its direction. The bell rang again.

Reaching the door, he started to jerk it open when a thought hit him. What if it was Lisa wanting her purse? It'd be just like her to lean on the bell. He decided that it wouldn't do to appear angry. Why give her a reason to miss out on a second helping of the Leonard love machine? He put on his best smile.

He opened the door. It wasn't Lisa; it was some man.

"What do you want –"

A blur of motion.

Hot pain tore through Leonard. He raised his hands and clutched the hilt of a knife protruding from his chest. He stumbled back, trying to yell, gaping at the man who lunged forward and pushed him further into the room. Leonard fell to his knees. He couldn't catch his breath. The man leaned over, grabbing at the knife. Leonard swayed and pitched forward to the floor, driving the knife deeper into his chest. He tried to rise, then darkness covered him and took the pain away forever.

CHAPTER TWO

Bernard sat on the stone bench outside the library, watching the police search the grounds. He still felt jarred almost as if someone had struck him on the head. At least my hands have stopped shaking, he thought. Now if my stomach would settle down, I'd be okay.

He was embarrassed by his reaction and even more so by Sims's sincere concern. Treating me like I was a child, he thought disgustedly, aware that he was being unfair. Of course, I'm not acting much better than one. Although anyone would be shocked by finding a dead person, he couldn't help feeling that he was being unmanly. But the way her throat gaped open –

The scene swam before him. He closed his eyes and took a deep breath. Carefully he placed his head between his knees, trying to remember if that was what you were supposed to do if you felt faint or did you do that if you felt sick? Either way, it applies right now, he thought.

"Are you okay?" a female voice asked.

Why yes, I'm fine. I always sit this way, he thought, but he said, "No, I'm feeling sick."

"Oh." Someone sat down beside him. "Do you need a doctor?"

"No, I need to be still." And be left alone, he added silently.

She was quiet for a moment, then asked, "Are you sure you don't need one?"

He sighed and raised his head slightly. A slender woman with straight brown hair was sitting beside him, watching him expectantly. She looked vaguely familiar.

"No, I'll be okay," Bernard said, trying to place her. "Thank you, though."

"What's wrong? Is it the heat?"

"No." He sighed again. "I had an upsetting experience."

"What happened?" She leaned forward.

"Do I know you?" he asked.

"I don't think we've met, but I'm Lisa Trent. I used to work for the *Ryton Journal & News*. I'm ... stringing for *The Oklahoma City Dispatch* now."

"I'm Bernard Worthington," he said. "I don't know if I can talk to you. I mean, I don't know what the procedure is in cases like this."

"Cases like what?" Lisa asked.

"I don't think I should answer any questions until the chief says it's okay," Bernard said, realizing that he was still leaning over. He straightened up, embarrassed.

"Chief Donaldson?"

"Yes, he's up there," Bernard said. "And I think I should have his permission first. I'm sorry."

"No problem. I'll go and talk to him and catch you later," she said, watching a policeman poking around under the shrubbery.

Bernard expected her to leave then, but she remained, leaning back on the bench and writing in a notebook she produced from a pocket in her faded jeans.

"What are you doing?" he asked, alarmed by the thought she might be writing about his refusal to talk to her.

"I'm setting the mood," she said. "Details bring a story alive. I wish I had my recorder."

"Where is it?"

"I ... left it in my purse, and I left that at a friend's house." She frowned. Her mouth twisted like she had bit into a lemon.

He noticed her eyes were deep brown. "The library has recorders you could check out."

"Really? That would be great." She turned to him. "Aren't you a librarian here?"

"Yes, I'm the assistant librarian."

"I remember now." She snapped her fingers. "I did the story when the City Council hired you. It wasn't that long ago. I can't believe how bad my memory is sometimes. I kept thinking I had seen you somewhere before."

"Don't feel bad. I was trying to place you, too."

He smiled at her. She smiled back. With something akin to panic, he realized he wanted the conversation to continue but could think of nothing more to say.

"Well, I guess I better go find someone to interview," she said, closing her pad and placing her pen behind her ear.

"Maybe you should go ahead and talk to me now."

She looked at him.

"You'll probably want to since I found her body," he added.

"Body?" Lisa flipped her pad open. "Go ahead."

After Bernard finished telling his story, he watched as Lisa sat in thought, her brow wrinkled.

"How bizarre," Lisa said. "I know the old lady was a witch, but I can't see someone killing her for that. Did you like her?"

Bernard could feel her studying him. "Frankly, no. She made this job a good facsimile of hell."

"I remember she wasn't too happy when they hired you."

She paused, obviously considering a question.

"No, I didn't kill her," he said.

"I didn't ask."

"You were thinking of asking."

"Well, maybe. After all, aren't most murders an inside job, so to speak? You know, the cheating spouse, the jealous boyfriend, the jilted girlfriend, and so on."

"What would be my motive?" he asked.

"Maybe you wanted her job?"

"Not really. I want to move away from Ryton, and I can get a better paying job elsewhere."

"So how did you end up here in the first place?"

The thought of Sherry intruded on Bernard's mind; as always, it hurt.

"I made a bad choice," he said shortly. "And the sooner I'm away from here, the better."

Lisa looked like she wanted to ask a question but didn't get the chance.

"Bimmer," Sims called from the library door. "The chief wants to talk to you now."

"I'd better go." Bernard stood, his stomach immediately tightening again.

"I think I'll tag along." Lisa followed Bernard. "What did he call you?"

"Bimmer," Bernard said. "It's my nickname because I have the same initials as the car. Bernard M. Worthington. B.M.W."

"Do you like it?"

Surprised, Bernard looked at her. "I think you're the first person who has ever asked. I guess so. At least it's better than Bernie." They walked up the library steps to where Sims waited.

"Hey, Lisa. What are you doing here?" Sims asked. "I thought the paper closed yesterday."

Bernard glanced at the reporter. Her face reddened.

"It did," she said. "I'm stringing for *The Oklahoma City Dispatch* now so you'd better be careful. You can't push me around now." She lightly hit Sims on the arm.

"Of course not, Your Hineyness. We'll treat you with TLC."

"What's that? You only hit me where it doesn't show?"

"No. It means we use the soft end of our sticks."

Their easy banter irritated Bernard. "Isn't the chief waiting?"

"Let's go," Sims said, opening the door.

Sims led them to Agatha's office. A man in gray coveralls knelt before the door, working on the lock. The chief frowned at Lisa. She smiled brightly.

"I thought the paper closed," the chief said.

"She's working for *The Oklahoma City Dispatch* now," Sims said. "She's a hot shot reporter."

"Congratulations," the chief said. "I always thought you were too good for the Journal."

"Thanks," Lisa said. "Do you have a statement yet?"

"No, but I will later today," the chief said.

"I've got it, Chuck," the locksmith said. "And it was a total bear and a half. That lady had a good lock."

"Thanks, Tommy," the chief said. The chief stepped forward and opened the door.

Bernard gasped.

The office had been Agatha's pride and joy. From the polished oak desk to the burgundy leather chairs to the large portrait of Eliah Ryton to the deep pile carpet, it was hers completely. Lax about other things, she kept her office immaculate.

Now, books and papers were strewn across the floor. The backs and the seats of the chairs were slashed open. The portrait lay on the floor, its glass broken, its frame pulled apart. The desk drawers were in a pile, and the desk overturned. But what captured everyone's attention was the east wall where a wall panel was slid aside to reveal the open door of a safe.

Sims stepped inside and went to the safe. "It's empty."

"What was in there?" the chief asked Bernard.

"I don't know," Bernard said, shaking his head. "I didn't even know she had a safe in here."

"Chief," Sims said. "Look over here." He pointed at the floor by the desk. A dark red pool glistened on the floor. Splatters of the same fluid were scattered around the room and spotted the carpet in large amounts.

"All that blood ..." Lisa said, her voice shaking.

"She probably thrashed around a lot," Dimes said, stepping into the room and kneeling beside the blood. "I'd say this was where she was killed."

"You going to tell me that without a lab test?" the chief asked.

"In this case, yes," Dimes said, holding up a pair of tweezers with a bloody object in it. "There's a chunk of her throat here."

Bernard barely made it to the restroom before he threw up bile.

*

"My car or yours?" Lisa asked Bernard.

"If you don't mind driving ..." Bernard said quietly.

"No problem. I just hope nothing grabs you." Lisa opened the door to her faded Topaz and slid behind the wheel. "Let me clean off the seat." She grabbed the books and papers in the passenger seat and tossed them on the already large pile in her back seat. Bernard silently got in the car.

She had convinced Bernard to telephone a pharmacy for anti-nausea medication, but he hadn't seemed in good enough shape to drive so she offered to take him. She needed some fresh air herself. So much for the reporter with nerves of steel, she thought.

Bernard slumped in the seat. She felt sorry for him. He'd been through quite a shock today, and all in all, he was handling it fairly well, she thought.

As she drove to the local Super Value Pharmacy, she worked on the lead paragraph of the story, stirring the facts around and deciding on their placement. The chief had promised her a statement around one o'clock today. She'd wait for that, then call the Dispatch and try to wrangle herself a job. She hoped Cameron Veit remembered her from the Oklahoma Press Association meetings.

Thinking of the story reminded her of her recorder. She hated going back to Leonard's, but she wanted the confidence her recorder gave her. She decided to stop on the way back to the library.

She glanced over at Bernard. "Are you okay?"

"Yes," he said. "Thanks for taking me to the pharmacy. I guess you must think I'm a flake."

"Why?"

"Getting sick like this."

"Not really," she said. "Lots of people get sick at the sight of blood. And finding her body would rattle anyone." She turned a corner. "Her office certainly doesn't make me feel too good, but I suppose I've got used to things like that."

"How?"

"I've covered several bad car wrecks," she said. "After the first one, I was shaky for days. Gradually, I stopped thinking about it. The ones after that didn't seem to affect me the same way or at least for not as long. If you can understand that."

"Yeah, I can," Bernard said, looking out the window. "I used to be an EMT."

"Really?"

"Yeah," Bernard said. "I wasn't always a librarian."

"What happened? I mean, why did you stop being an EMT? Was it the blood?"

"No," he said shortly. "I wasn't bothered by it then."

They drove in silence for a few moments.

"I wonder if there's going to be a second murder," he said abruptly.

Lisa glanced at him. Maybe being in the same car with him wasn't such a good idea. While her instincts said he was okay, they could be wrong. "What do you mean?"

"I'm not sure, but it all seems so weird." Bernard shifted in his seat. "Why would someone want to kill her?"

"Offhand, I'd guess about anyone who ever met her. The murder suspects will form a double line."

Bernard laughed. "No, seriously. Think about it. She's been an ogre for years – or so I've been told. Why would somebody decide to kill her now?"

"Maybe they finally got fed up," Lisa stopped at a light. "Besides, robbery was probably the motive."

"Now, that really bothers me. Robbery of what?" Bernard asked. "I didn't even know the safe was there. And what could be in there that was valuable enough to kill for?"

"Money. Stocks. Bonds."

"I don't see how she could have much of anything."

"I thought the library paid you pretty well."

Bernard looked at her.

"I remember from the story," she said.

"Well, I guess they do. But she wasn't paid as much as me. The Board wanted to hire someone with a masters, and that doesn't come cheap. Actually, the salary wouldn't have been enough to hire me, except I was already planning to move here." He grimaced. "Agatha always said my salary would have been better spent on books."

"Maybe old man Ryton left her some money. He certainly seemed loaded." Lisa remembered being told that he made his money in the stock market. Or was it the commodity market?

"I don't think she would have worked at the library if she had money. She liked working about as much as she liked me," he said.

"All right. If it wasn't money in the safe, what was?"

"Beats me. I'm just talking, trying to make some sense of this." He sighed. "I wonder if they've told her family yet."

Lisa turned into the pharmacy parking lot. "I didn't know she had any."

"I think a brother and maybe a sister. She didn't talk about them much. The brother lives in Oklahoma City. I think he has a bookstore there." He opened the door. "I'll be right back."

She watched him enter the pharmacy. She hoped the medicine would help. She had seen his obvious distress on the bench at the library and had immediately wanted to help, her reaction surprising her a bit. She enjoyed talking with him. He's a nice guy, she decided. And cute, too. Of course, I went to bed with Leonard Brewer, so what kind of taste could I have?

Thinking of Leonard reminded her of her purse again. She hoped he wasn't home. The thought of his leering grin made her feel ill. She looked in the mirror and winced at her reflection. No make-up, mussed hair, crumpled white sweatshirt, faded blue jeans, dark circles under her eyes. Bernard probably thought she looked like she had been rode hard around the track a few times and put away wet. She rummaged in the glove compartment and found an old comb and a rubber band. She combed her long hair back into a pony tail and snapped the rubber band around it to hold it. A little better, but not by much, she thought ruefully.

Bernard startled her as he opened the car door.

"That didn't take long," she said, starting the car.

"It was ready," he said, taking a brown bottle out of a white bag and staring at the label. "Well, here goes." He drank a mouthful and made a face. "Nasty stuff."

"Most medicine is. My dad used to say that they make it that way so people will think it's actually doing something."

"That sounds right," Bernard said. "What does your dad do?"

She paused. "He passed away five years ago."

"I'm sorry," Bernard said.

Lisa shook her head. "You didn't know. It's all right. My mother died of cancer, and he took it hard. I've always thought he died of broken heart." No matter what other people say. "The doctors said it was a blood clot."

"I'm sorry," Bernard said again.

"Where do your parents live?" she asked.

"My mom lives in Edmond," Bernard said. "Where are we going?"

"I have to pick my purse up from a friend's house," Lisa said. "It won't take long."

"Would I know her?"

"I don't think so. I used to work with him."

"Oh." He looked out the window.

Lisa began to feel uncomfortable. "He's not a good friend. I really don't know him very well," she said. Not that I owe you any explanations, Mr. Librarian. "He worked in the pressroom at the Journal."

Bernard nodded, still looking out the window.

Almost desperately, she asked, "Why do you think the murder is so weird?"

"Well, for one thing, I wonder where the murderer was taking the body," he said. "If she was killed in her office, why drag her body to the second floor?"

"Maybe he was going to drop her out a window?"

"Why not take her out the side door?"

"Maybe he stabbed her, and she ran up there before she died."

"Then why wasn't there blood everywhere? And something else. She was lying on her back with her hands at her side. If she fell, I don't think she would be so ... arranged. I think someone dragged her up there."

"Why?" Lisa asked.

"I don't know. I don't know why her office was trashed, I didn't know the safe was there, I don't know what could have been in it, and I have no idea why she was killed. To think I used to believe that I was fairly knowledgeable." He smiled wryly.

He had a nice smile. Sort of goofy and kind. And he had marvelous blue eyes. Steady, girl, Lisa told herself. Stay on point. "Let's say whoever killed her knew what he was looking for but didn't know where it was. She wouldn't tell him at first so he trashed the place looking for it. She finally told him it was in the safe. Then he killed her so there wouldn't be any witnesses. Was the library broken into?"

"No," he said, shaking his head. "Not that I could tell. All the windows and doors were intact."

"Maybe she knew him well enough to let him in. Or maybe he picked her up at her house and forced her to go with him."

"That would explain what she doing there so early if someone had forced her." Bernard paused. "I think she must have known him because he knew there was something valuable in the library. Whether or not he knew about the safe, he knew something was hidden there."

"Or knew Agatha had something valuable to hide. Or thought she had something. Or thought the library had something. That's plenty of 'or's'," Lisa said with a grimace. "Of course, the murderer could be a woman."

"I don't think so. Agatha probably weighed two-fifty. It'd take a fairly strong person to move that. And there are more strong men than women." Bernard rubbed his eyes. "I wish I had my contact solution with me."

"You wear contacts?"

"Yes. I'm near-sighted." He massaged his neck. "The whole thing doesn't make any sense."

"Probably it will turn out to be really simple," Lisa said. "It only looks weird because we don't know what happened." She pulled into the parking lot of an apartment building. "This won't take long."

As she walked up the steps, she noticed Leonard's car was parked in the lot. Great, she thought, the slug is here. Oh, what a wonderful day. If he says anything, I swear I'll kill him.

She knocked on his door. No answer. He might still be sleeping off last night, she thought hopefully. When she tried the knob, the door opened. She stepped inside. If luck was with her, she could grab her purse and go before Leonard noticed her.

Lisa had often been teased about her purse. It was huge and always crammed full of make-up, pencils, notepads, her recorder, some tapes, a couple of screwdrivers, and just about anything else she needed or thought she would need. It functioned as her supply room and security blanket. If she hadn't been so depressed this morning, she wouldn't have forgotten it.

She looked around and saw her purse. It was lying on the couch with its myriad contents spilled on the floor.

"You, jerk!" she shouted. "Going through my purse –"
Striding across the room, she flung open the bedroom door. "Leonard, I don't know what you thought you were doing, but let me tell you –"

He lay on his back by the unmade bed, a knife buried to the hilt in his chest. All Lisa could think about was that he couldn't tell anyone she had spent the night with him. She would have to do that now.

*

The chief sighed. Two murders in one day. The City Council would holler to high heaven. "You know," he said to the room at large, "being a police chief is like trying to applaud with your buttocks. It's practically impossible, and it rubs you wrong."

Lisa, Bernard, and Sims just looked at him. They were back at the police station in the chief's office. Lisa and Bernard were perched on his couch, and Sims was at a small writing desk, ready to take their statements.

The chief sighed again. "Lisa, would you go over this again so that Sims can get it down."

Lisa nodded. "Leonard and I went to Rochelle's Bar and Grill last night along with some of the other people from the paper. We stayed until about midnight. Leonard invited me over so I went. I stayed the night. When I left this morning, I forgot my purse. It had my recorder in it so I stopped by Leonard's to pick it up after Bernard picked up his medicine. That's when I found him."

"What time did you leave Leonard's this morning?" the chief asked, glancing at Bernard. He seemed to draw away from Lisa. She sat stiffly, not looking at him. Interesting, the chief thought.

"It must have been a few minutes before ten 'cause on the way home I saw your cars at the library."

The chief looked at Bernard. "Mr. Worthington, would you step outside for a moment?"

Bernard looked startled but nodded. "Is there a water fountain here?"

"Sims, show him where it is," the chief directed. "We've also got a pop machine back there. And some coffee."

Sims and Bernard left.

Lisa twisted her hands, looking nervous.

"Lisa, I wanted to ask you a few questions that I thought you might feel more comfortable about if they left," the chief began. "But first, are you okay?"

She nodded. "It shook me up."

"Were you and Leonard close?"

"No." Lisa looked away. "Actually, if I hadn't been drunk, I wouldn't have gone home with him ever. I thought he was sleazy."

"Did anything happen?"

"Like what?"

"Well, like maybe he was interested, but you weren't?"

"And in the struggle to preserve my virtue, I stabbed him? Is that what you're getting at?" Lisa asked.

"Not exactly, but is that what happened?" The chief leaned forward, watching her pale face and trembling hands.

"No. Leonard was alive when I left. We didn't fight. In fact, I don't think we did anything. I mean, nothing at all."

The chief raised his eyebrows in a silent question.

"Look, let me be blunt. We were both drunker than skunks. Leonard's car had a flat on the way home. When he got out to change it, I passed out. I woke up in his bed with my ... shirt and bra off, but my jeans were on. He was naked and passed out. I dressed and got out. I don't think we had sex, and we certainly didn't have a fight!" Lisa finished in an angry rush.

The chief sat there quietly, giving Lisa a few moments to calm down. "What do you think of Worthington?" he asked suddenly.

"He's okay," she said. "Why do you ask? Do you think he murdered Agatha?"

"Do you think he did?" the chief asked.

"No."

"Why not?"

She frowned. "I don't know. He doesn't seem the type."

"He disliked her, and he had opportunity. Why shouldn't I think he did it?"

"Do you think he did?" she asked.

"Off the record?"

She nodded.

"No, I don't. Same reason as you. But he might surprise us. Some people hide their bents pretty deep."

"Do you think I killed Leonard?" she asked.

"No." The chief shook his head. "His billfold was cleaned out of cash just like your purse. I'd say someone decided to rob him while he was in the shower and he caught them at it. But don't you go leaving town, you understand. Besides making you seem guilty, it would look bad on me. And you'd better be ready for what people are going to say about you around town."

She smiled grimly. "They've said it before. I'm used to it."

"Did Brewer fight with anyone last night?"

"No, I don't think so. Although I think the guy who helped change the tire was pretty irate. We were blocking his drive or something."

"Do you remember where you had the flat?" the chief asked.

"Not really. Maybe near Fourth Street," she said. "I'm not sure."

The chief thought for a moment. "Let's see. Coming back from the bar, you probably came straight down Main."

"I guess so."

"So you would have come right past the library. In fact, Fourth is right before the library. Did you notice anything?"

"I'm sorry I have to keep saying 'no' all the time, but I was totally wasted."

The chief picked up a letter opener and turned it in his hands. "You know, many a time your father was here."

"I know," Lisa said stiffly. "I bailed him out."

The chief pointed the opener at her. "So if I were you, I'd watch the drinking."

Lisa started to say something, then looked away.

"Give Sims a list of the people who went to Rochelle's with you," he said. "He's also going to fingerprint you so we'll know whose prints are whose at Brewer's apartment. You didn't touch the knife, did you?"

"No," she said curtly.

"Well, I'm finished for now unless you can think of anything else."

She shook her head and rose. "What about my purse?"

"I'm afraid it's evidence. If there's anything in there you just have to have –"

"My tape recorder. My wallet."

"I'll see what I can do."

She nodded and left.

The chief settled back to think. Leonard's death was easier on his mind than Agatha's. Leonard ran with a tough crowd, and the chief believed firmly in the old adage that if you lie down with dogs, you'll get up with fleas. It was a shame Lisa happened to be with him. She'd worked hard to gain some respect, and a lot of people would think bad of her for going home with Leonard. The chief had never understood why the children of alcoholics drank. You'd think they'd know better.

Agatha's death, however, seemed darker, more evil. Too many

puzzling things about it. Why was Agatha at the library in the middle of the night? Did she know her killer? Why did the killer drag her upstairs? What was hidden in the safe?

He wondered if it was too early to call Dimes. He checked his watch. Four o'clock. Dimes wouldn't have anything yet on Agatha and certainly nothing on Leonard. At least this day was nearly over.

The chief searched his pockets and found the number for Agatha's brother-in-law, Richard Storer. He dialed it. It only rang twice before it was answered.

"Hello?" A man's voice, deep and pleasant.

"Is this Richard Storer?" the chief asked, steeling himself to deliver the bad news. It was never easy.

"Yes, who is this?"

"This is Police Chief Donaldson from Ryton. Sir, I'm afraid I have some bad news for you. Agatha Ryton-Storer is dead."

"Dead?" There was silence for a few moments. Then Storer asked, "How did she die?"

"I'm sorry to say she was murdered," the chief said.

"Murdered?! What happened?"

"I'd rather discuss it with you face-to-face," the chief said. "Tell me, would it be possible for you to come up here tomorrow?"

"Yes, I can arrange that," Storer said. "Uh, Chief Donaldson, where is she? I mean, who do I call about arrangements?"

"Presently she's at the County Coroner's. When you decide on a funeral home, tell them. They'll arrange transportation."

"I'll have to get things worked out here. I should be there around noon. Where would you like to meet?"

"At her house if possible. Do you have keys for it?"

"Yes, I watched the house for her occasionally. Did you need anything else?"

"No. I'd like to say how sorry I am."

"Thank you." Storer hung up.

Sims stuck his head in. "They're gone."

The chief nodded. "Did you get Worthington's hometown?"

"It's Oklahoma City," Sims said.

"Call the police up there and see if they have anything on him. I keep thinking I've heard something about a Worthington before. And have we located Jones yet?"

"No. Hayden and Harris drove over to his place and poked around. They didn't find anything unusual, but his truck is gone. Do you want me to put out a bulletin on him?"

"Yeah, I think you should. I find it mighty strange that he would come up missing right now."

"You think he could be the killer?" Sims asked.

"That or another victim," the chief said.

Sims left. The chief leaned back in his chair. He wondered if his peaches were ripening as they should, but thoughts of the rosy pink peaches kept reminding him of Agatha's throat and Brewer's chest spattered with dark red blood. His stomach pained him. He reached into his desk and grabbed a bottle of liquid antacid. I'm going to catch whoever did this, he thought. And they're going to be really sorry.

*

"Would you like me to drive?" Bernard asked.

Lisa shook her head.

He could tell she was furious. She started the car as he closed his door. He wanted to ask what happened in the chief's office, but decided she would tell him if she wanted him to know. Besides, what business was it of his? He barely knew her.

Halfway back to the library, she burst out swearing. She cursed the chief, the city, the world, and everything in between. The tirade lasted about a minute and showed a real talent for creative profanity.

He waited for a few moments after she finished. "Feel better?"

"Not really," she said. "I'm so mad I could scream."

"What about?" he asked, hoping she wouldn't think he was prying. "Surely the chief doesn't think you had anything to do with that man's death?"

"No, he thinks I'm innocent. And although I think I'm not supposed to tell you this, he doesn't think you killed Agatha, either."

"Good. But that doesn't sound like something that would upset you."

"It didn't."

Bernard waited.

She glanced at him. "You see, my father was an alcoholic." She paused.

"You know you don't have to tell me anything," Bernard said.

"No, it's okay." She shrugged. "I got used to it, I guess. He was one of Ryton's two town drunks."

"I'm sorry."

"It's not a big deal," she said. "I loved him a lot, and he was a good father. A good man. He died about six months after Mama did. Everyone thinks that he drank himself to death, and that was how he did it. But he died because Mama was gone, and he couldn't live without her." She ran a hand through her hair. "Anyhow, whenever I drink more than I should, someone has to throw him up in my face."

"Who brought it up?"

"The chief."

Bernard thought for a moment. "I'm sure he didn't mean to be insulting."

"Oh, I know he didn't," she said. "I'm madder at me than him. I know better than to get drunk. I do dumb things when I'm drunk."

"Most people do," he said.

Lisa turned the car into the library parking lot.

"Yeah, I know. It doesn't make me feel any better."

She parked the car. A couple of police cars were still there, and a policeman was walking around the grounds.

"Would you like to go to dinner with me?" he heard himself asking.

She looked at him and frowned. "As long as you're not feeling sorry for me –"

"No, I'm not." He smiled at her.

She smiled back. "Okay, I'd like that. Where to?"

"How about The Señor? I haven't been in a while, but they make good food. Unless you'd prefer somewhere else?"

"No, that sounds great. Pick me up around seven-thirty. I need to call the Dispatch and file my story first." She gave him her address.

He watched her drive away. Absurdly, he was feeling good. Nothing like a couple of murders to brighten a day, he thought.

He went up the steps to the library. Inside he found the police had closed off the second floor and Agatha's office. He asked one of the officers how long the police would want the library closed. The officer shrugged.

Bernard went into his office and looked at the pile of work on his desk. He didn't feel much like working. He stuck his hands in his pockets and felt the shipping form he had picked up outside this morning. He dropped it on his desk. I'll take care of it tomorrow, he thought. With the library closed, I should have plenty of time.

"Bernard?"

Sherry's voice hit him like a kick in the stomach. She stood in the office doorway.

"Are you okay?" she asked.

"Yes." He suddenly found it hard to breathe. "What are you doing here?"

"I heard the news on the radio, and I know how things upset you," she said, coming into the office. "I told the officer that I knew you, and he let me in." She cocked her head to the side. "Are you sure you're okay? Maybe I should drive you home?"

"No, thank you." A terrible hope was inside him, tangling up his thoughts.

"Do the police know what happened?" she asked.

"No. They're working on it."

"Do they have any suspects?" she asked.

"I don't think so," he said. The awkward silence grew.

"Well, I just wanted to check on you," she said finally. "I hadn't seen you in a while."

"I thought that's what you wanted," he said.

"I'd still like us to be friends," she said.

He shook his head. "I don't know if that's possible. I don't think it would be good for either of us." Certainly not for me.

"Don't be silly," she said, walking over to him. "We were friends before we started dating. There's no reason we can't be friends now. Tell you what, why don't you come to dinner tonight? Mom and Dad ask about you all the time, and I know they'd love to see you."

"You moved back in with your parents?" he asked.

"Yes, I didn't like living in an apartment," she said. "They offered, and my old room sounded good to me. So are you going to have dinner with us?"

"Thank you, but I can't tonight," he said. "I have a date."

"Oh?" She raised an eyebrow skeptically.

"I'm taking Lisa Trent out."

Sherry frowned. "I don't think she's quite your type."

"Thank you for your opinion."

"Now, come on, Bernard, don't get upset," she said. "I just mean she runs with a rough crowd. That's all." She paused for a moment. "Wasn't her father an alcoholic?"

"I don't know," he said.

"You know, I've heard she makes a habit of dating guys with good jobs," she said.

"What does that mean?" He looked at her, angry and confused.

"Nothing. No reason to get upset," Sherry said, holding up one hand. "She seems to take care of herself, that's all. Well, I need to get going." She turned to leave, but looked back at him from the door. "Maybe tomorrow night?"

"I'll have to see how my work's going," he said. "I'm not sure how things are going to go here now."

"Yes, I bet you have a lot of work to do. And you'll have more soon." She smiled at him. "Daddy says you'd probably get the Head Librarian job. He thinks a lot of you. We all do." She left.

Bernard stood silently, his fists clenched. How could she do this to him? He could never be just friends with her. And how dare she criticize Lisa! Maybe she was jealous? And if she was jealous, perhaps she still loved him. No, he thought. I won't do this to me again. It's over between us. I've been hurt enough.

Even as these thoughts crossed his mind, he had already decided to call tomorrow and accept her invitation.

*

Lisa placed the phone on its cradle, then whooped with excitement. Everything had gone exactly right. As soon as she told him about the murders, Veit had hired her as a local correspondent, a stringer, for the Dispatch, and told her she would be paid by the word – not a full-time reporting job, but a beginning. Then she had dictated the stories of the murders directly to him. He only had a few questions when she finished, and for each one he asked, she had the answer. She could tell he was impressed. He wanted her to continue covering the murders and told her to fax any further stories to him since she didn't have a computer and couldn't email them.

Did the office supply store downtown have a fax machine? She would have to check tomorrow. She wondered what they charged to send a fax. Or maybe she could dip into her meager savings and purchase a fax machine. She had been saving for a computer, but that purchase didn't seem like it was going to be possible for a while. At least not until she had a definite job.

She had worried about Veit's reaction to her being in the story about Leonard's death. But he had only said that her byline wouldn't be on it. The story had been short by necessity; the chief hadn't had much to say about Leonard's or Agatha's death. The chief said that he would have more to tell her tomorrow morning.

Before then, she needed to get another recorder. Didn't Bernard say the library – Bernard! She looked at her watch. Six-thirty. She'd have to hurry.

Rushing up the stairs to her bedroom and bath, she nearly stepped on Obsidian who hissed and spat his displeasure. "Sorry, sweetie," she said, "but you're in the way." A quick shower and a hurried dress selection later, she sat at her vanity, applying her "party paint" as her father used to put it.

All in all, it had been a roller coaster day, she thought, and she'd come out on top. A stringer wasn't a reporter, but she was one step closer. The doorbell rang. She glanced at the clock.

Seven-fifteen. Bernard was early. Just her luck.

She hadn't intended for him to see how messy her house was, but that's the way things go sometimes. She hurried down the stairs and opened the front door. "Sorry. I'm running late –"

She had a blurred impression of a man in a ski mask, rushing toward her. He slammed against her.

She stumbled back and fell on the stairs, her breath knocked out of her. His body landed on her. His hands grabbed her throat. She struck at his face and pulled free.

He hit her on the side of the head. The room spun. She tried to kick. He threw himself on her, and his hands closed again on her throat. She couldn't get free, couldn't draw a breath. Her hands fell away. Her vision tunneled. Far away, she heard shouting. Then the pressure on her throat was gone. Someone was shaking her, but she was drifting away. She closed her eyes and let go of everything. It was surprisingly easy.

CHAPTER THREE

"You'll have to wait for the doctor," the nurse said and turned to answer the phone. The chief scowled at her back. He hauled himself off the counter and headed back to the waiting room, hoping that the doctor had come by in his absence.

As he turned the corner, he could hear Sims questioning Bernard again. The chief allowed himself a brief moment of pity for the librarian. It was obvious that Bernard was having a hard time. I'm not having it that easy myself, the chief thought.

"Are you sure you can't think of any other details?" Sims asked Bernard.

Bernard shook his head. "Like I've already said, it happened so fast I didn't get a good look at him. All I could tell about him was that he was wearing dark clothes and a red ski mask. We've gone over this twice. It's not going to change –"

"Did you notice anything about him when you fought?" Sims interrupted.

Bernard sighed. "We didn't fight. Not really. When I came in, he was on top of Lisa, choking her. I yelled, grabbed him, and pulled him off her. He shoved me against the wall and ran out the door. I stayed with Lisa, called the ambulance, and did what I could until they arrived."

"Could you tell how tall he was?" Sims asked.

"Maybe my height or a little taller," Bernard said. "But I can't be sure."

"Eyes?"

"Yes, he had two, and no, I didn't see what color."

"Any distinguishing features?" Sims persisted.

"You mean, like a biker tattoo or a deep-sea diving scar?" Bernard snapped.

"Give it a rest, Sims," the chief ordered. He dropped into a chair. "Has the doctor come yet?"

"No," Bernard said.

"They won't tell me anything up there," the chief said with a disgusted wave in the general direction of the nurses' station. "How bad did she look, Bernard?"

"Not good." Bernard swallowed. "She was beat-up. But she woke up in the ambulance and talked a little." Sims leaned forward eagerly. Bernard looked at him disgustedly. "She didn't say anything important. Just wanted me to take care of her cat."

"Who's the doctor?" the chief asked.

"I think his name is Osborne."

The chief nodded. "He's good. She's lucky you came early."

"Some luck," Bernard said shortly.

"It could have been worse," the chief pointed out.

"Just because it could have been worse doesn't make what happened better," Bernard said.

"She could be dead," the chief said sharply. "We can be grateful that she isn't."

After a moment, Bernard nodded.

Wearily, the chief put his head back on the chair and listened to the muted sounds of the hospital. Maggie once told him that no matter how quiet a hospital was, it still wasn't restful. He understood what she meant.

Bernard broke the silence. "I don't get it. Why would anyone want to kill her?"

"Maybe that wasn't his intention," Sims said. "He might have been intending to rob her – or maybe rape her. I watched this movie where this serial killer would capture women and put them in his basement ..."

His voice trailed off as the chief glared at him.

"We'll know more after we talk to her," the chief said. "Until then, Sims, keep your thoughts to yourself." He regarded Bernard. "How are you doing?"

Bernard let out a long breath. "Okay, I guess. I'm more angry than anything else. This isn't what I associate with Ryton. This seems more like something that would happen in New York City or Chicago or some big city like that."

As the chief nodded soberly, he could feel his ulcer beginning to burn. He fumbled in his coat pocket and brought out a roll of antacids, thinking glumly about the delicious dinner that Maggie had prepared and that his stomach would be in no shape to finish when he got home. He'd been right in the middle of enjoying the meal – despite the murders – when Sims called about the attack. And what with two unsolved murders, one that involved Lisa, the chief decided that he wanted to talk to her if it was possible.

"Chief, could this be connected to the murder of Brewer?" Sims asked.

"The thought has crossed my mind," the chief said. "Maybe someone thought she saw something."

"Like who the murderer was?" Bernard asked.

"Or his car," Sims said, excitedly.

"It could also be completely unrelated," the chief said. "Let's talk to Lisa before we get all carried away."

Deputy Harris entered and came over to the chief. "We looked around the neighborhood, Chief. Couldn't find anyone who shouldn't be there."

"Did any of the neighbors see anything?" the chief asked.

Harris shook his head. "For one thing, the house across the street from her is empty. It's up for sale. And so is the one next to it. The people in the house next door to hers on the south side weren't home. The other side is an apartment complex, and it faces the other street. Hayden and McGraw are talking to the residents now, but it didn't look good when I left."

"The way things have been going, I'm not surprised." The chief thought for a moment. "Listen, I want you to check every dumpster in that neighborhood. Look for a red ski mask and any dark clothes. Check any trash cans, ditches, and anywhere else you think someone could throw some clothes."

"Yes, sir."

"And get Hayden and McGraw to help you," the chief said. "It needs to be done before the trash trucks make their rounds tomorrow morning." Harris nodded and left.

"Do you think they'll find anything?" Sims asked.

"Maybe. If no one noticed him wearing a ski mask, he had to take it off, and he wouldn't want to be caught with it," the chief said. "Why don't you go up there and see if you can find out if we're going to get to talk to her."

But Dr. Osborne was already heading toward them.

"How is she?" the chief asked.

"Fairly good all things considered," Osborne said. "I'm going to keep her overnight. She has a slight concussion, and the left side of her face suffered severe bruising as did her throat."

"Can we talk with her?" the chief asked.

"Yes, if necessary, but keep it short. She needs rest. Sleep will help her the most." Osborne looked at Bernard. "Are you Bernard?"

"Yes."

"She wanted me to give you her keys so you could get in her apartment and take care of her cat," the doctor said, handing the keys to Bernard.

"I think I'll go in by myself," the chief said.

"I wanted –" Bernard started to protest.

"It would be less stressful if she only saw one person now," Osborne said.

Bernard nodded slowly. "Well, okay. Tell her I'll be by tomorrow. And the cat will be fine."

"Sims, drive Bernard back over to Lisa's and then help Harris," the chief ordered.

The chief followed Osborne into a room. Lisa lay in a bed, an IV attached to her arm. The left side of her face was swollen and reddened. The chief could see the heavy bruises on her throat. Her eyes were shut.

"Lisa, it's Chief Donaldson," the chief said. "Can you talk for a moment?"

Her eyes opened. Her voice was a soft, painful whisper. "Yes."

"Do you know who attacked you?" he asked.

She shook her head.

"Can you give us a description?"

She shook her head again and closed her eyes. Tears ran down her cheeks. The chief awkwardly patted her arm.

"You might try tomorrow," Osborne said softly. "We've given her something to make her sleep."

The chief nodded. He patted her arm again, shook his head, and left quietly.

*

"Lisa's a nice girl," Sims said, breaking the long silence in the patrol car as he drove to Lisa's house.

"Yes, she is," Bernard said.

"Man, I'd like to pound whoever did it."

"Me, too," Bernard said wearily.

"Hey, are you okay?" Sims asked, glancing at Bernard.

"Yeah, I'm fine. Compared to her, I'm doing great," Bernard said. "It's been a bad day. I feel like I've dropped off the face of the earth and ended up somewhere terrible."

"Yeah, well, a good night's sleep will help you out," Sims said.

"You'll feel better in the morning. And don't worry, Bimmer, we'll catch that guy. The chief is very good."

Bernard stared out the window. If only he had arrived a few minutes early. Lisa's door was ajar when he drove up. He walked up the sidewalk and into a bad dream. When he saw the attacker, he yelled and grabbed the guy. He pulled the man off her, but the attacker jerked free of his grip and ran out the door. Bernard dropped to his knees beside Lisa.

For a horrible moment, he thought she was dead. All the memories of his father's death came flooding in. Then she moaned. A moan was his salvation. He called an ambulance and the police. The second time today I've called the police about a crime, he thought. It'd better be the last. I don't think I could take a third time.

Sims pulled into Lisa's driveway. "Do you want me to come in with you?"

"Is there any reason for you to?" Bernard asked.

"Guess not."

"Is there anything I could disturb?"

Sims looked baffled.

"I mean, like evidence," Bernard explained.

"No, we already went over the place. He wasn't in there very long, and he didn't leave anything behind."

Bernard got out and walked up to the door as Sims drove away. He let himself in. It took him nearly thirty minutes to locate Obsidian. He finally found the black cat under Lisa's bed. It hissed, spat and struck at him, and wouldn't come out. Leaving the animal to sulk, he refilled its water dish in the bathroom. Canned cat food filled one of the kitchen cabinets, and as soon as he started the electric can-opener, Obsidian appeared, purring and weaving between Bernard's legs. After feeding the cat, he emptied the litter box. He found a bag of kitty litter under the kitchen sink.

Going into the living room, he sat down on the couch, pushing a couple of books and a pizza box aside. The room was filled with books that ranged from science-fiction to romances to grammar usage manuals and style books. He counted two bookshelves devoted exclusively to poetry. Her front window overflowed with plants. His own apartment was neat, and there had never been a plant he couldn't kill. I need to go home, he thought. Why am I still here? He couldn't think of an answer. He finally rose, locked her door, and drove home.

He pulled off his clothes and fell into bed. And surprised himself by going quickly to sleep and having no dreams.

*

Along with the coroner's report on Agatha, the chief had three surprises on his desk the next morning. The first was the coroner's report on Leonard, which was a surprise because he hadn't expected Dimes to get it to him until later in the day. The second surprise was what the report said. He read it twice to be sure he fully understood. The third surprise was the report from the Oklahoma City police department concerning Bernard M. Worthington. The chief read it as Sims looked on.

"Well, that's interesting," the chief said. "I thought I remembered a Worthington in the news."

"The guy who did it was never caught," Sims said.

"I did read the report," the chief said pointedly. His ulcer was bothering him, and he wasn't feeling friendly toward the world in general.

"Do you think maybe Bernard killed Agatha?" Sims asked. "Suppose what happened to his dad made him crazy –"

"You know, you must watch too much TV. I don't think Bernard could kill anyone, but I do think I'd like to talk to him. Call him and ask what time he gets to the library. We'll meet him then." The chief settled back in his chair. "I need a little time to try and make this all fit."

The chief was still working on it as he and Sims walked up the library steps. Sims rattled the door and knocked on the glass. After a moment, Bernard let them in.

"I wouldn't have answered your knock if I hadn't known you were coming," Bernard said, walking them to his office. "At least ten people have come by since I got here, trying to get in and look around. I never realized how ghoulish people are. Would you like some coffee?"

"Yes," Sims said.

"No," the chief said. "Doesn't help my ulcer."

"It's over on the table behind the circulation desk," Bernard told Sims. "Help yourself. There should be creamer and sugar if you use them."

The chief and Bernard sat down in Bernard's office. Sims, holding a steaming coffee cup, joined them.

"What did you need, chief?" Bernard asked. He fiddled with a pen.

"Well, I got some surprising news today," the chief began.

"But first, did you know Leonard Brewer? Did you ever meet him?"

Bernard shook his head.

"Maybe he came in the library?" the chief asked.

"I don't think so," Bernard said. "I know our regulars fairly well. I guess he could have before I came here, but I don't think he's been in during the last six months."

"Leonard probably didn't know how to read," Sims said, earning a sharp look from the chief.

"Why do you ask?" Bernard asked.

"Well, the coroner says the knife stuck in him was also the one that killed Agatha Ryton-Storer," the chief said.

"The same knife?" Bernard looked startled.

"Yes. The coroner found traces of her blood and tissue on it. Apparently the knife lodged in the bones in Brewer's chest, and the killer couldn't get it out. A lucky break for us, I guess. So right now I'm looking for a connection besides the one I think I've got."

"Which is?" Bernard asked.

"The other night, when Leonard and Lisa were driving to his place, they had a flat tire. Leonard got out to fix it. Lisa said some man helped Leonard change the tire. She thought Leonard's car was blocking the guy's drive. I think maybe it was blocking the drive into the library's parking lot."

"And the guy killed Leonard and tried to kill Lisa because they saw him here!" Bernard stood up in his excitement. "Wait, that doesn't make any sense."

"Why not?" the chief asked, confident he knew what Bernard was going to say.

"Why would a murderer help someone fix a flat tire?" Bernard sat down.

"Maybe he wasn't intending to murder Agatha," Sims suggested.

"That's what I think," the chief said. "For some reason, he was meeting Agatha here late at night. He wasn't intending to kill her. Perhaps they argued. He lost his temper and killed her without thinking. Then, because Leonard could place him here, he had to kill Leonard."

"So Lisa knows who did –" Sims started to say.

"No, she doesn't. Too drunk. She said she never got a look at him," the chief said. "She left her purse at Leonard's. When the murderer killed him, he found her address. He probably knew what she looked like. Just because she was too drunk to see him doesn't mean he didn't see her."

"We can use Lisa as bait," Sims said. "He doesn't know she didn't see him. He'll try to kill her again."

The chief shook his head in disgust. "You do watch too much TV. We don't risk her life. In fact, I've already sent someone down to the hospital to watch over her. He might try again, but we're not going to try to set him up by using her." At least not yet, the chief added silently to himself.

Bernard stood and began to pace. "So the real question is why was Agatha killed?"

"At the moment that seems to be the big one," the chief said. He watched Bernard for a moment. "But perhaps you should sit down because I need to ask you about something."

Bernard looked at the chief for a long moment and sat down. "What is it?"

The chief took a deep breath. "We've talked to the Oklahoma City police department about your father." Bernard became still. "I thought maybe you should tell us about it."

"Why?" The question was flat and hard.

"Because I think you should," the chief said, his voice just as emotionless.

Bernard looked away. "He was a jeweler. He sometimes carried a lot of money. One night in August about ten years ago, he was walking home from the store. We didn't live very far, but he didn't make it. Someone robbed and stabbed him several times. He was thrown into a ditch. A man heard his moans and called an ambulance. He died at the hospital." Bernard stopped.

"And they never caught who did it," the chief said.

"No, they didn't. He didn't live long enough to give a description."

"The report said you were at the emergency room," the chief said.

Bernard didn't say anything for a long time. Sims looked at the chief. The chief shook his head. He could wait.

Bernard finally said, "I was an EMT at the time. I was hanging around the ER with my partner waiting for our next run when another ambulance brought him in." Bernard looked at the chief. "They rolled him right past me. He was so cut up and covered in blood that I didn't recognize him. Not at first. But he reached for me. I realized who he was when I saw his eyes. He died in the ER."

Sims let out his breath.

"I'm sorry," the chief said.

Bernard closed his eyes briefly. "It was years ago. Why did you want to know?"

"Well, there was a chance it had unbalanced you," the chief said. Sims shot him a look that the chief ignored. "I wanted to see how you reacted."

"Did I pass the test?" Bernard snapped.

"I think so," the chief said. "Now, we need to figure out why the murderer was meeting Agatha. Any ideas?"

"No," Bernard said shortly.

"Could she have been meeting a boyfriend?" At Bernard's incredulous look, the chief said, "It's possible."

"If she had one, she never mentioned it," Bernard said. "And I can't see her having one. She had a low opinion of men."

"I wonder if that included her brother-in-law," the chief said.

"Who's that?"

"Richard Storer. Lives in Oklahoma City and owns a bookstore," the chief said. "Ever meet him?"

"No. She mentioned him a few times, but I thought he was her brother," Bernard said. "He never came here as far as I know. And she only mentioned him to complain about how badly he treated her, although she never explained what he did that was so terrible. I think Agatha had a sister, too."

"She does, but Evelyn Ryton left town years ago and I haven't been able to get a line on her," the chief said. "Tell me, can you think of any possible reason Agatha was killed?"

"No, I can't make sense of this," Bernard said. "But I don't see how it could have anything to do with the library other than she was killed here."

"If you think of anything, please let me know," the chief said. "I hope my questions didn't upset you too much. We'll be going now."

"Chief, how long will the library need to be closed?" Bernard asked.

The chief paused. "Do you need in her office for anything?"

"No."

"Let me make sure we're finished upstairs, but I don't see why you couldn't open Friday as long as her office stays shut."

"That will probably be exactly what everyone will want to see," Bernard said with a grimace.

The chief nodded and walked out, followed by Sims.

Once they were outside, Sims asked, "What do you think of him?"

"I still don't think he did it, but the boy may have a few problems," the chief said. "Let's try to keep a close eye on him for the next few days."

*

"I can't find any of them, Bernard," Millie said, handing Bernard the shipping invoice that he had picked up off the ground yesterday morning before finding Agatha's body.

"They have to be here somewhere," Bernard said. "We couldn't have lost an entire box of books."

"Maybe they're in there." Millie pointed at Agatha's office. "Can I go see?" she asked eagerly.

"You're dying to look inside there, aren't you?"

"No, of course not," Millie said, looking wistfully at the office door. "But she always unpacked the books in her office. That's all I was thinking."

"True enough," Bernard said. "I guess it won't hurt if we look inside. We'll stand at the door."

Millie followed him eagerly to Agatha's office. A yellow banner that read 'Police Line: Do Not Cross' hung across the door.

Bernard unlocked and opened the door. Millie leaned forward and gasped.

"Wow, it's really trashed," Millie said. "This is so exciting! Are those brown places her blood?"

"Yes," Bernard said. "Quite a little ghoul, aren't you?"

"I've never seen where anyone was murdered before," she said. "You know, this is like something off of Shadow Seekers. Do you watch it?"

"I don't watch soap operas very often," Bernard said.

"Oh, you should," Millie said. "Right now, Joshua has developed an evil second personality. And it's driving Kristin crazy – that's his wife – because she's attracted to them both."

"I'll have to try to catch it sometime," Bernard said. "Well, I don't see any boxes in here."

"No, unless there's one behind the desk. Should I go look?"

"That won't be necessary," Bernard said dryly. "It's sitting too close to the wall; the box we want wouldn't fit behind it."

"Oh," Millie said, disappointed.

Bernard closed the door. A night's sleep had lessened the

impact, and looking in her office hadn't bothered him. Maybe the shock of finding Agatha had undone what the shock of his father's death had done. And that's our pop psychology for today, he thought.

"Is it okay if I go to lunch now instead of at one?" Millie asked as they walked over to the circulation desk. "I'm supposed to meet my mother at the Fashion Fountain and try on clothes. I'll be back in an hour."

Agatha had always been a stickler on lunch times for the help. Bernard went at twelve and returned at one, Millie went at one and got back at two, and Agatha went at eleven and came back when she was good and ready. But Agatha was gone, and Bernard was in charge, at least for the time being.

"Sure," Bernard said. "After lunch, I want us to get caught up on our shelving. Since we're closed today, it'll be a good time to do that. And maybe we'll run across those books."

Millie grabbed her purse and hurried out of the library. Bernard locked the door behind her. He didn't want anyone wandering in for a look, and Millie had keys. In his office, he picked up the phone, dialed the hospital, and asked for Lisa's room. A woman who identified herself as Rita answered the phone and told her that Lisa was sleeping, but had been awake earlier and complaining about the hospital food. Bernard told Rita to tell Lisa that he had called and hung up.

He looked at the shipping invoice again. It was dated a week ago and listed fifty hardcover books, including four bestsellers that he had wanted Agatha to order for the library. Where could they be? he wondered. Could she have taken them home?

He thought about Agatha's procedure on checking in books.

She had always insisted all deliveries be brought unopened to her office where she could open them at her leisure. Sometimes books would remain in her office for two or three weeks before she gave them to Millie or Bernard to be cataloged and checked in. Bernard had simply put it down as another one of her bizarre eccentricities.

Could there have been something else besides books in the missing box? Something that someone would kill for? Man, I have completely lost it, Bernard thought disgustedly. Next thing you know I'll be making Agatha into a drug lord.

"Enough," he said, mentally shaking himself. "Time to get to work."

The book cart wasn't behind the desk. He looked around, then remembered he hadn't brought it back down after he found Agatha. He walked up the marble stairs. A yellow police banner was pinned across the aisle where he found Agatha's body. He looked at the white tape on the floor that outlined where her body had been. The book cart wasn't there, but was pushed all the way back down the next aisle. He pushed it out and picked up a book: *The Joys of Kite Flying* by Webster Bennings. He looked at its spine to read its Dewey Decimal number, which was 796.15a BEN.

He carried it to the 790's and was about to place it on the shelf when a thought occurred to him: What did the 'a' in the number mean? The 796.15 placed the book in The Arts classification under the subdivision of Recreation. The 'BEN' was the first three letters of the author's name.

Bernard pulled another book out of the shelves. No 'a' on its number, but there it was on the next book. He began to randomly check books. Most had a small 'a' after the number. He moved to the 600's. Nearly all of them had the letter. He checked other shelves. The 'a' showed up on all the newer books and most of the older ones.

Could the 'a' stand for nonfiction? He went downstairs and began to check the fiction stacks. The fiction books were grouped by authors, and their classification was simply the first three letters of the authors' names. Most also showed a small 'a' either at the top or bottom of the spine.

He went to the juvenile section. He knew a small 'j' marked all the juvenile books. Perhaps the 'a' stood for adult. He quickly discovered he was wrong as several of the books he looked at were marked with both letters.

Thinking over the past few months, he remembered that he had noticed the 'a' before and had meant to ask Millie or Agatha about it but hadn't done so. If I'm going to be in charge for a while, I should know how we classify books, he thought.

He heard a noise up front. Millie must have returned. But as he walked around the staircase, he saw a man in a blue sports jacket opening the door to Agatha's office.

Bernard stopped. Could this be the murderer? His heart raced. "What are you doing?" he demanded.

The man jumped, tried to turn around, and stumbled to the floor. He swore and got up. "You about gave me a heart attack, you know that," he said, brushing off his clothes.

"I'm sorry," Bernard said, not moving any closer. "But who are you? And what are you doing here? Why were you looking in that office?"

"I'm Neal Gibson," the man said, walking toward Bernard and extending his hand. "You must be Mr. Worthington."

Bernard backed away. "You haven't told me what you're doing here, and I'd rather you didn't get any closer."

Gibson looked baffled. "I don't understand."

"Someone was murdered here," Bernard said. "If I'm overreacting, I'm sorry, but I would like to know what you're doing here."

"Jumpy, aren't you," Gibson said. "But I guess I can't blame you. I own Skyways Real Estate. Mrs. Ryton-Storer asked me to do an appraisal of the library." He pulled a sheaf of papers from his coat pocket. "Here it is. She didn't tell me if it was for her or the library, and so I thought I would stop in and see if someone knew. I haven't been paid for it."

"Why were you looking in the office?" Bernard asked, indicating the yellow police banner.

Gibson looked abashed. "Well, I was just curious. I didn't go inside."

Bernard slowly relaxed. Gibson seemed harmless. He also realized the real estate agent must think he was paranoid. "I'm sorry about my behavior." He walked over to Gibson and put out his hand. "I'm afraid that the murder has left me a little edgy."

Gibson shook Bernard's hand. "It's okay. Actually I was feeling a little awkward myself. I mean, I don't want to seem uncaring about Mrs. Ryton-Storer, but if the library needs the appraisal, I need the money for doing it. I have the bill for it." He pulled an invoice out of his pocket.

"I'm afraid I don't know anything about an appraisal," Bernard said. "She didn't say why she wanted it?"

"No," Gibson said, looking disappointed. "I was hoping it was for the library."

"Not as far as I know," Bernard said. "I could call the city and see if they know anything about it."

"Thanks. I would appreciate it."

Bernard phoned the city offices but couldn't find anyone who knew why Agatha had ordered an appraisal.

"Well, I guess I lost out," Gibson said. "Thanks for checking. Here's my card. If you should find out anything about it, I'd appreciate a call."

"When did she order it?" Bernard asked.

"Last week," Gibson said. "I came by last Wednesday night and looked over the inside and looked over the outside Thursday. I had to check on a few things and was supposed to get back with her today. Of course, she … passed away yesterday."

"Millie and one of our part-time helpers work late on Wednesdays instead of me, or I would have recognized you," Bernard said. "I'm sorry I couldn't be more help. Maybe you could file a claim against her estate."

"That's an idea. Thanks." Gibson nodded and left, passing Millie who smiled and spoke to him cheerfully.

"You know him?" Bernard asked Millie as she dropped her purse and some shopping bags behind the counter.

"Oh, yes, I've known Mr. Gibson for years," she said. "I went to school with his daughter Georgia. She's married to Mike Carter now. Mr. Gibson owns Skyways Real Estate and, I think, some businesses in the city. He used to have lots of money, but when his wife left him, she took a big chunk of it. Or so I've heard. Boy, his daughter sure was a cow, I mean, a real heifer. And stuck up. I never did like –"

"Thanks," Bernard said hastily. "I've got some errands to run. Why don't you get started on the shelving, and I'll be back about two."

Bernard left the library, wondering why Agatha would want an appraisal and whether he should tell the chief about it.

*

The chief could see that Richard Storer, the brother-in-law of the late and so far unlamented Agatha Ryton-Storer, was shook up, but didn't know whether it was because the murder had rattled him or because he was standing knee deep in the wreckage of his late sister-in-law's house. Someone had systematically torn Agatha's small house apart. Her belongings were on the floor, most broken; the seat cushions of her living room couch were shredded.

"I found it this way," Storer said. "I can't believe someone would do this."

The chief nodded, mentally kicking himself. He should have sent deputies over to the house yesterday.

Sims came into the living room. "Chief, all the rooms are torn up like this."

"Figures," the chief grunted. "Mr. Storer, we had better go outside so that we don't disturb anything. There might be some evidence in here. Sims, you'd better call for some help and start dusting for prints."

Storer followed the chief outside to the covered porch and stood quietly. The bookstore owner was slight, with sandy brown hair and a crease in his brow. He looked rumpled with his tie loosened and his shirt wrinkled.

"Are you doing okay, Mr. Storer?" the chief asked.

"Yes." Storer sighed. "This is ... I'm taking this harder than I thought I would." He took a deep breath. "I took off work for a few days so that I could handle all the arrangements. I was planning on staying here, but I guess that won't be possible?" He looked questioningly at the chief.

"At least not for a couple of days until we're finished, if you don't mind," the chief said.

"No, that'll be fine. I have an uncle I can stay with." Storer watched as Sims went to the police car to use the radio. "Tell me how she died," Storer requested so quietly the chief could barely hear him.

The chief thought for a moment, looking for a gentle way to tell the story, but couldn't find one. "Sometime between seven and eight Tuesday morning, someone attacked her in her office in the library. Her throat was cut. She was found upstairs by her assistant around nine. Also that morning, the murderer killed a man who possibly could have identified him, and later that night, he may have attacked a woman for the same reason. She survived, but unfortunately she's unable to identify him. We don't know much more than that."

Storer never looked up, studying the unkempt lawn as if it was a tome of precious knowledge. Storer was so quiet and still that the chief began to get uneasy.

"Are you okay, Mr. Storer?" the chief asked again.

Storer sighed. "Yes, this has been quite a shock." He moved to the side of the porch and sat down on the old wooden swing. It creaked uneasily, and the chief decided he wouldn't test it by sitting down, too.

"I was wondering if you could tell me anything that would help me understand why this has happened," the chief said, leaning against the porch railing. He felt that something about Storer's reaction wasn't quite right, but he couldn't pin down what.

"I doubt that I would know much that could help you," Storer said, knitting his fingers around his knee. "Agatha pretty much lived her life, and I lived mine. We talked about once a year, usually on August tenth." He stared at the porch roof. "That's the anniversary of my brother's death. And we never talked long. To be honest, I always wondered why she called. I guess that I was the nearest thing to my brother she could find. And she did like to hold onto things."

He pulled out a pack of cigarettes and offered one to the chief.

The chief shook his head. "Never picked up the habit. Why did you have keys to her house?"

"Two or three years ago, Agatha went to California to attend a relative's funeral. She asked me to check on her house while she was gone. I came up and spent a few days here and visited some old friends. She had a spare set of keys for me, and I never gave them back. I forgot I had them until you called."

It occurred to the chief why Storer's reaction seemed off, so he said, "If you don't mind me asking: if you weren't close, why are you so upset?"

Storer laughed shortly. "Good question. It's hard to tell you how I feel about Agatha. She was rude, irritating, insensitive – pick your bad quality, she had it. Still, she was always there. Kind of like an old sofa that you hate and intend to move to the basement, but you never get rid of. It's hard to explain. But I'll miss her. And she was a connection to my brother."

The chief nodded. He could understand that. "Tell me, are you familiar with the library?"

Storer lit up the cigarette and took a long draw. "No. I haven't been in it since it became a library thirty years ago."

"Did you know there was a safe in her office?" the chief asked.

"No, though it doesn't surprise me," Storer said. "Old Eliah loved secrets, and Agatha was a lot like him."

"Do you have any idea what she would keep in it?"

"No. Agatha and I weren't that close."

The chief shrugged casually. "Just wondering since whatever was in there was gone."

Storer didn't reply.

The chief tried a different tack. "Could Agatha have had any jewelry or anything like that?"

Storer laughed shortly. "No, the Ryton family jewels were stolen a long time ago by Agatha's sister. Or at least that's what Agatha always said. Of course, she believed Eve was actually Satan in disguise."

"That would be Evelyn Ryton," the chief said, moving upwind from Storer's cigarette smoke. "We haven't been able to find an address for her."

"I might have an old one," Storer said. "We haven't stayed in touch. Not after –"

"Not after?" the chief prompted.

"My brother's death," Storer said.

The chief felt certain that Storer had almost said something else.

"Was there any particular reason Agatha didn't get along with her sister?" the chief asked.

Storer seemed startled. "Well, what do you know. Old scandals do die. I didn't think this town would ever forget."

The chief waited.

"My brother was killed over thirty years ago in a car accident," Storer said. "He was driving too fast on Watts Ridge and went off the side of the cliff. Just an hour before, he had told Agatha that he was leaving her and running away with another woman. The other woman, of course, was her sister Evelyn."

*

Lisa woke up in pain in a room she didn't recognize. Her throat throbbed, and her face felt numb and swollen. She started to panic and tried to rise, but the effort was too much. She slid off into darkness again.

When she woke again, a nurse was checking her pulse. "Where am I?" she tried to ask, but only a strangled noise came out.

"Ah, you're awake," the nurse said. "I'm Tina Hayden. You might know my husband, Deputy Hayden."

Lisa tried to talk again and did a little better. "Where am I?" she rasped. The effort created spasms of pain in her neck.

The nurse looked concerned and said, "You're at the hospital, dear. Dr. Osborne treated you last night, but you're going to be fine.

You have a slight concussion. That and the medication has you all mixed up right now."

Lisa nodded. She could remember her attack in startling detail, but after that, it was hazy, disjointed.

"Dear, we were wondering if you had any relatives that you might like us to call. Your friend Rita didn't know."

"Rita was here?"

"Yes," the nurse said. "She heard about it on the radio and came to see you. I'm afraid you were sleeping all the time she was here."

"She used to work with my mom at the truck stop," Lisa whispered.

"So is there anyone you'd like us to call?"

Briefly considering her elderly Aunt Stella, Lisa finally shook her head. Stella had enough health problems of her own without worrying about her grandniece.

"Well, Rita said she would be back later."

Lisa started to nod, but fell asleep again. It was afternoon before she opened her eyes again. Her thoughts were clearer, and the pain in her bruised throat had settled down to a dull throb.

"You're awake."

Bernard's voice startled her. He sat in a chair beside her.

"I only got here a few minutes ago," he said. "I didn't want to wake you."

"Obsidian?" she asked in a soft whisper.

"Oh, he's fine. I went around this morning and fed him again. How many times a day should I feed him?"

Lisa held up two fingers.

"Okay, I'll go around tonight. Rita was here when I got here. She went down to the cafeteria." He looked embarrassed. "I think she thinks we're … dating."

Lisa raised her head a little. "Did they catch him?"

"No. He ran away when I showed up, but the chief thinks they will soon," he said. "There's a policeman outside your door."

She leaned her head back and closed her eyes. She felt bereft and beaten. Tears welled up. Suddenly Bernard reached out and took her hand.

"I want you to know I'm here for you," he said.

For some reason, him saying that seemed funny. And it was even funnier that she saw Rita stick her head in the doorway and smile knowingly at them. She tried to laugh, but it hurt. She drifted off to sleep as he held her hand.

CHAPTER FOUR

The peach trees never seemed tall enough to the chief. Although he knew the semi-dwarf Harvesters and Loring Stark Brother varieties were designed to be ten to twelve feet tall, they looked like overgrown bushes that shouldn't produce anything other than their crescent-shaped leaves. But the trees' branches sagged gently with pastel-colored peaches in lush abundance. He smiled as he regarded the fruit. They'll be ready to pick in a couple more weeks, he thought.

He walked over to the irrigation pump and connected the main water line, which branched into several smaller pipes. Each pipe ran down a row of trees and had an emitter at each tree. Peaches required a lot of water. The chief started the pump. Its chug-a-lug faded in the background as he headed back to his car to sit while the pump pulled water from the well for the thirsty trees.

Although it was only the middle of May, the sun soon made the car uncomfortably warm. He got out and started walking the rows, something that he had done a lot lately, trying to make sense of Agatha's murder. Brewer's murder was easier to find a motive for; he'd simply been in the wrong place at the wrong time.

It had been over a week since the deaths, and the chief attended

Agatha's funeral this morning. Few people showed up: only Bernard, Lisa (sporting a new, even larger purse), Richard Storer, Mayor Brunson, a couple of councilmen, the chief and Maggie, and a handful of elderly ladies who seemed to show up at all the funerals of people of their generation. The funeral depressed the chief as it seemed to emphasize that he was no closer to catching Agatha's killer.

Once again he went over the few facts he had. The same person or persons had killed both Agatha Ryton-Storer and Leonard Brewer. That was established; the forensic report said the same weapon had killed them both. No motive yet for Agatha's murder. But Brewer was killed apparently because he had seen the murderer while changing his flat tire. And Lisa had been attacked because the killer was afraid she could identify him.

Mores the pity, Lisa had been too drunk to remember what the killer looked like or simply never saw him at all. Sims had even convinced the chief to have Lisa hypnotized by that dentist who used it for "painless" tooth surgery. She recalled nothing of value.

After some thought, the chief released the fact that Lisa couldn't identify the man. He hoped her attacker would realize that he was safe and not attack her again. So far it seemed to be having the desired effect. The chief was still having her house watched. He'd rather err on the side of caution in this situation.

Jay Jones, the janitor, remained missing. An APB was issued on him, but no sightings so far. The chief wished he could believe Jones killed Agatha and Brewer and ran when his attempt to kill Lisa failed, but he couldn't. Even if Jones had killed Agatha, too many questions remained. Why would he and Agatha be meeting in the middle of the night? What was in the safe? Why was Agatha's body carried upstairs?

The chief sighed. He couldn't find any answers. He had gone through Agatha's house thoroughly and discovered nothing. Same for the janitor's apartment. He read the coroner's reports until he could recite them. He questioned Bernard and Lisa until they dodged him on the street.

Bernard and Lisa. Now, there's an interesting couple, the chief thought. Bernard had visited Lisa at least twice every day she had been in the hospital, and when she got out the day before yesterday, he'd been the one to drive her home. Last night, Sims had seen them at The Señor restaurant and said they were holding hands and "makin' eyes" at each other. The chief hoped Lisa had finally found someone who would treat her decently. She hadn't had an easy life, and it would be nice if one good thing came out of this awful mess.

The chief looked at his watch. He'd better head for the house. Agatha's will was to be read today at one, and the chief intended to be there. He thought it would probably be a waste of time, but right now, he was clutching at straws.

After a quick lunch with Maggie, he arrived at Harold Hastings's office on time. Maybe being here isn't such a bad idea, the chief thought as he surveyed the people gathered to hear Hastings read Agatha's will in his quiet and too sincere voice.

Bernard sat on the leather-bound sofa, talking quietly to Lisa who was taking notes on a yellow spiral pad and looking around like a dog sitting under a barbecue grill. Richard Storer, looking tired and uncomfortable, sat in a chair across from him. Neal Gibson, on the other hand, looked relaxed and jovial as he sat chatting with Timothy Fiddler, vice-president of the First National Bank of Ryton. Hastings was at his desk, ostentatiously going through some legal papers.

The intercom buzzed. Hastings picked up the phone.

"Yes?" He listened for a moment. "Send her in." He replaced the phone on its cradle with the slow, deliberate speed that so grated on the chief's nerves.

The chief looked at the door as it opened, and a woman stepped in. She wore a plain white dress that emphasized her extreme thinness. A large white hair barrette firmly held her white hair. White hose, white shoes, and a large white leather-look purse completed the monochromatic outfit.

"Eve!" Richard Storer stood.

"Rich." The woman nodded in acknowledgment, glancing around the room.

"Come in, Miss Ryton," Hastings said. "This is Evelyn Ryton, Mrs. Ryton-Storer's sister." He introduced everyone else in the room. The chief noticed her gaze lingered on his badge a moment when he was introduced.

"Eve, I tried to get in touch with you, but you'd moved," Storer said. He looked even more uncomfortable.

Evelyn nodded. "Yes, I moved to Tulsa six years ago. I saw no reason to update you."

"Miss Ryton contacted me yesterday," Hastings said. "Very fortunate since we were already seeking her regarding the will. Now that we're all here, shall we get started?"

The chief squashed an impulse to say no.

"Mrs. Ryton-Storer recorded her last wishes in a legally prepared will and on this cassette." The lawyer held up a tape cassette that he placed in a player. "While the recorded version is not in the proper legal form, the will is. If everyone is ready ..." He pushed a button, and Agatha's sharp tones filled the office.

"I, Agatha Wilhelmina Ryton-Storer, being of sounder mind than most and certainly more sensible, do order my goods, wealth, and property to be disposed in the following manner:

"To Richard Storer, I leave all the photo albums and pictures of his brother and any of my books he might desire. We have been through harsh times together, and I hope his life is better for having seen how bravely I have held myself during these many long years of adversity and pain."

"I can't believe it," Richard Storer muttered.

"To my sister Evelyn Ryton, I leave our mother's brooch. Mother would have wanted me to have it and I had intended to be buried with it, but since Evelyn stole all the other jewelry, she should also have this piece. It could possibly be the very first precious thing she's ever received without committing theft. And, Evelyn, *he* would have come back to me. He would have."

Evelyn Ryton simply shook her head and looked at the floor.

"My other belongings, goods, house, and property are to be sold by the Gibson Auction Service. The money received from the auction of such items and the rest of my financial securities are to be given to the Ryton Memorial Library on the condition that it be renamed in my honor, the Agatha Wilhelmina Ryton-Storer Memorial Library, a fitting and deserved tribute for my many long years of faithful and devoted service to the library and to the community of Ryton."

Bernard looked pole-axed while Lisa scribbled frantic notes.

"I name Harold Hastings of the law firm, Hastings and McLadd, as executor of this will."

Hastings switched off the player and picked up some papers.

"These are copies of the will," he said as he passed them out. "I will be happy to answer any questions."

"No, thank you," Evelyn Ryton said, rising. "All of this is perfectly clear. She only placed me in the will so that she could have one more chance to attack me. Sell the brooch, too." She turned to leave. The chief rose.

"Miss Ryton, I would like to talk with you if you don't mind," the chief said.

Evelyn looked at him for a long moment. "I have some other calls to make today. Perhaps we could talk tomorrow."

The chief didn't like the way she made her last statement sound like an order but decided not to press it. "That would be fine. Would around ten in the morning be okay?"

"Yes," she said. "I'm staying at the Eagle Inn." She left, her heels clicking a staccato rhythm.

"I don't have any questions," Richard Storer said hastily and followed Evelyn out.

The chief could hear him calling after Evelyn. I wonder what they have to talk about, the chief mused.

Neal Gibson was talking to Hastings, and from the gist of the conversation, Gibson was being hired to appraise and auction Agatha's house and contents. Gibson seemed to find the whole will immensely funny and was chuckling as he left.

Bernard, however, was not laughing. "Mr. Hastings, I would have to consult with the Library Board about this, but I don't see any way they would agree to rename the library."

"Mrs. Ryton-Storer and I anticipated your response," Hastings said. "But I think when you have all the facts, you might reconsider. I asked Mr. Fiddler here because Mrs. Ryton-Storer banked with First National. Timothy, if you would give Mr. Worthington a financial report on the estate now."

"Well, this was on short notice," Fiddler said, opening a briefcase and pulling out a sheaf of papers. "But I prepared this for you." He handed the papers to Bernard. "Of course, you must understand that much of Mrs. Ryton-Storer's monies are in certificates of deposit, bonds, and other investments of that nature, some of which have not reached maturation. She was conservative in all of her financial dealings, but she knew when to take the proper risks. I think you will find –"

Hastings cut in. "I think Mr. Worthington would be more interested in the value of her investments, Timothy."

Fiddler looked annoyed. "Harold, he should also be made aware that some of the investments are not fully realized as of yet and that it would be in the library's best interest if care was taken in handling the estate and liquidating the assets."

Now, this is interesting, the chief thought. It appeared to him that Fiddler was worried that the library might want all of Agatha's money immediately. How much did she have?

Bernard apparently had the same thought. "Mr. Fiddler, exactly how much money are we talking about?"

"Actually, it's impossible to say exactly," Fiddler said. "As I was saying, many of her investments have not been realized fully in the way of financial –"

"Your best estimate would be fine," Bernard said.

"Well, at the moment, in our bank ..." Fiddler wiped his brow. Bernard leaned forward as did the chief. Hastings watched them with a vaguely superior smile while Lisa's pen hovered over her notebook like an eagle over prey.

Timothy Fiddler told them how much money the late Agatha Ryton-Storer had in the First National Bank of Ryton.

The chief broke the silence first. "Well, I'll be dipped in vinegar. She was rich!"

*

"Imagine that," Lisa said as she and Bernard drove to her place. "All this time, Agatha was a multi-millionaire. This is going to make a great story!" And she needed to sell another one to the Dispatch. Her checking account was getting a bad case of anemia.

She had worried that Veit would assign another reporter to cover the murders while she was in the hospital, but the Dispatch editor had not – probably due more to being short-handed than her writing skills, she thought ruefully. If he had known about the attack, he probably would have, but he didn't learn of it until the morning of the second day after it happened when Bernard had faxed her story to the Dispatch.

"What I'd like to know is where that money came from,"

Bernard said, turning onto Owens Street. "It doesn't make any sense. More than once she told me that Eliah Ryton left her nothing. She was very bitter about it."

"Eliah was her grandfather, right?" Lisa asked. At Bernard's nod, she continued, "So what happened to her parents?"

"Well, this story is from Millie, who says her mother told her, so your guess is as good as mine concerning its truth, but Millie says Agatha's mother, Margaret, was pretty wild, at least by the standards of that time. She ended up getting pregnant. She never told anyone who the father was, and he never showed up. Margaret died giving birth to Agatha and Evelyn – fraternal twins if you haven't guessed. Old Eliah raised the girls, but he could never forgive their mother. So he took it out on them."

"Good lord, it's like a soap opera," Lisa said. "I actually feel sorry for her. It's no wonder she was such a crone."

"Yeah, maybe. In some ways, I guess life does shape us, but it's still not an excuse to let it make you mean," Bernard said. "What she said to her sister in that will was vicious, pure and simple."

"Sometimes it's hard not to be bitter," Lisa said slowly. "It's easy to say you shouldn't let things affect you, but it's a lot harder to do when you're the one they're happening to. And when you're pushed around a lot, there comes a point where you start getting mad at the world because its sole purpose seems to be to dump on you and then you decide to start dumping back." Lisa realized Bernard was looking at her strangely. "I'm not saying it's right. I'm just saying it's understandable. And maybe her sister really did steal the family jewels. We don't know that she didn't."

"I guess so," Bernard said, pulling up in Lisa's drive.

Lisa thought about it for a moment, thought about it some more, and asked, "What exactly does 'I guess so' mean? Does that mean: 'Yes, I agree' or does it mean: 'No, I don't agree, but I'm too polite to say so.'"

"What kind of question is that?" Bernard asked.

"One I want an answer to," Lisa said, looking squarely at Bernard.

"I guess it means I don't know for sure," Bernard said. "Does it matter?"

"Yes, it does," Lisa said. "One way, you're being judgmental, and the other, you're being understanding. There's a big difference."

"I don't understand what we're talking about or why you're getting upset," Bernard said. "Why is this a big deal?"

Lisa sat quietly. She realized why she had started this and gathered her courage to tell him. "Because I couldn't get deeply involved with someone who saw the world in such a bleak and black-and-white fashion."

A long silence.

"Are we getting deeply involved?" Bernard asked.

"I don't know," Lisa said. "I'm confused about us, about if there's even an 'us' to be confused about. What exactly are we to each other?"

Bernard didn't say anything.

"We've been together a lot these past few days," Lisa said. "And we've done some making out so I know this is a more than just friends. I'd like to know if we're going to try to be more than that."

"Do you want us to be more than just friends?" Bernard asked, looking out the side window and apparently finding Lisa's garbage can endlessly fascinating.

"I don't know. Do you?" Lisa asked, seemingly finding the shrubs that lined her drive as interesting as Bernard found her trash can to be.

"What does being more than friends mean? Are we talking about going steady, having sex, getting married, or all or none of the above?" he asked.

"Some, all, or maybe none," Lisa said.

"That's not much of an answer."

"Sorry. I don't know. But I think we need to talk about it," she said, looking at him. "I don't know if we have something good here or not, but I think it might be. I'm willing to find out if you're willing."

Bernard looked at her.

"Well?" she asked, feeling her pulse in her temples.

"I don't know what you want me to say," Bernard said. "I think if something happens between us, it'll happen. I don't think we can force it."

"That's not what I meant," she said. "But if we don't make some choices toward that direction, it won't happen because circumstances aren't going to allow it."

"What circumstances?" he asked.

"Look, I'm having to make some decisions here," she said. "I don't have a job, and my money is getting low –"

"I'll loan you some," Bernard cut in.

"Thanks, but no thanks," she said. "That's not good for any

relationship. What I'm trying to say is that if we have something good here, I'll try to find a job in Ryton. If not, I'm probably going to try to get one somewhere else."

"I think you should do what's best for you and not worry about our relationship," Bernard said. "I mean –"

"Never mind," she said getting out of the car quickly. "Good night." She walked to the house, hoping he would come after her. He didn't.

She closed and locked the door. Picking up Obsidian, she walked up the stairs to her bedroom. When she looked in the vanity mirror, she realized tears glistened on her cheeks. She wiped them away. This is stupid, she chided herself. I've barely known him for a week. We come from entirely different backgrounds. He's only being friendly. And if it's anything more on his part, it's because he's on the rebound from Sherry what's-her-name.

She took a deep breath. Obsidian purred as she scratched his head gently. Placing the cat on the bed, Lisa sat down at her desk. It was unlike her to become attached so quickly to someone. Since the attack she seemed unable to control the swings of her emotions. Sometimes she became afraid for no reason.

The chief had told her yesterday that he was no closer to finding whoever attacked her and murdered Agatha and Leonard. It made her angry that her assailant was still out there, literally getting away with murder, while she jumped at every unexpected noise and strange shadow.

Yesterday she had spent a large amount of badly needed money on a handgun. She had never owned a gun in her life. Now, a blue-steel weapon rested in her top desk drawer. The man at the sporting goods store had shown her how to load it and told her that the YMCA had a shooting range she could use.

She walked downstairs and mixed herself a rum and Coke. Sitting on the sofa, she took two sips before she stopped, appalled at her unconscious response to the situation.

What am I doing? What. Am. I. Doing? She poured the drink down the kitchen sink.

"I'm too strong for this to break me," she said, listening to the sound of her words and pulling strength from them. Tomorrow, she would see about talking to that friendly minister at the United Fellowship Church. She knew he counseled people and didn't charge for his services. Rita thought the world of him. She nodded to herself. Talking to someone would be a good idea.

She went back upstairs and sat down at her typewriter to write a story about Agatha's will. Those mysterious millions will certainly pump new interest into the story, she thought.

Tomorrow I'm going to type up my résumé and see about getting on as a reporter for the Dispatch. I'm not going to be able to live on what they pay a stringer. If Veit doesn't want to hire me, maybe he can suggest another paper that will, but I'm finished with Ryton. She nodded firmly and began to type. She became immersed in the story and only thought of Bernard occasionally.

*

"You don't have to rush off so early," Dolores Hyatt said.

"I'm really tired, and I have a lot to do at the library tomorrow," Bernard said, rising from a chair in the Hyatt's living room. "I'm going to go in early and get started on some paperwork that should have been done a month ago."

"I guess being the acting Head Librarian is keeping you busy, especially since Agatha hadn't been doing her job," Michael Hyatt said as he put his arm around his wife.

Sherry was sitting on the floor near her mother and father and smiled up at Bernard. "Mom would probably let you have more of that cake if you asked her nicely."

"Tempting offer, but I've got to go," Bernard said. "Thank you for the meal. It was delicious."

"You're always welcome, Bernard," Dolores said. She rose and headed for the kitchen. "Mike, if you would help me, I think we could get most of the clean-up done tonight, and I wouldn't have to worry about it tomorrow."

Michael rose with alacrity. "Be right with you, dear." He shook Bernard's hand. "It's been good seeing you again, Bernard. Don't be a stranger." He promptly followed his wife into the kitchen and closed the door behind him.

"Obvious exit, if I've ever seen one," Sherry said, smiling.

Bernard laughed.

Slowly the smile left her face. "You know, Daddy was very upset with me when we broke up. Of all my boyfriends, he liked you the best. He says I made a mistake."

Taken aback, Bernard couldn't think of anything to say.

She looked up at him. "Why don't you stay and talk for a while?"

Bernard sat back down, and they talked for an hour or so more.

Or actually he listened as she told him in exhaustive detail about a clerk in some store who had attempted to convince her that burnt orange was her color. While she talked, Bernard watched the lights glisten off her auburn hair. He studied the shape of her face, her perfect blue eyes, the expressions she made as she imitated the clerk, her quick gestures; once he had been content to simply be with her. To his surprise, he found himself stifling a yawn.

Finally he stood. "I've simply got to go and get some sleep. I can barely keep my eyes open."

"I had no idea I was that boring," Sherry said with mock dismay.

"You know that's not it," he said, wondering if it was. "I've not been getting enough sleep lately with all this stuff going on."

"You shouldn't worry so much," she said as she walked him to the door and then paused at the threshold.

"You're right. Thank your parents again for me, and thank you for inviting me," he said. He was outside and at his car before he realized she had been waiting for him to kiss her good night. She had already closed the door. Stupid, you missed a chance, he chided himself, but for some reason, he couldn't get worked up about it. Too tired to think straight, he decided.

Bernard drove home, his mind drawn back to his conversation with Lisa earlier in the day. What did she expect me to say? he wondered. I don't know how I feel about her. I like her, but I don't want her making decisions about her life based on our relationship – whatever it might be. Things go wrong all the time. Look at Sherry and me. And after what Sherry had done to him, he didn't think he would be ready for a deep relationship for some time – supposing, of course, he and Sherry were finished.

A few days ago, he had no doubts that their relationship was over; now, he wasn't sure. Since that day in the library, he had eaten dinner with her family three times counting tonight, and she had called at least once every day. He couldn't decide if Sherry was attempting to start over or was only trying to be friendly. After all, she might have hesitated at the door because she was trying to avoid kissing him, not because she wanted him to. He wasn't sure how to interpret her actions.

And he didn't understand his, either. Barely a week ago he would have given anything to have Sherry back, and now he wasn't sure how he felt about her. Can a person change that much in a week? he wondered. And where does Lisa fit into my life? Is she a friend or something more?

It occurred to him that he had not mentioned the meals or the calls to Lisa. And why should I? he asked himself. It's not like I'm cheating on her. But it still bothered him that he hadn't.

As he passed the library, he turned in on an impulse. I've wanted to read that new Carolyn Hart book, and maybe it will get my mind off all this.

He walked to the doors, unlocked them and entered, still wrestling with Lisa and what she represented. He flipped on the lights and walked back to the shelves. He found the book quickly and noticed a small 'a' adorned its spine. He shook his head in exasperation. Millie and the other library aides had no idea what the 'a' meant. He would have dismissed it as simply an outdated classification except it also appeared on the most recent books, apparently inked in by Agatha herself.

He checked the book out and flipped the lights off. He stopped dead. Out of the corner of his eye, he could see a thin strip of light beneath the door to Agatha's office. He caught his breath. Was someone – the murderer – in there? Could the police have left the light on? Yesterday morning, Sims had told him that the office could be cleaned and used again, but Bernard hadn't got around to telling Franklin Kane, the new janitor, yet. The yellow police banner still hung in place, not that it would keep people from simply going underneath it if they wanted in the office.

Bernard listened intently. Suddenly the air conditioner clicked on, its humming sounding like thunder to Bernard's over-sensitive hearing. He started, nearly dropping his book. He swallowed. Should he call the police? He'd feel ridiculous if no one was in the office. Still, wouldn't it be better to be ridiculous than dead? He gave himself a mental shake. He was letting the events of the past few days make him paranoid. He flipped the library lights back on and walked over to the office door. He pulled the police banner down and turned the doorknob.

The light in the office went out! Bernard stumbled back, panicked. Someone was in the office.

Backing into the circulation desk, Bernard suddenly realized he was a perfect target. He scrambled over the counter, knocking pencils and papers everywhere. He grabbed the phone and dialed 911.

"Emergency services."

"Get the police over to the library now!" Bernard whispered.

"Sir, you'll have to speak up. I can barely –"

"Get the police to the library now," Bernard said. "This is an emergency. Someone has broken in. I think it may be the murderer!"

"Sir, stay calm. Your call is being relayed. Who is this?"

"Bernard Worthington. Please send the police."

"Help is on the way. Are you in any danger now?"

"I don't know."

"Can you leave the building safely?"

"I don't know. I'd have to go past whoever is in there," Bernard said. "But the door is closed –"

"Don't chance it. Stay put. Help is on the way. Do you know if the intruder is armed?"

"No."

The dispatcher continued to talk to him, but Bernard was no longer listening. He thought he heard someone move in the office. Cautiously, he peered around the corner of the counter.

He couldn't see anyone, but the office door was slowly opening!

He pulled back.

"Sir, are you there? Sir –"

"I'm here," he whispered. "Where are the police?"

"They're on their way. Where are you at in the library?"

"I'm behind the circulation desk. In the lobby."

He was still there when Sims and another officer, guns in their hands, entered the library.

"Bernard," Sims called softly.

"I'm here," Bernard said.

"Has he left the office?" Sims asked.

"No," Bernard said.

"Okay, you stay there and keep your head down."

I think he's enjoying this, Bernard thought. He carefully glanced around the corner of the desk and watched as Sims and the officer slid along the wall to Agatha's office.

"This is the police," Sims said. "Come out with your hands over your head."

Silence.

Two more officers came in and took up positions around the lobby.

Sims slowly reached around the doorway and turned on the lights in the office. He jerked his hand back. Nothing happened.

"I'm going in," Sims told the officer. He crept around the doorway, crouched over. Absurdly Bernard thought about the Hunchback of Notre Dame. He waited for a shot or a shout or some noise.

Sims came out of the office. He looked both disgusted and relieved. "There's no one here. Bernard, are you sure no one came out?"

"Yes, he would have had to come right past me." Bernard got up, went over to the office, and looked inside. It looked the same as when he last saw it. "Did you check behind the desk?"

"Yes," Sims said curtly and turned to the other officers. "Why don't you guys look around outside and then go call in."

The officers holstered their guns and left.

"The windows?" Bernard asked with a sinking feeling.

"Both locked."

"Someone had to be in here because the lights went out when I touched the door," Bernard said.

"Maybe it has a short." Sims flipped the light switch up, the lights went out, flipped it down, the lights came on. He repeated the action a few times. "Doesn't seem to be anything wrong."

"But the door opened," Bernard said.

"You must have turned the knob," Sims said. He looked at Bernard's stricken face and sighed. "Hey, don't take it so hard. You've been through a lot this week. It's no surprise you're a little edgy. Why don't you go home and get some sleep. You'll feel better in the morning, Bimmer."

"I guess you're right. I'm sorry about this. But when the light went out, I thought ... Well, never mind." The worst thing, Bernard thought, is that I *won't* die of embarrassment.

Sims helped him pick up the scattered papers and other items Bernard had knocked onto the floor earlier.

"I've got to get back on patrol," Sims said.

"Why are you working tonight?" Bernard asked as he turned the library lights out. "I thought you were on day shift."

"I am, but I'm covering for Philip Owens this week. He's on vacation. Nice guy but really crazy about fishing."

Bernard locked the doors and walked to his car, only half-listening to Sims. He felt like a fool. And he knew that the story would be all over town tomorrow. With my luck, Lisa will sell it to the Dispatch. At least I won't be here much longer. He remembered the Carolyn Hart book. He had left it on the circulation desk. It's just as well, he thought. I don't think I feel like reading a thriller right now.

Sims waved and drove off. Bernard paused at his car door and looked back at the Ryton Memorial Library. In the darkness, its turrets, tower, and Gothic trimmings gave it an evil air that a haunted house would envy. Bernard couldn't suppress a shiver.

He drove home, thinking of unsolved murders, undefined relationships, and unexplained lights.

In the dark and quiet library, the office door closed firmly.

*

"I do not think I can help you, Chief Donaldson," Evelyn Ryton said as she glanced around the lobby of the Eagle Inn. "My sister and I haven't spoken in years. I have no idea who could hate her enough to kill her, but, knowing Agatha, I imagine your list of suspects is rather long – quite possibly the entire city." The morning sun, beaming through the tall windows, glared off her red pantsuit and red shoes. Her hair was pulled back by a red barrette.

The chief had always believed that environment played the largest factor in determining the personality of a human being. After having spent a few minutes questioning Evelyn and comparing her with Agatha, he was beginning to think there could be a genetic factor for meanness. Of course, they did slither out of the same environment, he thought.

"Do you have any idea what could have been in that safe?" he asked, squinting in the sunlight and wondering if she always dressed in one color.

"As I've already mentioned, Agatha and I were not in communication. So I have no way of knowing what she kept in there."

She settled back. "When we were children, it contained our great, great uncle's Civil War journal and a few other war souvenirs that Grandfather considered priceless. I wonder what became of them."

"I believe they're in a display in the library," the chief said. "On the second floor."

Evelyn seemed amused. "Grandfather would have liked that. I imagine that's why Agatha put them there. She spent a lot of time attempting to win his favor. Even after he was dead, she couldn't break the habit."

"If you don't mind me asking –"

"Would it matter if I did?" she cut in.

"No." The chief was developing a real dislike for the woman. "As I was saying, why didn't you and Agatha get along?"

"Surely you've heard the story," Evelyn said with a sly twist to her voice. "About how the evil sister Evelyn stole the shining, pure husband from the good sister Agatha and about how the husband went off a high cliff in a fast car." Suddenly she looked tired. "It was a long time ago."

The chief waited.

"It was a long time ago," she repeated. "Is it important now?"

"Could be."

She looked at his face and then down at her hands. "There's not much to tell. Agatha married Kenneth Storer. They weren't right for each other. He fell in love with me, and we decided to run away together. On his way to pick me up, he lost control of his car, and it went off Watts Ridge. He was killed. Agatha never forgave me." She paused. "I left Ryton soon after."

The chief nodded. "Sometimes it's best to leave places that have painful memories."

"Oh, that wasn't why I left," she said. "Grandfather gave me no choice, thanks to dear Agatha. His house – the library now – was broken into the day after Kenneth died, and Mother's jewelry was taken. Agatha convinced Grandfather that I was the thief. He told me to leave town, or he would have me arrested. I went to stay with an aunt. I never saw him again." She paused and made an impatient gesture. "How could this possibly be important?"

"Maybe it isn't. I have to check everything I can."

The chief shifted in his chair so that he could see without the sun in his eyes. "Can you tell me where you were the night Agatha was killed?"

"I believe I was home. Alone. Watching TV." She smiled. "I don't know if I could prove it, however. Will I have to?"

"I'm not accusing you of anything," the chief said. "I'm trying to find out who killed her."

"She'd like it if I went to jail for her murder," Evelyn mused. "She blamed me for her bad marriage, the theft, everything that went wrong in her life. I believe she always thought that if she could blacken me enough, Grandfather would love her. What she couldn't understand – what took me years to understand – was that the old man couldn't love anyone. I think our mother's death killed it in him." She shook her head. "I have always wondered why he didn't send us to the orphanage."

"Perhaps he actually cared about you," the chief suggested. "Some people have a hard time in showing their feelings."

"If you had known him, you would realize what a completely asinine statement that is," she said. "I think he simply couldn't bear to see anything that belonged to him escape. Agatha was a lot like him. It nearly killed her when he left the house to the city. Even worse was losing all that money. I wasn't surprised she became librarian; it was the closest she could get to the fortune."

"She seemed to have quite a bit of money herself," the chief said. "A millionaire several times over."

"Yes, that surprised me when Hastings told me this morning," she said. "I think he's hoping that I'll contest the will so that he can prove what a good attorney he is. He and I grew up together. Do you know he's never married? I don't think he will ever find anyone who loves him as much he does."

The chief couldn't keep from smiling. "You know him all right. Are you going to contest the will?"

"No, I'm sure it would be a waste of time and money. Narcissistic as he may be, Hastings knows what he's doing." She shrugged. "Let her buy her memorial. It's the only way she'll ever get one." She paused, the hard lines of her face softening. "I shouldn't say that. She's dead now, and she was my sister. I wish I had known about all this sooner. I only learned of her death because a friend of mine in Oklahoma City read about it in the paper and called me. I would have liked to have attended her funeral. Did you go?"

The chief nodded.

"Was it a nice service?" Evelyn asked, looking old. "I took some flowers out to the grave. She's buried next to Mother."

"It was a nice service," the chief said, gently.

"Well, good. I'm glad for that." Evelyn checked her watch. "Will you need me much longer? I have an appointment with Hastings at eleven. He's going to give me the brooch. I've decided to keep it."

"One more question. Do you know where her money came from?" the chief asked.

"I have no idea. She certainly didn't inherit it. Grandfather left us nothing. You might ask Rich. He told me that he had kept in touch with her somewhat over the years." She sighed. "Poor Richard. If he had been more exciting, perhaps none of this would have happened."

Looking at the chief's puzzled face, she barked a short laugh. "I thought you knew. Admittedly, it is ancient history, but I expected you to be familiar with the whole sordid story."

The chief gave her a hard questioning look.

"If Richard had been a little more exciting," she said, over-emphasizing each word, "I might have never left him."

"You were ..." The chief was taken aback.

"Yes, I was married to Richard, but unlike Agatha, I took back my maiden name." She smiled bitterly. "Are you surprised? It was practically a French farce. While Kenneth was cheating on my sister Agatha with me, I was cheating on his brother – my husband, good old Richard Storer – with him. You should have seen it. Everyone sneaking around and trying to hide from everyone else. It must have been very funny."

The chief thought about what it had cost the people involved and said, "No, I think it must have been very sad."

The smile faded from her face. The chief rose, excused himself, and left her sitting alone.

CHAPTER FIVE

Bernard watched Benjamin Rivers intently, hoping that the fat little councilman wouldn't say anything else. The Ryton City Council had already sat through two of Rivers's mind-numbing speeches, and Bernard wasn't sure if he could endure another one. Or actually if his rear could. Bernard decided that if he was ever a councilman, the first thing he would do was get padded chairs in the city hall auditorium.

"Any other business?" Mayor Otis Brunson asked.

Bernard sent a silent plea upward, promising to teach Sunday school, or feed the poor, or do some other selfless service, but his bribe was ignored.

"Yes, I have something I think we should discuss," Rivers said, his jowls shaking as he nodded his head vigorously, looking like those toy nodding dogs Bernard occasionally saw in the back windows of cars. "For some time, we have needed a new system to allow us to maintain better control of the city's finances." He held up some papers. "I believe I have formulated a plan that will accomplish that and also correct some problems that our treasurer seems unable to do anything about."

The other councilmen sighed, exchanged glances, and resignedly listened as Rivers expounded – in numbing detail – his plan for a new accounting system for the city. City Treasurer Merriman Smith glowered at Rivers.

Bernard shook his head in exasperation and leaned back in his seat, stretching his legs under the seat in front of him. He was waiting for the Library Board meeting, which would follow the Council meeting. The Board meeting was scheduled to begin at seven-thirty, but Rivers had apparently decided to launch another offensive in his ongoing war with Merriman Smith. The two men had battled for years.

When Bernard first moved to Ryton, he had started attending the City Council meetings, fascinated by the interplay and workings of city government and by the rivalry between Rivers and Smith. Even now he might have enjoyed watching the fight except he was eager to discuss Agatha's will with the Board. Bernard was certain they would approve the name change – in fact, he had decided to recommend it; whatever his personal feelings about Agatha were, she had served the library for thirty years – and he wanted to discuss a couple of ways that the money could be spent, the chief of which was finally computerizing the Ryton library and making Internet access available to the patrons.

But first on the agenda was a recommendation to appoint Bernard as the new Head Librarian. Bernard checked his shirt pocket to make sure his short acceptance speech was there. The mayor had called him this afternoon to tell him to prepare one.

"I don't think you'll have any trouble being appointed," Brunson had told Bernard. "The Board recognizes your ability and skills. And several people have called me to express their support. Why, Michael Hyatt's even called twice."

Thinking about the call, Bernard found it bothered him that Sherry's father had spoke to Brunson. Although he had always liked Michael Hyatt, Bernard had never been close to him. He felt like he was supposed to be grateful for the support. I don't want to owe him anything, Bernard thought. My relationship with Sherry is already too complicated as it is.

Bernard looked around the auditorium. It was empty other than him and a couple of elderly men who always attended the meetings to give their opinions on any and all issues. Occasionally the auditorium would fill up when a controversial subject was on the agenda, but for the most part, the Ryton City Council operated without citizen input. Which seemed to be the way the Council liked it and might explain why the chairs were so uncomfortable.

A movement at the back of the room caught Bernard's eye. He could see a woman standing outside in the hall, but she was too far back for him to identify. He hoped it was Lisa. He tried to call her twice today and received no answer either time. He thought they needed to talk, although he didn't know what to say that would mend the rift that had developed in their relationship last night. He hoped she would.

Rivers finished his speech, and Bernard's attention was drawn back to the meeting. Smith was obviously intending to respond but didn't get a chance as Mayor Brunson hastily said, "We should certainly look into the matter. Do I have a motion to adjourn?"

Almost as one, the councilmen said, "Aye." Smith subsided

with an angry look at Rivers who pointedly looked everywhere except at Smith.

After shuffling papers, Brunson, who also served as the Board's chairman, finally called the Library Board meeting to order. The last month's minutes were read and approved as Bernard waited impatiently, unconsciously tapping his fingers on the arm of his seat. Brunson favored him with a smile.

"Bernard, come up here and sit down," Brunson said, pulling back a chair.

The various councilmen nodded their greetings to Bernard as he seated himself at the table. A woman walked into the auditorium, but it wasn't Lisa. A camera hanging at her neck, Sherry waved at Bernard. Disappointed, Bernard still smiled back and thought it was nice of her to come to see him become Head Librarian. She sat down in the front row and adjusted her camera.

Brunson reached over to turn on a cassette recorder. It was an election year, and Bernard was certain the tape of this would find its way to the local radio station where its one-person news staff would accept it gratefully and give the mayor some free publicity in the form of a news story.

Reading from a paper and leaning toward the recorder, Brunson began. "As you know gentlemen, we have a position to fill at the Ryton Library, that of Head Librarian left vacant by the tragic and senseless death of Mrs. Agatha Ryton-Storer. We are fortunate, however, that we have a trained person already on the library's staff who I believe will be able to handle the job with the professionalism and efficiency that Ryton residents have come to expect during my administration. I'm talking about Bernard Worthington, of course. I would like to go on record now as recommending him for the position based on his experience, education, and knowledge – three attributes that I place above all else in hiring our city's employees to serve our fine citizens."

Smith rolled his eyes at that statement. Bernard tried to not grin. He glanced away for a moment and realized someone was still standing in the hall. He couldn't see who. He focused his attention back on the mayor who, after asking if there was any need for discussion and finding that there wasn't, was now calling his recommendation to a vote.

"All in favor of Bernard Worthington being employed for the position of Head Librarian of the Ryton Memorial Library say 'Aye' and be counted," Brunson said, being unnecessarily formal and long-winded for Bernard.

A chorus of aye's.

"All opposed, say 'Nay' and be counted." The mayor barely paused. "The 'ayes' have –"

"I'm sorry to interrupt you, Mayor Brunson, but I think I should save some of your time in case it is valuable," a woman's voice cut in, startling the entire Board.

The woman that Bernard had glimpsed in the hall now walked toward the front. With a sinking feeling, Bernard recognized her.

Evelyn Ryton smiled brightly as she said, "I am Evelyn Ryton, and as a direct descendent of Eliah Ryton, I claim the job of Head Librarian of the Ryton Memorial Library as per the terms of his bequest to the city. I believe I should join you now, gentlemen. I'm sure we have many things to discuss." She reached the front, walked up the steps of the stage, and sat down next to Rivers.

The mayor shut the recorder off.

*

Lisa drove into the city hall parking lot. Bernard's car was still parked in it. She frowned and looked at her watch. Nine-thirty. The Board meeting should have been over an hour ago. Belatedly, she remembered Bernard was to be hired as Head Librarian. I didn't mean to miss that, she thought. I know what I'll do. I'll take him out for coffee and a burger to celebrate. Besides, that will give us time to talk. And she felt they should talk, although she didn't know what to say. She hoped he would. She had gone by his house earlier, intending to speak with him, but he was out. She found herself driving past the Hyatt's home, almost afraid to look and see if his car was parked there. She hadn't realized how good an empty driveway could look until then. It was practically art.

She had considered calling him a couple of times today but put it off, reluctant to face the emotional problems he raised. He, however, remained on her mind most of the day as she went about her various tasks: faxing her story to Veit, typing her résumé, calling newspapers in the area and getting addresses, picking up another ribbon for her typewriter, and so on. She had also set up an appointment with the United Fellowship minister, Lewis Morgan. Talking with someone would help her, she believed, and he seemed nice and knowledgeable over the phone.

John Towers, her former editor, had taken her to dinner and told her that a group of local businessmen were trying to raise enough money to buy the defunct *Ryton Journal & News* and pay off its debts. He asked her if she would come back to work for him when and if the paper resumed publication. Barely a week ago, she would have jumped at the chance, but a lot had happened since then. She was beginning to feel if she didn't make something happen for herself now, she would never have another chance. Let's face it: I'm not getting any younger, she thought ruefully. And I can't see me staying in Ryton all my life. She had told Towers she'd think about it. He assumed she had been hired as a fulltime reporter with the Dispatch. He didn't know she hadn't gathered together enough courage to ask Veit for a job.

Tomorrow, I'll ask him, she promised herself as she walked up the sidewalk. Entering city hall, she immediately saw Bernard talking with the mayor and one of the councilmen. Not wanting to interrupt, she glanced around and saw Merriman Smith at the drinking fountain.

"Merriman, how are you doing?" she asked, moving over to him but keeping an eye on Bernard.

"Lisa, my girl, how are you?" Merriman asked, a rare smile flowing across his face like desert rain. He had known her for more years than she could remember, and Obsidian was one of the offspring of his cat Slate.

"I'm doing okay," She said, frowning as she watched Bernard who seemed upset.

"Good. I was wondering how you would make out when the paper closed, and then I hear you're working for the Dispatch. I knew you had it in you."

"Thanks," she said, smiling at him. "But I'm just stringing for them right now, and that's a ways from a job yet."

"You'll be one of their reporters soon, I bet."

"What's going on over there?" she asked, indicating Bernard and the mayor.

"Oh, boy, you missed a good meeting tonight – at least, the Library Board meeting was," Smith said. "In the Council meeting, that fool Rivers proposed the stupidest fiscal plan I've ever heard in my entire life, which is saying a lot when you consider that I vote Republican."

Lisa couldn't care less about Rivers, but during the years, she had learned not to push Smith. He would get to the Library Board meeting in his own sweet time. She listened patiently as he unfavorably compared Rivers to bathroom bacteria and told her what he would have told the City Council had he been given a chance.

Finally he got to the Board meeting. Lisa listened in amazement as he detailed Evelyn's entry and how it had completely thrown the entire Board.

"You should have been here," he said. "I felt sorry for your boyfriend, but you should have seen the look on Brunson's face. I just about split a gut."

"What happened after that?" she asked, shifting so she could get a better view of Bernard's face. No wonder Bernard is upset, she thought. First, he suffered through Agatha, and now there's Evelyn to carry on and take what should be his job.

"Well, they all got into a big debate about what they should do, and they decided to ask the city attorney for an opinion on her request. It was so late that they adjourned without covering another thing on the agenda. Basically they put her off until the next meeting so your boyfriend is in charge until then." Merriman leaned close. "I think they're going to have to give the job to her, but they're afraid since they offered it to Bernard, he might sue."

"Bernard wouldn't do that," she said, shaking her head. "He's not that type of person." She looked back at Bernard and the mayor. The mayor patted Bernard on the back and moved off.

"Thanks for the information. I'll see you later." She quickly hugged Merriman and headed for Bernard.

Before she reached him, Sherry Hyatt stepped out of the ladies' restroom. Lisa stopped. Sherry glanced her direction, casually took Bernard's hand, and spoke to him. Bernard looked at Lisa and dropped Sherry's hand like it had burned him. Lisa struggled with a sudden impulse to jerk Sherry Hyatt bald-headed.

He came over to her, Sherry trailing behind.

"I heard," Lisa said flatly before Bernard could speak. "What do you think they're going to do?"

"Probably give the job to her," Bernard said. "Brunson told me that I could continue on as assistant, but he thinks they'll have to honor the terms of old man Ryton's will if they want to keep the building."

"Can't they reduce her authority or something?" Lisa ignored Sherry, who was standing way too close to Bernard as far as Lisa was concerned.

"Ryton's will detailed the job duties," Bernard said. "He was a cagey old coot, I'll give him that."

"What are you going to do?" Lisa asked.

"I don't know," Bernard said.

"Surely you don't plan to stay here now," Lisa said. "Not after this. What about your other job offers? Do any of them look good?"

"I haven't followed up on them," he said. "I was waiting to see what happened."

"Well, now you know. Ryton doesn't have much for you anymore," Lisa said. She realized she was pushing, but she was angry and didn't care.

"He might have more here than he thinks," Sherry said, smiling even though her voice had an edge in it that could cut bone.

Lisa glanced at her, then looked back at Bernard. "I was going to take you out for coffee to celebrate your promotion. We could still go and talk."

Bernard looked uncomfortable, glancing at Sherry.

"How nice," Sherry said, still displaying those white teeth that Lisa was thinking about making into a necklace. "But Bernard and I already have plans."

"Some people from church are getting together tonight at the Pizza Shack," he said. "It's late, though –"

"I'm sure they'll still be there," Sherry said. "Joan told me that they weren't going to get there until nine."

"You're welcome to come," Bernard said.

Sherry's smile became strained.

Lisa looked at him, marveling at the stupidity of men. "No, thank you." She walked away.

"What about tomorrow?" he asked.

"Thank you, but I'm busy," she flung back over her shoulder.

"I'll call you," he said.

She went out the door without answering. She stalked to her

car, talking angrily to herself. You blew it, Bernard M. Worthington. That was the last time I humiliate myself for you. You can go to –

"Lisa, wait," Bernard said from behind her. "I want to talk to you."

Lisa whirled around. "I thought you were going with Sherry," she bit out.

"I told her that I needed to talk to you," he said. "I thought it was more important."

She took a deep breath. "Okay, let's talk."

"Don't you want to go somewhere else?"

In way of a reply, she walked over to a stone bench by the sidewalk and sat down.

He followed her.

They sat in silence and watched the parking lot empty. Sherry looked over at them, hesitated, and drove off in a flurry of gravel. They listened to the night sounds for a while.

When he spoke, his voice was quiet. "I don't know why you're so mad at me. I thought we had become friends. I need to know what you're thinking."

"That's exactly what I was going to say to you," Lisa said. "What are you thinking?"

"About what?"

"About the situation in the Middle East, of course," she snapped.

Silence.

"I need to know what we're talking about," he said tightly. "I don't think I deserved that."

Lisa sighed. "No, you didn't. Sorry."

He considered her for a moment. "It's okay. I think we've both had too many shocks this week."

"I'd like to talk about us," Lisa said.

"I'm all ears. Although I think I ought to see a plastic surgeon about that."

"Be serious."

"Sorry," he said. "What do you want to talk about?"

"Well, for one thing, is there an 'us' to talk about?"

Bernard was silent for a moment. "I don't know. I think there is, but I don't know. Do you think there is?"

"Haven't we had this conversation before?" she asked wryly.

He smiled. "I believe so. And it was so much fun the first time, too." His smile faded. "I don't mean to be avoiding the question. I honestly don't know. This is all very different for me."

"In what way?"

"I guess it's different because I keep feeling like I need to make a decision about it." He looked at her. "It's like this. All my life, it seems things have always worked out for me. I mean, I didn't so much choose to be a librarian as it chose me."

"You're not about to tell me about a bright light coming from the sky and the voice of Dewey speaking to you, are you?"

"Now, who was telling who to be serious a few moments ago?"

"Sorry."

"Actually, I like your idea, but that's not how it happened." He looked down at the ground. "After my father ... died, I started finding it hard to make decisions. Everything seemed pointless. Why decide to do anything when you could end up in a drainage ditch? I drifted along, and it seemed like all my decisions just happened." He shrugged. "My mother was a librarian. I guess libraries may have seemed safe. I certainly knew a lot about them. When I went to college, I drifted through it. Don't get me wrong, It's difficult work, and I had to work hard for my degree, but I don't know if I really chose it."

"What about Sherry?" Lisa asked quietly.

"Almost the same thing. We ran around in a group together. Everyone assumed we'd be a couple." He slapped at a gnat." This is kind of sick, but in a way, I was glad when all this happened because it meant I didn't have to make any decisions about a new job."

"Well, that explains why you worked six months with Agatha," Lisa said.

"Yeah, I guess most people wouldn't have lasted that long. Of course, for the first few months, I was staying for Sherry."

Lisa shook her head. "You know, it's funny in a weird way. You and I have exactly the opposite problems. You have trouble making decisions, and I make them too fast. I rush around a lot, changing things, readjusting my life to suit my mood, and never considering all of the consequences. I've ... wrecked some things that way. I push too hard. I guess it's because I feel like I've never had anything so I want everything. And I want it right now."

"What do you want, Lisa?" Bernard asked, turning to face her. "What do you want right now?"

Lisa paused, then the answer came clawing out. "I want to catch the bastard who attacked me!" She burst into tears. Bernard reached out, placed his arms around her, and gathered her to him. He held her until the tears passed.

"Okay," he said softly. "We will."

*

The chief was at the station at eight the next morning. Sims was sitting in his office as he entered. The chief grunted a hello.

"Chief, we caught Jay Jones last night!" Sims exclaimed.

"I know," the chief said. "The scanner woke me up."

"Oh." Sims looked crestfallen. The chief decided to give him a chance to crow, and besides, he was interested in the details. He had nearly come to the station last night, but Maggie had pointed out he wasn't needed. She wasn't too keen on him leaving the house at two in the morning.

"Tell me about it. I only caught the tail-end." He settled back, enjoying Sims's excitement.

Sims began eagerly. "Harris went by Rochelle's Bar about one o'clock just to check it out." And to see his girlfriend, I bet, the chief supplied silently. "When he went in, he noticed Jones sitting in a side booth, just as bold as a bare butt. He called me, and we went in the front while Hayden and Edwards covered the back. But he wasn't in the booth when we got there. We walked around, and I thought we had lost him. We were leaving, but I needed to use the john. And there he was." Sims paused. "Of course, I waited until he was finished."

"Good work," the chief said. "Did he give you any trouble?"

"No, he just acted surprised. He didn't resist at all." Sims sounded a little wistful. "He was carrying a hunting knife, but he didn't try to draw it."

"Well, maybe next time," the chief said, keeping his face straight. "He was carrying a knife?"

"Yeah, is that important?"

"Maybe." The chief frowned. "It's unlikely if he was the murderer that he'd be carrying the same type of weapon that killed Agatha and Leonard. But then again, some murderers take a likin' to what they use. Pigs to their slop." The chief pushed away from his desk and rose. "Let's see if he'll talk to us. Remind him he can have an attorney if he wants one."

"We read him his rights."

"Remind him again. But before you get him, I have an idea I'd like to try out. Here's what I want you to do." The chief told him and waited while Sims did it and went for Jones. He wondered how the peaches were doing. He needed to water them later. The county agent had said he was going to drop by and check the trees today, also.

Sims brought Jones in. The janitor, dressed in camouflage pants and an orange hunting vest over a gray sweatshirt, looked frightened and angry. Sims sat at the writing desk, opened a drawer, and pulled out his new toy: a voice-activated tape recorder that he had convinced the chief to purchase. The chief had agreed but insisted Sims had to continue to take the statements, also.

"Have you been advised of your rights, Mr. Jones?"

"Yes." Jones sat slumped over in the chair.

"Would you like an attorney present?"

"No."

"We're going to record this, for your protection and ours," the chief said, motioning to Sims.

"Do anything you want." Jones stared at his handcuffed wrists.

The chief studied him for a moment. "Take the cuffs off him," he ordered Sims.

Sims looked like he wanted to protest but obeyed the chief. Jones rubbed his wrists.

"Would you like some coffee?" the chief asked. Jones nodded slowly. The chief looked at Sims again who reluctantly went to get it.

"Aren't you afraid to be alone with me?" Jones asked. "They told me everybody thinks I'm a killer two times over."

"Should I be afraid?"

"No!" Jones burst out. "I didn't kill the old bat! I didn't kill anyone."

"Okay," the chief said. "So tell me, where have you been?"

"I've been squirrel hunting. Around Muldrow if you know where that's at." The chief shook his head. "It's about ten miles west of Fort Smith, but in Oklahoma. Got some nice woods over there."

Sims brought in the coffee. The chief noticed Sims's holster flap was unsnapped. He hid a smile.

Jones took a sip of coffee. He seemed to be relaxing.

"Did anyone go with you?" the chief asked.

"No. I know that looks bad, but I've found the best way to not bag anything is bring some noisy idiot along." He looked earnest. "Besides, I really like to get out there alone in the woods. It's peaceful and quiet. I got back about eight last night. I dressed out some squirrels I got, and then I went to Rochelle's to kick back."

"What about your job?"

"I quit. Last Tuesday, I guess it was."

"Why did you quit?"

"Didn't she tell anyone?" Jones started to look scared again. His hand played with the empty knife sheath at his side.

"No."

Jones swallowed. "She called me about seven that night and wanted me to come out and move some boxes for her. She said she couldn't get them herself, but I think she was just being mean. I told her I couldn't. She said she would fire me if I didn't." He shrugged helplessly. "Before I knew what I was doing, I told her that I quit."

"You worked there for twenty years, and you up and quit like that?" Sims asked in disbelief.

"I got unemployment. And I was sick and tired of her chewing on me all the time." He hastily added, "But not enough that I'd kill her. You've got to believe that. You do, don't you?" Sweat beaded on his forehead.

"We're trying to find out what happened," the chief said. "No one is accusing you of anything. What did you do that night?"

"Well, I was already planning this hunting trip 'cause my vacation started next week – this week, I mean. So I decided to go ahead and leave. I threw my stuff in my camper, and I left about six the next morning. I figured it was no big deal." He stared into his coffee cup. "No big deal."

"Did you know there was a safe in her office?" the chief asked.

"No. She didn't let me in there except once a month. And when I cleaned, she'd be in there watching me, telling how I was leaving streaks on the windows or missing some dust somewhere." The janitor took a deep breath. "I know this sounds bad for me, but I'm not going to lie and say that I'll miss her. She was mean all the way down to the bone. When I quit, I felt like a load of bricks fell off my back."

"She was hard to get along with, that's a fact," the chief said. "Do you know of anyone who would want to kill her?"

Jones hesitated, a sly look coming momentarily to his eyes. He shrugged. "Not really. But I think you should talk with Worthington. He's always seemed a little odd to me."

"In what way?"

"Don't know. He strikes me as strange." Jones frowned. "Like he's never interested in 'guy' stuff. I've asked him a couple of times to go hunting or fishing, and he's always turned me down. Doesn't pay much attention to sports either. Hard to talk to him about anything. And lately he's been down 'cause he broke up with that Hyatt girl."

"So you think he killed her?"

"I'm not saying that," Jones said. "I'm saying maybe you should check him out."

"Perhaps so." The chief paused, apparently in thought, then said, "I think that's all the questions I need to ask you now."

"I can go?"

"Yes, but don't leave town. I might need to talk to you again." The chief pulled open a desk drawer and brought out a white box with Jones's name penciled on it. "Here are your personals. If you would go through them and make sure they're all there, Sims will sign you out."

Jones nodded and started putting things in his pockets as Sims checked the items off a list. Jones pocketed his billfold and some change. He deposited a comb, which the chief decided Jones had never used, in a vest pocket.

"Wait a minute," the chief said, leaning forward. "Sims, I think that's the wrong knife."

"Couldn't be," Sims said.

"It looks like the one P.C. left here after his last drinking spell." He looked disgustedly at the lieutenant. "Can't you keep anything straight?"

Jones picked up the knife and looked at it. "Chief, this one is mine. See it's got a nick in the blade from where I dropped it on concrete."

"You're sure that's your knife?"

Jones looked puzzled. "Yeah, but I thought I took my double-edged ..." His voice trailed off. He stared at the chief, suddenly horrified. "Oh, no –"

"Afraid so," the chief said. "That's the knife that killed Agatha Ryton-Storer and Leonard Brewer, and it belongs to you."

"I want a lawyer," Jones said, his face white.

"I expect you do."

*

Bernard stood in the center of Agatha's office. Under the guise of helping Franklin Kane, the new library janitor, clean up the debris, he and Lisa had thoroughly searched the office. With the broken items removed, the only reminders of the murder were the empty safe (which wasn't closed because no one knew the combination), the dark patch on the wall where the portrait of Eliah Ryton had hung, and the brown stains in the carpet that Lisa noticed Bernard was careful to avoid. Frank would take some carpet cleaner to the stains after lunch.

"What's next, Sherlock?" Lisa asked brightly in an extremely bad British accent. She was sitting cross-legged atop Agatha's desk, which was pushed against the inside wall so that they would have room to work.

"Let me think, Dr. Watson," Bernard said in an accent that was even worse. "Ah, yes, I believe I shall have to ... tickle you!" He rushed her, and the next few moments passed in frantic movement and laughter.

"Okay, okay, enough," Lisa said, breathless, after he trapped her in the corner. "We don't want Mrs. Hudson to catch us."

"I sent her out to get us some kippers and chips," Bernard said. He pulled her close.

"I'm very glad we talked last night, Sherlock," she said.

"Me, too."

He kissed her for a long moment. "I had no idea crime solving was so interesting. No wonder people enjoy it." He kissed her again.

"Hmm, don't you find that its greatest enjoyment lies in its intellectual stimulation?" Lisa asked.

"Oh, certainly." A kiss on her cheek. "You are positively correct." He nibbled at her neck. "In fact, I was thinking my intellect will need a cold shower soon."

"And we know what a great problem over-heated intellects are," Lisa said. "But wouldn't you be taking a chance to quickly expose your intellect to sudden cold? If I remember my high school physics, it could be dangerous. Didn't the surgeon general release some warning about it?"

"If he hasn't, I'm sure he will." Bernard nodded. "I believe you're correct. The best course to follow is to cool off gradually."

"I assume you have a plan, of course," Lisa said.

Bernard didn't answer.

"Bernard?"

"Oh. Sorry. I just realized that we were kissing in the same room that Agatha was murdered in."

"You do know how to kill a mood."

"Sorry." He pulled away and circled the room again. "I don't know what I was hoping to find here. Especially after the police went through it."

"It was a good idea," Lisa said. "Sometimes people miss things because they're looking with preconceived ideas about what they'll find."

"In that case, we should do well because we had no idea what we're looking for." He sighed and walked over to the light switch. "I wish I could figure out how this light turned off the other night." He flipped the switch down, turning off the light, and then up, turning it back on. "If it's a short, it must be a really short *short*, if you know what I mean."

"Maybe it wasn't the lights in here," Lisa said. "Could it have been car lights shining through the window? Maybe from the parking lot or the street."

"I think the windows are too high off the ground, but it wouldn't hurt to find out. Let's come back tonight and try it."

"Okay." Lisa nodded. She heard a noise from the lobby. "I think someone wants to check out a book."

"Be right back." Bernard went out the door.

Despite her banter, Lisa felt depressed. We spent all morning in here and didn't find a thing, she thought. Not that I really expected us to. After all, the police went over this office inch by inch. If there were anything to find, they would have found it. Who are we fooling? We have about the same chances of catching the murderer as Agatha does of being posthumously named Miss Congeniality.

Lisa walked to the door and watched Bernard talking to a couple of kids as he checked out their books. She caught his eye, and he smiled at her. She found herself smiling back. The day seemed better. Oh, girl, you've got it bad this time, she told herself.

As the children exited, they passed Evelyn Ryton, dressed in yellow from head-to-toe, coming in. She stopped a few feet from the circulation desk and looked around with a strangely sad expression on her face.

Bernard looked up and saw Evelyn. He stiffened. "Good morning, Miss Ryton."

"Good morning, Mr. Worthington," Evelyn said. She seemed amused by Bernard's expression. "I didn't mean to startle you. But surely you weren't so foolish as to think I would become your superior without familiarizing myself with the library first, did you?"

Bernard stared at Evelyn. His fists clenched. Lisa moved to stand beside him.

"Although I know this place too well." One side of Evelyn's mouth twisted up. "I spent many a horrid day here. Or upstairs where Agatha and I shared a room and I planned my escape from this mausoleum." She looked at Lisa. "Lisa Trent, isn't it? I remember you from the reading of the will. Richard told me that you're a reporter or something dreadful like that."

"I see you have face recognition down pat," Lisa said brightly. "Perhaps you can master politeness next."

Evelyn glared at Lisa, but ignored her comment. "Is that where she died?" she asked, pointing at the office. She walked over and looked inside. "Well, after the carpet is cleaned, I think I will enjoy working here."

Although Evelyn pretended seeing the site of her sister's murder did not affect her, Lisa noticed that the older woman's hands shook and that she briefly leaned against the doorframe as if she needed the support.

Evelyn turned back to look at Bernard for a long moment, then sighed. "I really don't mean for us to get off on the wrong foot. I know I'm taking your job, and I am sorry. But I think you will find that I work hard and learn quickly. I was always quite different from Agatha. We might, in time, even become friends." Her face hardened. "But make no mistake about it; I am going to be Head Librarian. You might as well get used to it."

"Why are you taking this job?" Bernard asked evenly. "It's not like we're talking about being the head of some multimillion dollar corporation. This is a library in a small city. It doesn't even pay that much." His voice rose. "Do you have any training at all? This library could offer Ryton many more services that it does now. Does that matter to you? Why would you even want to come here?"

Evelyn drew herself up. "What does what I want have to do with anything?" Her eyes snapped fire. "And as for money, what might not be a lot to you might very well be quite a bit for me. Agatha certainly did well for herself here. She died a millionaire. Perhaps I will do the same. It comes down to this: I need a job, and this one is open." She regarded Bernard coldly. "And if you were wise, you should start looking for another position now because I can already see that we are not going to be friends."

Bernard studied her. "You didn't answer my question. Why do you want to work here?"

Evelyn tried to meet his eyes, but he stared her down.

"Perhaps I do not. But I am going to be Head Librarian here." She paused and smiled slowly. "If you must have a reason, let's say I like the ambiance." She turned and left swiftly.

Lisa looked at Bernard. "Whoa, tiger, you sure lit into her," Lisa said, amazed that anyone could be that passionate over a library.

He let out his breath. "Yeah, I probably shouldn't have. But this library has really suffered under Agatha. In other communities, the library is part of the social and educational structure. It should provide a place where people can be exposed to new ideas and information. But this library is as isolated from the community as Agatha could make it. I've already been making plans to change that, and now Evelyn comes along ..." He shrugged. "Well, that's that, I guess."

"It's a shame," Lisa agreed. "But you know, I think it's odd that she would show up wanting this job. Most people don't want to be a librarian. I don't mean to be rude, but it's not the most exciting job in the world."

"It's had its moments lately, but you're right," Bernard said.

"So what I'd like to know is this: What's so important about the library that someone would kill for?" Lisa walked to the center of the small lobby and looked at the high ceiling, up the marble stairs, at the decorative scrollwork on the walls, and finally at Bernard. "When we know that, we'll know who the murderer is."

Bernard snapped his fingers. He pulled out a phone book and began to leaf through the pages. "I just remembered. Agatha hired Neal Gibson to do an appraisal on the library. He came by here to see if we would pay him after she died." He found the number. "I'd like to know what that appraisal said."

Not a whole lot, Lisa decided two hours later, as she sat in an imitation leather chair in the office of Skyways Real Estate and half-listened to Neal Gibson babble on about lowered land values and the lack of interest in large buildings during the "present state of our depressed economy," to use the real estate agent's words.

Lisa tried to focus on what Gibson was saying, but her mind wandered. Bernard hadn't been able to accompany her because Millie became sick at lunch and didn't return to work. Lucky him, she thought. I'm learning quite a bit more about real estate than I really wanted to know.

"When it comes right down to it, exactly what is the library worth?" Lisa asked, cutting into an explanation of perceived value as opposed to loan value.

Gibson frowned. "Well, wait, why don't you take the appraisal." He rummaged through the papers on his cluttered desk. "It's not like I'm going to use it. And it's apparent I'm not going to be paid for it. I thought about submitting a claim to Agatha's estate, but who knows when probate will be finished? It's not worth my time to pursue it." He pulled out several papers stapled together and gave them to Lisa. "Values are on the last page."

Lisa skimmed through it, impressed with the details. Gibson had faithfully cataloged every feature of the library. She found the figure noted for the library's market value and made a quick calculation. The library was worth about a fourth of Agatha's fortune, which would disappoint Bernard who had wondered if Agatha had planned to use her money to buy the library. She could have bought it four times over, Lisa thought. Maybe she not only wanted to buy back her family's home, but also wanted enough money to live in a style that I'm not accustomed to.

The phone had rung while she was reading, and Gibson was giving various home listings to the caller. Noticing the gray in his carefully combed hair, she realized he was about the same age as the Ryton sisters.

He hung up and turned to her. "I hope I've been able to help. And perhaps you could mention to Mr. Worthington that if he finds the appraisal useful, I'd appreciate something for it."

"I'll pass that on," she said. "Did you know Agatha well?"

He looked startled at the question. "Not really. She was difficult to get to know. Why do you ask?"

"I was wondering why she chose you to do the library appraisal and why her will chose you to sell her house," Lisa said without thinking how it would sound. She looked up to see Gibson regarding her with a tight smile.

"I do pride myself on having a good reputation," he said.

"I'm sorry," Lisa said. "I didn't mean that the way it sounded. It's that she didn't seem to like anyone."

"Well, I can understand that," Gibson said, apparently

mollified. "Actually, it surprised me, too, because I thought she disliked me. About six or seven years ago she was looking at selling her home. She called and asked me to look it over. Unfortunately, there was no way that she could get what she wanted for it, and when I told her so, she threw me out. I thought that perhaps she felt bad about the way she treated me, and that's why she asked me to do the appraisal and why her will specified me. Maybe she had a conscience, after all." He adjusted his tie.

"I wondered if maybe you knew her when she was younger," Lisa said, suddenly uneasy for some reason she couldn't define.

He settled back in his chair. "I guess I did in a way. Agatha and Evelyn were a few years older than I was so we weren't in the same classes at school, but I knew about them. Everyone knew about them. They were the biggest snobs in Ryton. Man, they were mean." He looked like he was thinking. "Mean to each other, too. I remember once Agatha mixed up Evelyn's clothes so that Evelyn came to school wearing a blouse and skirt that clashed violently color-wise. Agatha started making fun of her out on the playground. Evelyn lit into her, and it took three teachers to separate them. Evelyn kept saying, 'I'm going to kill her.'" He leaned forward. "Just between you and me, when I heard about the murder, I wondered if maybe she finally had."

"Do you think she did?" Lisa asked, absorbed by the story.

"I don't know." He shrugged. "But I do know bad blood ran deep between them. Particularly after that business with Agatha's husband." He picked up some papers. "I have an appointment in a few minutes. Is there anything else I could help you with?"

Lisa rose. "Thank you for your time." A sudden thought hit

her. "But I don't understand something you said. How did Agatha mix up Evelyn's clothes?"

"Oh, that," he said. "Evelyn is completely colorblind. I bet that's hard to live with."

"I bet it is," Lisa said. She smiled and left. As she drove away, she kept running over what he said. For some reason, she felt she was missing something, but she couldn't figure out what it was.

CHAPTER SIX

"So, Chief, do you think Jay did it?" Bernard asked, pulling the shade to cut the glare of the setting sun. From behind Bernard's desk, Lisa studied the chief. Bernard walked over to stand beside her.

"No, not really," the chief said, shaking his head slowly. "For a couple of reasons. One, I don't think he's the type. Two, he isn't stupid enough to come back as plain as he did if he had murdered her. And even if he had murdered her, it wouldn't matter."

"Why wouldn't it?" Bernard asked.

"Because we don't have any real evidence against him," the chief said. "I talked to the DA, but he thinks a good attorney would get an acquittal quick. Even if he got a conviction, we'd lose on appeal." He looked at Lisa. "Unless you can identify him?"

Lisa stared at the floor. "No, I don't think he's the one. I don't think he's tall enough."

Bernard slid his arm around her shoulders. He could hear the frustration in her voice and feel the tension in her neck. "But it is Jay's knife, isn't it?" he asked.

"Jones says he lost it a couple of weeks back." The chief

shrugged. "Who's to say he didn't lose it at the library? The murderer could have picked it up there. There were no prints on the knife, and it had been dipped in bleach before it got stuck in Leonard. All we have is circumstantial evidence."

"So we're no closer to finding the murderer than when this all started," Lisa said flatly.

"Well, I do think Jones knows more than he's saying," the chief said. "We don't have enough to charge him with anything, but we're going to keep him locked up overnight and hope that it rattles him into telling what he knows. You're right, though; we aren't any closer. I think the reason is there's somethin' about this case that we haven't figured out yet. Something that got Agatha killed."

"But what?" Bernard asked, spreading his hands. "Since we don't know what we're looking for, we could be looking right at it and not know."

"Maybe, maybe not," the chief said. "We can figure out a few things about it. For instance, it's got to be worth some money. And it's got to be small enough to have fit in Agatha's safe. Otherwise, the murderer wouldn't have looked for it there."

"Maybe he found it," Lisa put in. "It may not be here anymore. It could have been at Agatha's house. For all we know, he could be halfway to France now."

"Could be," the chief said. "But I'd bet he's still here in Ryton." The chief rested his palms on his knees. "This is what I'm thinking. On that night, Agatha met someone, someone who wanted something she had. Perhaps they met at her house, then drove here."

"Couldn't the killer have forced her to come here?" Lisa asked.

"Maybe, but I don't think so. Otherwise, why would he help Leonard change a tire? There weren't any rope burns or other signs that Agatha had been tied up. I can't see her meekly sitting in the car if something was wrong."

"No, meek wasn't the word for her," Bernard agreed.

"Also, we found some prints in Agatha's car that didn't belong to her," the chief said.

"I don't suppose they match up to Jay's, do they?" Bernard asked.

"No. Do you think he did it?" the chief asked.

"Not really, but I will admit he has always given me the creeps with all his hunting," Bernard said. "It seems his idea of enjoying nature is blowing holes in it."

"The prints aren't Jay's, but they do belong to a man so I think we can safely assume our murderer was a man," the chief said. "Especially since Agatha wasn't in the habit of consorting with men."

"Or anyone else," Bernard threw in.

"But why would they come to the library?" Lisa asked.

"That, I can't even begin to answer, and I think it's very important." The chief paused for a moment, apparently recapturing his thoughts. "So they come to the library together. The murderer wants something from Agatha, but she refuses to give it to him. They argue. He loses his temper and kills her. He searches the office for whatever it is that Agatha wouldn't give him. He doesn't find it, not even in the safe, but he does take whatever is in the safe. Which could be anything."

"So either he knew the combination to the safe or it was

already open," Bernard said. Open … He had the nagging feeling he was missing something. Or forgetting something. He shook his head in exasperation.

"Good point," the chief said. "Where was I? Yes, okay. He was taking Agatha's body upstairs for some reason when Bernard arrives early. While Bernard rides the elevator up, the murderer goes down the stairs and out of the library."

"Why didn't he take Agatha's car?" Bernard asked.

"Remember that he didn't plan on this happening," the chief said. "Perhaps he panicked and ran. Or maybe he was afraid her car would be easy to trace or that you'd notice him driving it. Ryton's not that big. He could walk to anywhere his car was. Also, that would explain why Leonard wasn't attacked until ten. He had to walk to his car and then find Leonard's address in the phone book –"

"Or maybe he knew Leonard personally!" Lisa said. "Leonard knew everyone in town."

"I hadn't thought of that," the chief said. "And I should have. I'll set a couple of men onto finding out who Leonard's friends were."

"So he kills Leonard." Bernard prompted the chief to continue.

"Yes, and he opens Lisa's purse and gets her address. He may have even gone there, but she's not home. He drives to Agatha's house and searches it – for what we don't know. He may have found it then, but if so, why was every room in the house trashed? If he found what he was looking for, he would have stopped searching. So I don't think he found it. He's still worried about Lisa so he tries to kill her. Why would he try to kill her?"

"Because he thought I could identify him," Lisa said,

puzzlement plain in her voice. "I don't understand where you're going with this."

"If the murderer had been someone from out of town, why didn't he leave?" the chief asked. "If he found what he was looking for, why not leave? I see him killing Leonard because Leonard got a good look at him. But, you, you never saw him, which probably means he didn't get a good look at you, either. And if he did, he would have seen you, uh, sleeping. The odds of you giving a description of him were slight. But why stay around town and take the chance? Unless he had ties here and didn't want to leave. Then he'd have a reason to want you dead."

"He couldn't take the chance she would run into him and recognize him," Bernard said.

Bernard and Lisa exchanged a glance.

"That could still happen," Lisa said. She looked at the chief. "I'm a target, aren't I?"

"Well, he may think he's safe," the chief said. "After all, you haven't identified him yet, and we've released that you can't. There haven't been any other attacks on you. The danger may have passed."

Lisa stared at the chief. He sighed.

"Yes, it is a possibility," the chief said.

"Great. Just great," Lisa said.

Bernard pulled her closer. "Do you think she should leave town?"

Lisa sat up. "I'm not going to let some creep run me off."

"Better safe than sorry," Bernard said. "I like you in one piece, and I think it would be good if you stayed that way."

Lisa didn't smile. "I'm not leaving town."

"I don't think that will be necessary," the chief said. "For one thing, he hasn't tried anything else. I think if I was him, I'd lie low for a while. Especially since your house is being watched by the police."

Lisa swore. "Sorry, all this makes me so mad, and ... I don't know." She walked across the room and stood in the doorway, her back to the two men.

Bernard looked at the chief. "Is there anything we can do to help?" Bernard asked.

"I want you to find out why this library is so important," the chief said. "And I have a theory about that. Embezzlement. I think she's been stealing money from the library for years. That's where her money came from."

Bernard shook his head regretfully. "I don't think so, Chief." He went over to his desk and picked up a ledger book. "I had already thought of that so I went through the books for the past couple of years. The only monies Agatha controlled were the book fund and the office fund. And she didn't even write the checks for those. Mayor Brunson as the Library Board chairman has to sign all of them. I don't see any way that she could have got her hands on the library's money."

"Brunson signs the checks?" the chief asked thoughtfully.

"After the Board approves them," Bernard said. "It would be very difficult for anyone to embezzle money."

"Hmm, well, I'm open for suggestions now," the chief said.

Lisa went to the desk, dug her notepad out of her purse, and sat back down. "Maybe it would help if we wrote down all the things we don't know."

"A good idea," Bernard said. "I hope you have plenty of paper."

"First, who killed Agatha?" Lisa said, writing. "Second, why was she killed? Third, what was the murderer looking for? Fourth, why is the library important? Fifth, where did Agatha's money come from?" She paused. "Did I leave anything out?"

"Sixth, why was the murderer taking Agatha's body upstairs?" the chief said. "Seventh, are we correct on why Leonard was killed? And on why you were attacked?"

"I think that would be the eighth question," Bernard said. "Another thing that's been bothering me. Why did Agatha have the library appraised?"

"She had the library appraised?" the chief asked.

"Yeah. She hired Neal Gibson to do it," Bernard said. "He came by here, trying to get paid. It wasn't legitimate library business so he was out of luck. I meant to tell you about it earlier, but I forgot."

"Don't know where that fits, but it's interesting." The chief scratched his head. "I think that's all I can think of."

"Me, too," Lisa said.

"One more," Bernard said. "Where do Evelyn Ryton and Richard Storer figure in this, if they do?" He looked at Lisa. "How many questions is that?"

"Ten," she said.

"I think if we answer any one of them, we will be very close to figuring this out," the chief said.

After the chief left, Bernard sat down on the couch. He patted the place beside him. "How about joining me over here? So we won't get cold. It's important to conserve body heat in inclement weather."

"It's close to ninety outside," Lisa said as she slid under his arm.

"See how well it's working," Bernard said.

"Oh, the wonders of modern science," Lisa said.

A sharp knock sounded on the doorframe. Sherry stood at the door. Bernard jumped up.

"Hello, Bernard," Sherry said.

"Sherry," Bernard said.

"I wanted to remind you that we were going to eat at six-thirty tonight, instead of seven," Sherry said, ignoring Lisa. "Daddy has a meeting later."

"Thanks, I forgot," Bernard said.

Sherry nodded, clearly reluctant to leave. "Do you need a ride?"

"I have my car," he said.

"You could leave it here, and I could drop you back by later," Sherry suggested.

"No," Bernard said. He could feel sweat on his brow. "I'll see you there in a few minutes."

"I'm free tonight," Lisa said brightly.

Sherry looked at Lisa. "I'm sorry. It's a family dinner, but we really must get together and talk sometime."

"Oh, let's," Lisa smiled. "I think I would enjoy that."

"Bernard, don't be late. Mom's made pot roast," Sherry said. She nodded curtly at Lisa and left. Bernard still had his back to Lisa.

"Well," Lisa said, "I'd better not keep you."

"Lisa –"

"Don't even –" She held up her hand. "Just go to your dinner. "And don't be late. We wouldn't want 'Daddy' to miss his meeting."

Bernard faced her. "Lisa, you said you were busy tonight. I don't see how it hurts to go over there. She's just a friend."

"Oh, give me a break," Lisa said. "Sherry will never be just a friend, and you know it."

"What does that mean?"

"Bernard, you two were going to be married!"

"You're jealous."

Lisa went to the desk. "No, I'm hurt. Bernard, I told you things last night that I've never told anyone. I thought we had something special. Do you and Sherry talk like we did? Do you still make love to her?"

"Lisa, I wouldn't –"

"No." She grabbed her purse. "I don't want to know." She went to the door. "But I've figured out what your problem is. It's not that you're afraid of making decisions; it's that you want to keep all your options open. Well, you'd better listen to me. If you keep trying to keep all the doors open, you're going to find them all closed someday."

"That's one of the dumbest –"

"You think about it," Lisa said. "Because my door isn't going to stay open forever." She strode out.

Bernard shook his head. "Wonderful. I don't know how the day could get worse." After a pause, he looked upward. "And I'd just as soon not find out, thank you."

He walked over and dropped onto the couch. To be honest, he didn't know why he had accepted Sherry's invitation. When she called, he said he would before he even thought about it. And he didn't know why. He was finding her company less and less desirable, her concerns about clothes and gossip less and less appealing, but still he went over there. And the way her father somehow always turned the conversation to the murders bothered him. Bernard thought it was morbid curiosity carried too far. So why am I going over there? he wondered. Am I really just trying to keep that door open?

He did know one thing; he didn't want to lose Lisa. While he wasn't certain what they had together, he didn't want to lose it. He sat there for a few more moments, then went to the phone, telling himself that enough was enough.

*

Lisa left the library, furious and strangely depressed. One part of her wanted to scratch someone's – anyone's – *Sherry's* eyes out. Another part of her wanted to do the same to Bernard. And finally to herself. She swore. Why would Bernard go over there? Wasn't she enough? Why did everything she attempt turn out badly?

She knew she wasn't being fair to herself; she had accomplished many things in her life as evidenced by her success in journalism. After all, she was almost certain that Veit was going to offer her a reporting job. He had hinted enough. So why didn't she ask for one and be done with it? She certainly needed it. Why was she staying in Ryton?

Part of the answer to that was the unsolved murder, she admitted. She wanted the murderer and her attacker caught. She didn't want to leave it unfinished, and she felt she could contribute while she was in Ryton. But the most important answer involved Bernard. She didn't want to leave him. She couldn't figure out why Bernard was so important right now. With everything that has happened, am I just trying to hold on to something? Create some stability in my life? Do I ... love Bernard?

She knew she liked Bernard. He made her laugh, and he was – for the most part – sensitive to her moods and needs. But love? And even if I did, a fat lot of good it would do me with him running over to Sherry's house!

The thought rekindled her anger. She drove home, taking the turns savagely and cursing at anyone who got in her way. She was so caught up in her fury she didn't notice the police car that had sat across the street from her house for the past several days wasn't there.

*

"So what you're saying is that you're no closer to catching poor Agatha's killer than you were when you started," Mayor Otis Brunson said. "Is that correct?"

The chief regarded Brunson sourly. After leaving the library, the chief had stopped by the office to catch up on some paperwork. He was about three days behind. He had started looking at expense reports when Brunson waltzed into his office. The mayor had basically spent the past thirty minutes blabbering about concerned citizens, and the chief wasn't buying it.

"No, I wouldn't say that," the chief said, evenly. "While we haven't closed in the killer yet, we have made progress."

"But very little, right?"

"Yes, I'm afraid so," the chief said. "Why are you so fired up about this?"

"Many people have expressed their outrage with Agatha's murder," Brunson said, self-righteously. "Why, Mike Hyatt called me today –"

"You know, that surprises me," the chief said. "My impression was that most people detested Agatha and were tizzy-toed happy that she was dead. Now you tell me that they actually cared. I tell you, it warms my heart."

Brunson stared at the chief, his mouth open. He asked sharply, "Do you think this is funny?"

"No, I do not think this is funny!" the chief snapped. "I intend to find Agatha's murderer, and I will. I'm doing everything that I can think of doing. But why don't you tell me exactly what you're doing here 'cause I've known you too long to buy any of this load."

Brunson bridled and then laughed. "I have had more calls than you might think about her death, but you're right on the mark. Listen, we've had an offer on the library. Or actually on the land."

"Really?" The chief sat back in his chair. "When did this come about?" he asked, thinking of Agatha's appraisal.

"I learned about it yesterday," Brunson said. "Mike Hyatt called me and said that a company in Oklahoma City is interested in opening a small computer-assembly plant here."

"Why?" the chief asked.

"What do you mean? Ryton has plenty of benefits –"

"No, that's not what I meant," the chief said. "Why the library land?"

"That, I don't know," Brunson said, frowning. "But it doesn't really matter. The plant would mean about fifty local jobs. That would help the economy in a major way."

"Can the city sell the land?" the chief asked. "I thought Ryton had it pretty tied up in his will."

"Oh, the money from the sale would have to go to building a library and maintaining it, which is a shame considering how much street work we need to do around town, but old man Ryton was smart enough to realize that someday his house might not be large enough. His will stipulates that if the library is ever sold, the monies must go into building another library. We think with Agatha's bequest and the library fund, we can buy that old Cox property and build a new library there. It would have more parking, and it would be closer to downtown and to the school."

"Sounds good," the chief said. "But what does that have to do with the murder investigation?"

"In a weird way, the murder is responsible for the offer," Brunson said. "Apparently the publicity, negative though it was, sparked the interest. But people don't want to come to town where they're not safe. So we'd like to get this cleared up quick. If you need more men, I don't think you would have any problem getting extra funds from the Council." He paused for a moment, then hastily added, "As long as it was a reasonable amount, of course."

"Of course," the chief said. "Sure wish I could take you up on the offer, but I really can't think of any way that more money would help."

The mayor nodded and looked so relieved that the chief

couldn't help but add, "I'll keep it in mind, though." His good humor deserted him. "I'll tell you honestly, Otis. What we need right now is some good old-fashioned luck."

"Then I hope we get it," Brunson said as he left.

Listlessly, the chief pushed a couple of papers around his desk. It had been a long day. He decided the paperwork could wait until tomorrow. As he drove home, he made his usual detour to the orchard. He wouldn't stop as he was already late for dinner, but like most people in tree-scarce western Oklahoma, he took a deep enjoyment in seeing trees. While the wheat fields had a beauty that the chief wouldn't trade for that of any forest, there was something satisfying about a tree.

He frowned as he noticed a pickup parked inside the orchard entrance. It looked like Jerry Wilson's. Jerry was the county extension agent who had seen the chief through these five stressful years of peach farming. The chief pulled in and parked beside the pickup. He watched as Jerry walked over to the car.

The chief rolled his window down. "What's up, Jerry?" he asked, feeling his stomach churn as he waited for bad news.

"Maybe nothing," the county agent replied. "But I was driving by, and when I looked at the trees, for some reason, they didn't look right."

As far as the chief could tell, the trees were as green and fruit-filled as always. "What do you mean?"

"Don't really know," Jerry squinted at the chief. "It's probably my imagination working overtime, but is it okay if I take some peaches in to sample?"

The chief nodded his assent and watched as the agent pulled a few peaches down. "I sure hope nothing's wrong with them. We're close to picking time."

"They're probably fine, but it won't hurt to check," Jerry said. "When you've been at this as long as I have, you get a feelin' sometimes. Actually, this may just be a way for me to get some free peaches!" He laughed.

"You're always welcome to help yourself," the chief said. A thought occurred to him. "Hey, you've been around here for a while. Did you know old man Ryton?"

"Shoot, no, I've not been around that long," Jerry said, spitting some tobacco juice off to the side. "Exactly how old do you think I am?"

The chief grinned at him.

"Don't answer that," Jerry said, grinning back. "I did know the girls. Poor Agatha and ... what was her name?"

"Evelyn," the chief supplied.

"Yeah. They sure were a pair," Jerry said. "Are you any closer to catching who did it?"

"We're making some progress, but it's not coming together," the chief said. "What do you remember of them?"

"Not too much. They were a little younger than me and pretty stuck on themselves. I did get invited to one of their birthday parties once because my dad was a minister. I can still remember how grand that old house was." He paused to spit again. "The girls had their own playroom upstairs, and the maids sent up the birthday cake on a dumbwaiter. I'd never seen one of those before and I've never seen one since. About halfway through the birthday party, old man Ryton came stumping in the room with a bunch of Civil War stuff. Did you know he was barely five feet tall?"

"No," the chief said. "From the way people talk about him, I always imagined him to be about nine feet tall with fangs."

Jerry chuckled. "Oh, he was mean, all right. But sometimes the short ones are the meanest, I think. Anyway, he must have rambled on about the war for an hour or so. The girls made faces behind his back the whole time, but we were too scared to laugh." He sighed. "Thinking about it now makes me feel old. I guess all this just goes to show you."

"'Show you' what?" the chief asked.

"Nobody knows when the good Lord will call them home."

In the warm sun, the chief suddenly felt a chill run down his spine, and for some reason, he thought of Lisa.

*

Lisa pulled the sheet of paper out of her typewriter, a frown creasing her brow. The opening to the story still didn't read right. If she started by saying that it had been nearly two weeks and the police were no closer to catching Agatha's and Leonard's murderer, it sounded like she was criticizing the police department. She didn't want to give that impression since she felt the chief was doing all that could be done.

But if she started by describing the murders, it read like sensationalism. And it was old news. Lisa sighed. A good story angle would have been to interview someone close to Leonard or Agatha whose life had been touched by their murder. Unfortunately, all of

Leonard's family refused to be interviewed as did Evelyn Ryton.

"I have nothing to say that you could print or that I would want printed," Evelyn had said. "Don't bother me again." And she had hung up as quickly as that.

Thinking of Leonard's family made Lisa sigh again. The woman she briefly talked to was Leonard's sister, but the woman didn't seem to be grieving. In fact, she didn't seem to care that her brother was dead. Everybody should have someone to miss them when they're gone, she thought. I wish I had known the good things – surely there were some – about Leonard.

She looked at the story again. The body and conclusion seemed solid if she could get the lead right. She wanted this story to be one of her best. Veit had suggested she write a round-up story about the murders for the Dispatch and bring it to Oklahoma City tomorrow herself. He was going to take her out to lunch and, she hoped, offer her the position of a full-time reporter or give her a chance to ask for it.

She had decided tonight to work for the Dispatch if she could. Although she wanted to stay in Ryton until the murderer was caught, she needed the job, not only for the money but for the career opportunities it offered. She had told John Towers that tonight; her former editor had called to see if she had considered his offer. He had been disappointed, especially since he was close to raising enough money to get the Journal going again, but he said he understood.

"This is your chance, Lisa," he said. "I couldn't be happier for you. And I want you to know, if it doesn't work out, this job will still be open for you."

She almost changed her mind then. Towers had been her

mentor and friend, and she would miss him. But she had already made her mind up to give herself the best possible chance she could. She thanked him, feeling nervous about turning down a sure thing but more certain than ever that her future was not in Ryton.

As for her and Bernard, she had decided that if they wanted to continue to date, they would only be an hour away from each other. But she didn't know if they would make the effort. Perhaps their relationship could do with a little space, a little time to sort things out. One thing she did know was that she was not going to get involved in some sort of competition with Sherry Hyatt. If Bernard lacked the intelligence to see how much Lisa was worth, it was his loss. She intended to tell him so at the first opportunity. But all this wasn't getting the story finished. She needed a strong lead.

She stretched, feeling her back muscles pull and release. It occurred to her that she hadn't seen Obsidian since she returned home. She glanced around her room.

"Here, Obsidian, come here, baby," she said, as she looked under the bed and the closet. As she slid the closet door shut, she heard a muffled noise downstairs. The hair rose on the back of her neck. Her heart raced. She looked out the window. She didn't see the police car. She tried to remember if it had been there when she got home but couldn't recall if it was.

Opening her nightstand, she took out the gun. As she slid a clip in, Obsidian darted up the stairs and ran under the bed.

She gasped. "What's wrong, Obsidian?" she whispered, feeling her pulse pound in her temples. "Is someone down there?" Straining to hear any noise, she slid along the wall to stand beside the door.

Kneeling, she risked a glimpse down the empty stairs. She couldn't see anyone.

The only phone in the house was in her living room – downstairs where the noise came from. She thought of the times she had intended to have a phone installed in her bedroom and promised herself that she would at the first chance she got. If she didn't move to Oklahoma City, that was.

Why wasn't a policeman out there? She thought it was Hayden's night to sit outside her house. Where was he? If he's gone for coffee, I'll kill him, she thought. Of course, it might be nothing. Obsidian could have knocked something over in the kitchen; it wouldn't be the first time she'd had to clean up a mess caused by the curious cat.

Crawling over to the stairs, she started cautiously down. Why didn't I leave the lights on in the living room? Was that a movement? She froze and held her breath. Nothing moved. She thumbed the safety off on the gun and continued on down. At the foot of the stairs, she paused, trying to decide what to do. The front door was in full view of the living room. Should she make a run for it?

Of course, she'd feel pretty silly if she ran outdoors and no one was in her house. In fact, she hadn't heard or seen anything else. She had her gun. Surely she was safe. Raising the gun, she stood and slowly walked around the corner. Shadows from the trees outside filled the living room with moving shapes.

She reached over and turned on the light.

The doorbell rang.

She jerked, and her finger twitched.

The gun fired.

The front door burst open.

Lisa whirled around, fired again, and realized too late that it was Bernard.

*

The telephone rang, startling the chief who was caught up in the colorful adventures of Travis McGee. After dinner, he had determined to give his mind a rest from the puzzle of the murders. Although he didn't usually like mysteries, he had been given couple of MacDonald's books for Christmas a couple of years ago and had quickly become a fan of that author's modern knight errant. He turned the page.

"The phone's by you, dear," Maggie said pointedly. "If you wouldn't mind."

He sighed and reached for the phone.

"If that's Darla, tell her that I've decided to make strawberry-cream cake for the church dinner," Maggie said, looking up from her book. "I was supposed to call her this afternoon, but I forgot. Oh, and tell her that Edith is going to be out of town so we need someone else to bring a meat dish. And Mary is going to bring a spinach salad and a Mississippi mud pie."

"If it's Darla, you can talk to her yourself," the chief said as he picked up the phone.

"Chief, this is Sims. Sorry to bother you, but we've got a problem," the lieutenant said. "Hayden called, and his boy is real sick. They're at the hospital."

"Do they know what's wrong?" the chief asked.

"Maybe just the flu, but his temperature was really high," Sims said. "Their doctor told them to bring him to the emergency room. Anyway, Hayden was supposed to be watching Lisa tonight. Should I reassign someone?"

The chief considered. It had been almost two weeks, and there had been no new attacks on Lisa. Despite Brunson's offer, the department didn't have the funds or the manpower to continue watching Lisa's house indefinitely. Still, the murder remained unsolved, and the chief firmly believed that someone local was to blame. Other than the murders, Ryton had been pretty quiet lately. In for the penny, in for the pound, he decided.

"Yeah, I think we'd better," the chief said. "Why don't you send Harris. He's been complaining about patrolling so much lately. This'll give him a little rest and might let him appreciate –"

"Wait a minute, Chief," Sims cut in and then was quiet for a moment, listening to someone – Julie, the night dispatcher, the chief thought – talk to him. "Chief, we just had a call. Shots have been fired at Lisa's house!"

"I'll meet you there," the chief said. He rushed into the bedroom, grabbing on his clothes and explaining the situation to Maggie who calmly helped him button his shirt and find his shoes.

"Be careful," she said. "I'll wait up for you."

He knew she would be. She always did. He took a moment to kiss his precious wife of forty years, then he was in his car, racing down Collier Road.

*

The shot echoed through the house. Bernard stared at Lisa,

turned away, and crumpled to his knees, his hands searching his chest for blood. He couldn't seem to breathe. Lisa was at his side, saying something that he couldn't hear over the roaring in his ears.

He couldn't find any blood. He looked at his hands, expecting to find them bloody, but they weren't. No blood on his chest or his stomach. He looked up the wall. His gaze stopped at a half-inch hole.

"You missed," he said. He staggered into the living room and dropped onto the rocking chair, trying to catch his breath. He looked at Lisa who was still holding the gun.

"What's going on?" he asked. He slowly focused on what she was saying.

"Bernard, are you okay?! Are you okay?!" Lisa sounded hysterical, which Bernard could certainly understand.

"I'm all right," he said. "Why did you shoot at me?"

"I didn't mean to," Lisa said. "I heard a noise. I thought someone was in the house. I came down to see. The doorbell rang and I fired. When you came in, I didn't see who it was until after I shot again. Oh, Bernard, I didn't mean to – to shoot –" She started to cry.

"It's okay," Bernard said. "I'm okay. You missed." His breath was coming easier. "You missed. When did you get a gun?"

"A couple of days ago," Lisa said, wiping her tears with one hand. "I thought it would ... I was scared ..." The tears started flowing again. She dropped the gun on the floor. Bernard flinched, but it didn't go off.

"Come here," Bernard said, holding out his hand.

Lisa started over, then stopped. "What's that?" she asked, sounding frightened.

Faint police sirens grew louder.

"Oh, no," Lisa moaned. "The police are coming."

"It's all right," Bernard said, soothingly. "It was an accident. Nothing was hurt. Nothing except for your wall."

They both stared at the hole in the wall for a moment.

"They won't give back my deposit now," Lisa said mournfully.

They looked at each other. Bernard considered the absurdity of her statement. He couldn't help it; he started to laugh. Lisa looked at him like he had lost his mind, and then slowly she started to laugh, too.

They were still laughing when Sims burst through the open door, revolver in hand, followed by four other deputies and, a few moments later, by the chief. Bernard and Lisa sobered up fast.

Lisa, her voice only quavering occasionally, told the chief what had happened. Bernard verified her account where he could.

The chief didn't find it as amusing as they had.

"You know, he could have been killed," the chief said, his face hard. "He could be dead right now, and I would be arresting you for manslaughter. Do you hear me? Manslaughter."

"I know," Lisa said quietly. "I know. I shot before I saw who it was. I didn't mean to."

"She was scared," Bernard said. "It was an accident."

"Accidents with guns kill people," the chief said. "Even though Bernard doesn't want to press charges, I should write you up for discharging a firearm in city limits. A night in jail might do you some good."

"Chief –" Bernard started to say.

"But I'm not going to," the chief continued, holding up a hand to forestall Bernard. "In a way, this is my fault. If we'd caught the murderer, you wouldn't be so scared. And for that, Lisa, I'm sorry." The chief motioned to Sims who had picked up Lisa's gun. "Give it back to her. Make sure the safety's on."

"No," Lisa said. "I don't think I want it. I don't want it in the house. It was a mistake to purchase it in the first place."

"There's nothing wrong with having a gun in the house – if you know what you're doing," Sims said. "I'd be glad to show you the basics."

Lisa shook her head.

"You think about it," the chief said. "If you don't change your mind, I'll help you find someone to buy it."

"Thank you," Lisa said. "I would appreciate it."

The chief looked at her as if impressing her with the seriousness of the night's events. He said a gruff farewell. As the deputies left, Bernard heard the chief assign Harris to watch Lisa's house the rest of the night.

"Well," Lisa said, finally breaking the silence. "This has not been one of my better nights, that's for sure." She looked around the living room. "So that's what the noise was." She went over and picked up a plant off the floor and sat it back on the window sill. "Obsidian must have knocked it over. He can't leave my plants alone." She turned and looked at Bernard.

"What are you doing here, anyhow? I thought you were going to have dinner with Sherry."

"I called her and canceled," Bernard said. "I decided I wanted to spend the evening with you."

"And tomorrow evening, you'll spend with her?" Lisa said tightly. She shook her head. "I'm sorry. That wasn't fair."

"Yes, it was," Bernard said. "I deserve it. I have treated both of you badly. I apologized to her. And I'm apologizing to you. Both of you deserve better. But I'm hoping you will settle for me." He met her eyes. "I don't know what we have. Maybe after all this is over, we can sit down and figure it out. But I know this: You're bright and beautiful and I want you in my life." He paused. "I do have one request."

"What?"

"You have to promise to not shoot me."

"Deal." She laughed, and Bernard decided he could happily drown in that smile.

CHAPTER SEVEN

Ryton was well patrolled the next day. Officers were more than willing to get out of the station and avoid the chief. Last night's events had soured his stomach and his disposition.

As the chief sat at his desk, he felt restless and angry. He was beginning to doubt his ability. As he saw it, the truth was he simply didn't have much experience in murder. He had always seen himself as a shrewd judge of people and their motives, and he had figured that would be enough. I guess I was wrong, he thought glumly. Maybe I'd better retire soon. Maybe just kill peaches to pass the time. And when I get tired of that, maybe put some apples in and kill them. There are probably plenty of crops I could kill.

A tentative knock came at his door.

"What?" the chief snapped.

Sims stuck his head in. "Uh, we're about to let Jay Jones go. I thought you might want to talk to him again."

The chief considered it and shook his head. "Tell him not to leave town without notifying us, or he'll be in trouble. Besides, he said he wouldn't talk to us anymore without an attorney so why are you bothering me?"

Sims started to say something else but, after examining the chief's face, apparently thought better of it.

The chief swiveled in his chair and stared out his window at the downtown. Merchants were arriving to open their stores. He watched the sharply-dressed owner of the Fashion Fountain park her car in front of her store and enter the building. Great, she parked on the street again, he thought. That means Roberts will be calling soon.

The downtown merchants wanted all the employees and owners to park behind the stores so that the parking places on the street would be left for the customers. Lawrence Roberts of Ryton TV and Appliance had appointed himself the downtown traffic cop, and when some hapless owner violated the rule, he called the chief and complained. The chief would usually wander down to the offending merchant's store and remind him or her of the rule. Not that he could do anything if the owner didn't want to move the car – after all, it wasn't like they were breaking a law – but most merchants cooperated. But the chief didn't feel up to dealing with it today.

Jay Jones came into view, heading down the street. The chief watched him idly, wondering why Jay hadn't taken his pickup, which had been brought to the station when Jay was picked up.

The former janitor seemed to be walking with a purpose. He crossed Oak and Ash and kept going straight down Main. The chief frowned and moved so that he could see better. Suddenly he was curious about Jay's destination. He grabbed his field glasses and focused them on the janitor.

Jones walked a half-block more and stopped in front of the law offices of Hastings and McLadd. He lit a cigarette.

"Sims," the chief called, not looking away. "Sims, come in here." Could Jay be consulting with Hastings? If so, how could he afford it? Hastings didn't come cheap.

"Yes, chief?" Sims asked, coming into the office and moving over to stand by the chief.

"Why didn't Jay Jones take his pickup?" the chief asked.

"It wouldn't start," Sims said. "He said it needs a new battery. I offered to drive him to the auto parts store, but he said he'd walk."

"Did Jay have any visitors last night or make any phone calls?"

"No visitors, but he called someone about nine."

"Any idea who?"

"No, he didn't talk long. I think it was a local number, though. Doesn't he have some family around here?"

The chief grunted noncommittally.

A gray Lincoln Continental pulled up in front of Hastings's office and parked. The chief's eyes widened in surprise. He recognized the car. A plump, well-dressed man got out and shook hands with Jay. Both men entered the building.

"Well, well, well," the chief said. What would Jay Jones, Harold Hastings, and Ryton's Mayor Otis Brunson be meeting about? He looked at Sims. "I feel a sudden need to consult with an attorney."

*

Millie had already opened the library and was halfway through updating the overdue book file by the time Bernard arrived. He came in, attempting to whistle "Oh, What A Beautiful Morning" and doing a poor job of it. He never had been able to whistle.

"I was about to call you and see if you were sick," Millie said.

"Nope, I had some errands to run this morning," Bernard said, picking the mail up off the desk.

"I've never seen you in your glasses before," Millie said, looking curious.

"I don't wear them very often, but I had my contacts on fairly late last night," he said. "My eyes were tired this morning. We haven't been busy, have we?"

"No. There's a college kid upstairs who needed some information, and that's been it."

Kid? Millie couldn't be older than twenty-one if that, he thought. The 'kid' must not be good looking or ...

"I showed her how to use a card catalog," Millie said. "You know, I can't believe someone is going to college and doesn't know how to use a library. That seems like something you should learn in high school. I did."

Straight-faced, Bernard agreed. Ordinarily he found Millie's endless chatter annoying, but he was feeling sociable and generally pleased with the world despite being tired. He and Lisa had talked until three in the morning. He felt that their relationship was on solid ground, maybe for the first time.

"Did you stay up late watching TV?" Millie asked.

Perhaps she should help the chief investigate, Bernard thought. "No. Wasn't your show on last night?"

"Oh, you mean Shadow Seekers? Yes, and it's really getting exciting! It turns out that Joshua – remember I told you he had an evil second personality? – didn't really have another personality. Actually it was his evil twin, Jeremy, who was lost at birth when a nurse stole him and gave him to a poor family whose baby had died. And now Jeremy has kidnapped Kristin, and he left Joshua a note that said he was going to kill her unless Joshua gives up the family fortune, but the worst thing about it is that Alice, Kristin's cousin who hates her, lied to Joshua and told him that he wasn't the father of Kristin's baby so he may not even want to save her now!"

"How do you keep it all straight?" Bernard asked, fascinated in spite of himself.

"Oh, I've watched it from the very beginning," she said. "It's not that hard. If you watched it a few times, you'd pick it up easy."

"I'll have to do that sometime," Bernard said, taking the mail and heading for his office. He had never watched much TV, and it didn't sound like he was missing much.

A sudden thought hit him. "Twins?"

"What?" Millie asked.

"Twins. You said twins." Bernard turned to look at her. "Duplicates!"

"Yes," Millie said. "Joshua has an evil –"

"That's not what I'm talking about." Bernard thought a moment more, his excitement rising. Could he have stumbled on Agatha's secret? If what he was thinking was correct, he might even know who Agatha's murderer was! He had to check it out first. He wasn't going to call the police about nothing again like he did with the light. "Where is that packing invoice I gave you a few days ago?"

"Invoice?"

"I gave it to you the day after Agatha was killed so that you could find the books on it."

"Oh, yeah, but I gave it back to you," Millie said.

"That's right," Bernard said. "I wonder what I did with it." He didn't think he threw it away. He went to his office and rifled through the papers on his desk, hoping he hadn't tossed it. There it is – on the bottom naturally, he thought.

The publisher's telephone number was listed at the top.

"Millie," Bernard called.

She came to the door. "What?"

"I want you to try to find any other invoices that we have," Bernard said.

"I don't know where any could be," Millie said, frowning. "Mrs. Ryton-Storer kept those."

"Yes, I know, but I think there were a few in the blue file cabinet. Under 'Returns' maybe," he said. "Look and see. And check in those boxes under the counter. There may be a few in them. Check the storage closet, too. Oh, I'm going to be on the phone for a while so handle the front desk, please."

"Is there something wrong?" Millie asked.

"No," Bernard said. He started to tell her his idea then changed his mind. After all, he could be wrong. "I have a project I've got to finish." And maybe a murder to solve, he thought. What a story that would make for Lisa. For a moment, he indulged in a daydream of telling her. He set to work.

*

Lisa drove slowly down Meridian Avenue in Oklahoma City, ignoring the honking cars passing hers as she searched for The Bookworm, the bookstore owned by Richard Storer. She had left

Ryton early this morning so she could drop in on Agatha's one-time brother-in-law. She felt slightly guilty that she hadn't told Bernard about her plans but had decided that it wasn't necessary. After all, I just want to see if there's a story angle here, she thought. That's all. Of course, it would be nice if I discovered something that would help solve the murders, but I'm really only going to get some more background.

Amused by her inner justification, she almost missed The Bookworm. She swung her car into a parking place directly in front of the store. Hmm, not very busy, she thought. It might help if that sign was redesigned a bit.

Poorly done in Old English letters, the sign also sported a pale green worm winding around and through the words, which only made it even more difficult to read.

The store itself was clean, neat, and small. Make that very small, Lisa thought, as she stepped around two displays and threaded between two tables laden with bestsellers to get to the counter where a young woman was using a price gun on a stack of hardcover books.

The young woman looked up and smiled. "Do you need help in finding anything?"

"No, well, actually I guess yes," Lisa said. "I'm looking for Richard." Always ask for people by their first name whether you know them or not, her former editor used to say, and you have a better chance of getting to talk to them, an old reporter trick that had been successful for Lisa on more than one occasion.

"I'm sorry. He stepped out for a few minutes. Would you like to leave a message?"

"Is he going to be back soon?"

"I don't know, but I do expect him back before lunch," the woman said.

"Well, I think I'll just look around for a few minutes and wait if that's okay," Lisa said.

"Just ask if you need help." The woman smiled brightly at Lisa and went back to pricing the books. From the prices, Lisa could see that she wouldn't be buying any new books soon – not unless Cameron Veit hired her for the Dispatch.

Wandering down an aisle, Lisa noticed an open doorway at the back of the store with a sign over it that read "Used Books." She entered, then stopped, overwhelmed by the sight. The used book section part of the building stretched before her.

While the front was small and neat, the used section was large and overflowed with thousands of books. Black wooden shelves climbed all the way from the floor to the ceiling, covering all the walls. Four long rows of standing shelves divided the room and extended towards the back of the building.

She wandered among the shelves, breathing the old, wonderful, slightly musty book smell, picking up a book here and there and flipping through the pages. While a few of the books were in poor condition, most were in good shape. Not perfect, she thought, but at these prices, who cares? She found a long section of dictionaries and writing books and gleefully selected several volumes, including a Webster's New World Dictionary and a first edition of Strunk and White's *The Elements of Style*, one of Lisa's favorite books.

Turning the corner, clutching her treasures, she found one

whole row of shelves devoted to poetry. I have died and gone to heaven, she thought, scanning the titles. Archibald MacLeish, e.e. cummings, William Wordsworth, the Brownings, and many others that she wanted. She would always be thankful that Mrs. Moore, her senior English teacher, had introduced her to poetry and helped her learn to appreciate it, especially since Lisa hadn't been receptive at first and Mrs. Moore had taken the extra time necessary to convey to a slightly rebellious – all right, very rebellious – teenager the joys and beauties of poetry.

Thinking of time reminded Lisa to check her watch. It was already eleven-fifteen. She needed to get going if she wasn't going to be late for her meeting with Veit. She promised herself that she would come back and go through the poetry books another time. She took her selections to the counter and paid for them, telling the woman that she would catch 'Richard' some other day.

As she pulled out on Meridian, she glanced down the alley that ran along aside the book store. A man and a woman were getting out of a late model car. Lisa slammed on the brakes and was nearly rear-ended by a truck behind her. She hastily drove on, wondering what Richard Storer and Evelyn Ryton were doing together.

*

"What I discuss with anyone who comes into my office – even with you, Chief Donaldson – is protected," Harold Hastings said coolly, his elbows on the leather armrests of his desk chair, looking at the chief over the steeple of his fingers. "I have nothing to tell you. And I am very busy today."

Ignoring the hint, the chief took a moment to look around the office. A huge framed photograph of an oil rig dominated the wall behind Hastings. The talk around town was that most of Hastings's money was tied up in unproductive oil and gas leases, and that Hastings was in financial trouble because of his expensive tastes. A lawyer friend of the chief's had told him that Hastings wasn't turning down any cases that came his way, a radical break in his former policy since Hastings was well-known to turn down business from what he considered to be the lower classes.

"Well, no matter really," the chief finally said. "I'll catch up with Otis or Jay later."

"You may do that," Hastings said. "Mayor Brunson can tell you what he wishes as can Mr. Jones. As their attorney, I cannot."

Aha, so you are representing Jones, the chief thought. Now, I wonder just who is paying your fee? Brunson? Why would he? He can't be that desperate for voters.

Hastings continued. "And in the case of Mr. Jones, I suggest you ask him politely. You had no evidence to support locking him up. I believe that places you perilously close to a false arrest charge."

The chief started to reply but realized that Hastings was probing for information. He contented himself with a grunt.

"Perhaps you do not see that as a serious matter," Hastings said. "Then know this: I do not appreciate you watching my office. I do think a court could possibly see that as harassment, particularly if it discourages people from consulting with me."

"Well, I wouldn't want that," the chief said, realizing that while he had intensely disliked Hastings for years, he had never known until now that Hastings returned the feeling and apparently as fervently. The chief decided he could live with it. "I'll be sure to give your concern the consideration it deserves."

Hastings frowned at him. "If there isn't anything else, I have an appointment for which I need to prepare."

"Actually, there is," the chief said levelly. "I wanted to discuss the Ryton will."

"The will is filed in the county courthouse at Vessel," Hastings said. "Other than what is public record, I cannot discuss it."

"Not Agatha's will, old man Ryton's," the chief said.

"It is also at the courthouse," Hastings said. "I believe they stay open until five."

"I'd think a firm like this one would keep a copy so that I wouldn't have to drive over to Vessel," the chief said. "Although it would be nice to talk to Sheriff Jackson. We were talking the other day, and he was telling me about how the courts were looking at obstructing justice these days. He said you can practically charge anyone with it."

"Is that a threat?"

"Good lord, no," the chief said, acting surprised. "I was telling you what Jackson said. Of course, he does talk a lot. Don't know what to believe half the time ..." The chief let his voice fade away as he locked stares with the attorney.

Hastings looked away. "It would take some time to locate in our files. It would probably be faster if you drove –"

"That's all right," the chief said. "I basically just needed to ask a couple of questions about it. Are you familiar with it?"

"Although my father prepared it – I was only a junior partner in

168

the firm at the time – I have read it once or twice," Hastings said.

Considering the money it involved, I bet you know it by heart, the chief thought. "What I would like to know is whether it makes any provision for a member of the Ryton family to buy the library back from the city."

"What a curious question," Hastings said. "I don't see how it could have anything to do with Agatha's death."

"Maybe it doesn't," the chief said, "but I'd like to know if you don't mind." And even if you do.

"If you wish to waste your time with trivia, certainly." Hastings shrugged. "The will provides that any direct descendant of Eliah Ryton may purchase the library at fair market value if she desires to do so."

"Why did you say, 'she'?" the chief asked.

"Simply because Evelyn Ryton is the last descendant of Eliah Ryton," Hastings said with a superior smile. "Neither she nor her sister have any children. I would have thought that you would have at least known that from your investigation."

"Maybe so," the chief said, biting back a retort. "I'd also like to know if Agatha or Evelyn received any money."

"No," Hastings said. "He was not close to either of them. All of his fortune went to found the library, other than the monies set aside for the execution of the will, of course."

"Of course," the chief unconsciously echoed, wondering if Agatha had intended to buy the library. She certainly had enough money to do so, but why hadn't she? Why would she wait?

After a moment, Hastings asked, "Are there any other questions that I can answer for you?"

"No," the chief said regretfully. "Wait, there is, too."

Hastings sighed.

"Do you have any idea where her money came from?" the chief asked.

"With proper investment, you would be surprised how much a small nest egg can grow –"

"You could have just said no, you know," the chief said, rising. "Thanks for all your help. I'll return the favor someday." He closed the door behind him before the attorney could say anything else. And although the chief knew it was childish, he was delighted that he got the last word.

*

"So you're positive?" Bernard asked.

"Yes, Mr. Worthington," the woman on the other end of the phone replied. "I have it right here on the computer."

"Could you send me a copy of that? Our copy has been lost." Intentionally, he added to himself.

"Certainly."

Bernard thanked the woman and hung up. He picked up his list and checked off the last publisher's name. At first he had been delighted that his idea was checking out, but as each one of the publishers confirmed his suspicions, he became appalled by the extent of the fraud. No wonder Agatha had a fortune, he thought. She stole it from the library.

And he was discovering the smallest part of it, he realized. He and Millie had only been able to find a half dozen packing slips. Without the rest of the records – if they even existed – there was no way to tell exactly how much Agatha had stolen. Agatha and someone else, he thought. She had to have had help. And I bet it was Richard Storer.

Bernard found it almost unbelievable that Agatha hadn't been caught in all these years, but he could see how it happened. Other than the Library Board, Agatha had no one to oversee her, and the Board, which was also the City Council with other interests, wasn't overly concerned with the library. Agatha would turn in a report every six months, complain about not having enough money, and go on her way. If anyone attempted to check up on the library, Agatha would, of course, make life miserable for that poor individual. Besides, Agatha had no control over any funds. Why should anyone suspect her of stealing? What could she take? Books?

And the funny thing is, Bernard thought, that's what she took. Books. Lots of books. When she ordered books, she ordered them in pairs. One book stayed in the library. Its twin went somewhere else to be sold, probably Richard Storer's bookstore. If anyone asked, she could always say that she always purchased duplicates in case one book was damaged or stolen.

Another idea hit him. "Millie," he called, then remembered she was gone for lunch. He went out to the counter and pulled the list of damaged books and stolen books. He'd lay odds that many of the books listed as damaged had never been placed in the library shelves at all. He had always wondered what the citizens of Ryton had against books that would cause them to destroy them in such numbers. He checked the list.

Since Agatha's death, seven books had been listed in the

damaged category, three placed there by Bernard, one by Millie and the others by one of the part-timers. Last month's list had over sixty books on it, he remembered. Most of them had been placed there by Agatha.

While he was standing at the counter, the front door opened. Absorbed in the list, Bernard glanced at the door and back at the list before realizing it was Sherry. He looked up.

She walked over to the counter and slowly looked around the library before meeting his eyes.

"Hello, Bernard. Busy?"

Bernard could hear the anger in her voice. "No, not really."

"Good," she said, nodding her head once. "Maybe we can talk for a minute. I'd really like to talk. I'd like to know what I and my family did to deserve being treated like that."

"Sherry –"

"My mother went to a lot of trouble for you," Sherry said, her voice rising. "She made that roast just for you. And a coconut cream pie. We were all waiting for you. I guess we should consider ourselves lucky that you called when you did. And when you do call, what do I get? 'Sherry, I can't see you any more. I'm sorry.' That's it. That's all I get."

"I told you I'm involved with Lisa now," Bernard said. "You wanted to just be friends, remember?" Bernard's temper flared. "That's what you wanted, right? Or did you want me to hang around until you made your mind up?"

"You certainly didn't wait very long until you found someone else, did you?"

"That's none of your business."

"I guess if I want your attention now, I need to be drunk and sleep around."

"Lisa neither drinks nor sleeps around, but better that than a shallow, selfish –" Bernard stopped himself. He drew a deep breath. "Look, I think you'd better leave. This isn't good for me or you. It's over between us." He felt something twist inside him and then release. He repeated what he said, more for himself than her. "It's over." He looked at her. "I don't want there to be hard feelings –"

"Oh, shut up. You've always been a loser, and you'll always be one." Sherry stalked to the door. She stopped and turned. "You know, you wouldn't even have this job if it wasn't for Daddy. He has a lot of influence in this town, and if I was someone who wanted to keep working here, I'd remember that."

Bernard shook his head in disbelief. "I can't believe you said that. Do you realize how dumb it sounds? I only came to this town because of you. That was my only reason. Do you think that I can't get a job somewhere else? You know, Ryton is not the whole world. Why, I think there might even be a few other cities out there."

"You're a complete waste of time, you know that," Sherry said coldly. "I told Daddy this was –" She stopped and looked flustered suddenly.

"What does your father –"

"Drop dead. Just. Drop. Dead." She flung open the door and stormed out, her attempt to slam it frustrated by the automatic door closer.

Millie entered. She looked outside and then at Bernard.

"I'm going to lunch," he said quickly, to forestall the inevitable questions. Matching action to words, he walked out, his mind busy with the implications of why Michael Hyatt would send his daughter to talk to Bernard. He wished Lisa was with him so that they could discuss a very paranoid idea that had just occurred to him.

*

"No, really, this is very good," Lisa said. "I'm just not hungry. A late breakfast. I've never had French food before. Chicken, of course, I understand, but what does *cordon bleu* mean?"

"It's been years since my high school French," Cameron Veit, the editor of *The Oklahoma Dispatch*, said, "but I think it means 'blue ribbon' or something like that."

"I wonder if it's hard to make," she said, picking at the chicken dish. She was too nervous about this meeting to eat much. She sat her fork down and decided to approach the matter of a job directly and be done with it. Veit beat her to it.

"Lisa, I've been very impressed with your work over the past couple of weeks," he said. "I have a new position that I'm looking to fill, and I think it might be right for you."

"What type of position?" Lisa asked, hoping he wouldn't mention obituaries or headlines. She didn't enjoy the former and wasn't good at the latter.

"We're looking to expand our coverage at the Dispatch," he said, taking out his pen and starting to doodle on his napkin. "We're the number one newspaper in Oklahoma City, and we're number one because we have the best coverage of city events and issues. I'm not bragging. Well, maybe I am, but it's true."

Lisa nodded. *The Oklahoma City Dispatch* had won more national awards than any other paper in the Southwest.

"But we're weak in covering regional items," Veit said. "Like these murders in Ryton. It was a great story, but if you hadn't brought it to our attention, we wouldn't have got it until it hit the news services. And while the Associated Press does a good job of covering stories, they wouldn't have had the local color that you've provided." He coughed, waved apologetically, and took a drink of water.

"I appreciate that," Lisa said, trying to stay calm. "I worked hard on the stories." This was sounding better and better. But what was the job?

"It showed," Veit said. "Anyhow, several television stations in the city are sending their crews around the state to get human interest stories. They're doing a good job, but we think we can do better. We intend to be Oklahoma's newspaper. We're going to hire you and a couple of other people as 'roving reporters' to write stories about interesting people and places in the state. Now, this won't be all fluff – although I don't believe good human interest is fluff – if something big goes down in your part of the state, you'll be expected to cover it." He cocked his head. "So what do you think?"

"It sounds wonderful, but ..."

Correctly understanding her unspoken question, he then discussed salary and benefits. Lisa was pleased with both. She would start about a couple of thousand more than Dispatch regularly started the rookies so apparently her experience did count. And she had never before worked at a job that paid for health and life insurance.

"We'll also pay mileage and reasonable expenses," Veit

continued. "And we'll supply you with a laptop so you can email your stories."

A computer! She wouldn't have to spend her savings on one.

"Of course, you'll be expected to keep a travel log and receipts." He paused to take a bite of his lunch. "I know the money isn't great, but you would be eligible for a raise in six months. I think you would find it a real opportunity to gain more experience and build a good portfolio." He smiled at her. "So what do you think?"

"I think you have yourself a roving reporter," Lisa said, smiling.

"Good," Veit said. "Can you start June fifteenth? That'll give us enough time to gear up for this."

"No problem," Lisa said, feeling her appetite return. She picked up her fork and dug into her chicken with gusto.

"Until then, I'd like you to continue to follow the murder and anything else interesting that happens around here," Veit said as he opened his briefcase on his lap. "In fact, I found this for you. I thought it might give you a fresh angle." He handed her several photocopies of some newspaper stories. "These are the stories that covered the theft of the Ryton jewels and the founding of the library. The old man was fairly prominent back then so he made news."

Lisa flipped through the stories. Most of them covered the theft and the lack of progress in catching the thief. One of them quoted Agatha accusing her sister and saying that the theft caused her an attack of the "vapors." I bet, Lisa thought. The founding story included a photo of the mansion. It was even uglier then, Lisa decided, mostly caused by a tall row of thin windows covered with heavy bars that ran all the way across the front of the mansion. The black metal bars gave the old house all the charm of a mental institution. A small sign was in front of the house, but Lisa couldn't make it out.

"I thought a story about the history of the Ryton family might be interesting, particularly if you can get an interview with the remaining sister."

"I'll try, but she's tough," Lisa said.

"Give it a whirl," he said. "Do you think they're close to solving the murders?"

Lisa thought for a moment. "No," she said finally. "I don't think they are. The only one who knows who did it is the murderer." But, some way, somehow, I'm going to find out, she vowed silently.

*

The chief had never liked the mayor's office. The Brunsons had vacationed in Japan a couple of years ago, and it had made a big impression on Brunson's wife. Regina had decorated her husband's office with little jade ashtrays, little jade figures, several golden Buddha statues, and a large Oriental screen. She had reportedly wanted to have cushions on the floor for people to sit on, but Otis wouldn't let her so she compromised on expensive bamboo furniture that she buried in silk pillows.

The chief found the decor ridiculous and the furniture uncomfortable. As he sat on the couch waiting for the mayor to get off the phone, he felt like he was being swallowed by the pillows. It'll take a crane to get me off of this, he thought as he shifted uneasily.

Brunson hung up the phone and turned to the chief. "You're here to ask me about my meeting with Jay and Hastings."

"Hastings called you," the chief said. He briefly toyed with the idea of accusing Hastings of having violated his rights when the lawyer told the mayor of the chief's interest but regretfully realized he wasn't a client.

"He wanted to be sure that I understood my rights," Brunson said, pouring himself a cup of coffee from the pot on a shelf behind his desk. "Coffee?"

The chief shook his head.

Brunson scooped two spoonfuls of sugar into the hot coffee, followed by a heaping spoonful of creamer. "You know, he doesn't care much for you."

"He's not my dream date, either," the chief said.

"I felt he did have a point or two," Brunson said. "For instance, I'm not sure if I appreciate being spied on."

"It's hardly spying when I see you out on the street," the chief said. "It's not like I'm havin' you followed."

Brunson nodded his head. "Good point. And I can understand your interest. Tell me honestly, do you think Jay killed Agatha and that other man?"

"No," the chief replied. He wondered if the mayor realized how uncomfortable the couch was. "But I could be wrong. I do think he knows more about all this than he's telling. My turn. What's your interest in Jay?"

"Frankly, I couldn't care less about him," Brunson said. "But he's Regina's second or third cousin."

"Oh." The chief nodded. It made sense now. Regina was a Davenport, and it sometimes seemed that the Davenports and their relatives made up half of the population of Ryton. A lot of folks said that Brunson's only real political skills were his wife and her numerous voting relatives.

"They're not what you'd call close, but she doesn't want to see any of her family go to jail so I've arranged for Hastings to represent him if necessary."

"It probably won't be," the chief said. "What do you know about Jay?"

"Not much. He has a bad attitude toward authority," Brunson said. "It got him into a lot of trouble when he was younger, but I guess he's settled down. He hunts a lot and hangs out at Rochelle's Bar more than he should. Today was the first time in about five years that we've talked any, and we didn't do a lot of that."

"Considering how many relatives your wife has, it just occurred to me that maybe she's related to the Rytons," the chief said. It was an idle comment by the chief so he was surprised to see the mayor stiffen.

"I believe they are distantly related," Brunson said coolly. "Did you have a point?"

"No," the chief said, surprised. "I was making conversation."

"Well, I have a lot to do so if you will excuse me."

With difficulty, the chief pulled himself from the embrace of the couch. "I guess I'll be on my way."

The mayor grunted, apparently absorbed in a paper he had picked up from his desk.

The chief left. He stood outside the mayor's office for a moment, baffled by Brunson's reaction. What was going on? He was tempted to step back in and try to get to the bottom of it, but if Brunson had wanted to tell him, he would have. He had locked horns with the mayor enough to have a healthy respect for Brunson's willpower.

"Could I help you, Chief?" the mayor's receptionist asked.

Bemused, the chief shook his head. He walked out and down the stairs, heading for his office. Maybe Brunson knew that most people thought Regina's relatives won his elections for him and had thought the chief's remark was a reference to it. Pretty far-fetched, the chief admitted to himself, but he'd rather think that than the mayor being involved with these murders. Brunson wouldn't do anything criminal?

Or would he?

*

Where was that phone book? Jay Jones shoved a few hunting magazines off his beat-up coffee table onto the floor of his small house. He could call the operator, but he hated to pay the phone company for the number. The phone company already gouged him with high rates. Like most big corporations, they were out to get the little guy. He wouldn't even have a phone, but he needed it to call his buddies and set up hunting trips. He sure wouldn't ever have one of those stupid cell phones. Of course, calling the operator would really be an investment this time, he thought. He chuckled but kept looking. After all, this might not turn out the way he wanted.

He finally found the phone book under the couch beside an empty potato chip bag. He nervously dialed the number and swore when he got a busy signal. Maybe I oughtn't do this, he thought. He hesitated, then picked up the phone again and punched a button. This time it rang.

The call was answered after the second ring. "Hello."

"I know you killed Agatha," Jay blurted out.

There wasn't a reply.

"Hello?" Jay wiped his sweaty palms on his jeans.

"I don't know what you're talking about."

"Maybe I should call the police, huh?" Jay said. "And tell them I seen you at the library with Agatha when I sneaked in to get my coveralls that night. Y'all were in her office arguing and didn't see me. Then she turns up dead. I bet the cops would be real interested."

A pause.

"What do you want?"

Inwardly Jay jumped with excitement. "Money. Not a lot, but some money. I'm not greedy."

"How much?"

Jay thought of a number, rejected it, picked another, and rejected it, also. Start small, he thought. "Ten thousand. In twenty dollar bills. And I'd like it tonight."

"Where?"

"At Rochelle's Bar and Grill. About eight. I think I'd rather have people around us, if you know what I mean."

"Yes, I do. Do you realize that if I'm caught, you could be named as an accessory? Or at the very least, charged with withholding evidence. Are you sure you want to be seen with me? I know I don't want to be seen with you. I'd rather no one started to wonder what we were talking about. We need somewhere more private."

Jay turned it over in his mind, trying to sense the trap if any. "Where would you like to meet?"

"Why not outside Rochelle's? On the right side, near the oak tree. That should be both private and close enough to people for you to feel safe."

Jay thought fast. He needed more insurance. "Okay, but you listen. Nothing better happen to me. I left a letter with a friend. You wouldn't like it if he read it. Understand?"

No reply.

"I said, do you understand?"

"Yes."

"Good. You remember that." Jay hung up the phone, pleased with himself. He had handled it like a pro. He went to the fridge for a beer, ignoring his shaking hands. Something nagged him about the call, but he couldn't figure it out. It don't matter, he thought. Tonight, I'm going to have some real money. And it's just the beginning.

For the next couple of hours, he flipped through the hunting magazines, picking out the new equipment he intended to buy. Ten thousand didn't go as far as he thought it would. Well, I'll ask for more next time, he decided.

Something still worried him about the call. He replayed it in his head, trying to see what he could have missed, but came up with nothing. He decided that he'd better take a pistol to the meeting.

Yeah, that's it, he thought. That's what I need. And I'll go early and scout it out!

Excited by his smart decisions, he rushed around and got ready to go. He selected a small handgun and shoved it in the waist of his pants. It was too hot for a coat, he realized. He was frustrated for a moment. He thought of his hunting vest. He could place the gun in one of the pockets, and it wouldn't look that strange for him to be wearing it since he wore it a lot.

He was anxious by this time so he decided he might as well go on to Rochelle's. He could get a couple of beers and play some pool while he waited. He carefully locked his side door. He didn't want any of his guns stolen. He looked around, noticing how shabby the houses on his block looked. My neighbors are nothing but lazy bums, he thought, ignoring the waist-high weeds that filled his lawn. The house next door had sold a couple of weeks ago. Maybe he'd sell his and move somewhere nicer. Or get one of those camper-trailers.

Still holding his keys, he walked over to his pickup, skirting around the piles of junk that filled his driveway. Suddenly it came to him what had been wrong about the phone call; he hadn't been asked for his name. Why didn't the murderer ask? Cold fear clutched his guts. That had to mean that the killer already knew who he was!

Jay had often hunted deer. He had seen them start for no reason as he started to pull the trigger. He wouldn't make a sound, and yet they would gather their legs to run. He had wondered more than once if some survival instinct had warned them of death, had warned them that Jay was about to end their lives.

He began to run to the house. Inside he started to wail. He only made a few steps toward the door before an impact knocked him to the ground. He hit the ground hard, but he didn't feel it. He didn't feel anything. He turned his head in the dust. He watched the wind move the weeds until he couldn't see anything ever again.

CHAPTER EIGHT

D imes gave his preliminary "guesses" to the chief without their usual ritual. Perhaps he could sense how upset the chief was. Whatever the reason, the chief appreciated it. After viewing Jay's body, the chief wasn't in the mood for sparring. Unfortunately, Dimes didn't have much to say.

"I'd guess that he was shot by a rifle – probably a .30-30 or something similar," Dimes said. "It's popular around here."

The chief acknowledged the information with a nod. He owned a .30-30 himself. So did half of the deer hunters in Ryton. Maybe half the hunters in the world.

"Judging from the size of the wound and the lack of powder burns, and considering that it was a rifle, he was probably shot from a distance. Of course, it looks like you already figured that."

The chief looked across from Jay's house to where a vacant lot lay covered with chokeweed and scrub-brush. He could see McGraw and Edwards searching the area. If this was a movie, they would find a matchbook or maybe a clear impression of tire tread marks in some mud. With the way things had been going lately, he'd lay odds that they would find nothing other than a few signs – crushed underbrush and grasses – that the murderer had been there. The chief couldn't decide if it was because he was too dumb or the murderer was too smart. He was beginning to think it was a little of both.

He became aware of Dimes's scrutiny. "Something else?"

"Nothing about this. But you look like you could stand to get some sleep."

"I need a vacation," the chief said. "I'm getting too old for all this. Three murders, and I'm no closer to catching who did them than when I started. Josh, if you find anything ..."

"I'll do my best," Dimes said. "And you'll catch him."

The chief shook Dimes's hand. He leaned against the hood of his car and waited for Sims to make his report. As he watched the lieutenant question some of Jay's neighbors, he could feel depression wrap its damp arms around him. Three people had been killed in his town, and he couldn't seem to get a handle on the business. His stomach churned, but he was almost too down to notice. He popped a couple of antacids into his mouth and crunched on them.

Sims came over to him.

"Anything?" the chief asked.

"Not much, Chief," Sims said. "They heard the shot but didn't see anyone. A couple of kids found his body when they cut across his lot. Their mother called us."

The chief swore. "No one saw anything?! He was shot in broad daylight not more than fifty feet from their house. And no one saw a thing?!"

Sims stood there, looking uncomfortable. The chief closed his eyes and exhaled. It wasn't the officer's fault. It wasn't the neighbors' fault. If anyone is to blame, it's me, the chief thought, his anger exhausted.

The chief gave himself a mental shake. He couldn't afford to be depressed; he had to catch this murderer. He had to before anyone else was killed. He was positive the murderer had killed Jay because Jay had known too much about what was going on – whatever that was. He took the notebook out of Sims's hand and looked the notes over, hoping to find something he had missed.

Jay had been carrying a handgun. Interesting, the chief thought. Did that mean Jay had known he was in danger? Jay had been shot between the house and the street. It looked like he had been running to the house. His keys were found not far from his body; he had probably dropped them when he fell. The chief looked at Jay's truck, parked on the street in front of the house, apparently because the driveway was filled with junk. Had Jay been going to the pickup and saw the murderer and ran, or had he been returning from somewhere?

"Come on," the chief said to Sims. They walked over to the pickup. "Pop the hood." The chief waited for Sims to open the hood and then tripped the latch. The chief felt the engine. It wasn't hot. So Jay had been going to the truck. Of course, Jay could have been returning from a walk and had out his keys to open his house. The chief recognized it was a possibility, but discarded it since Jay had been packing a gun. Most people don't carry guns to go on walks. He was also wearing a vest that would have been too warm to wear while walking.

Okay then, Jay had been going to his truck. What did that mean? Obviously, he was going somewhere that made him feel like he needed a gun. The chief mulled it over. Could he have been going to meet the murderer? And the murderer ambushed him? What if Jay had been the murderer's partner? The chief considered it, then rejected the thought. Jay had seemed genuinely surprised about Agatha's death. Of course, that didn't necessarily rule out the possibility, but the chief felt sure if that was the case, the murderer would have informed Jay of her death. And why would Jay leave town like that? If he knew of her death, he would know his leaving would only make him look guilty. Could the murderer have been trying to frame Jay by leaving the janitor's knife embedded in Leonard Brewer? If Jay had known something about this, why hadn't he told the chief?

The chief's mind leapt to another possibility. Perhaps Jay had been a partner in whatever had been going on but didn't know about the murder. Could the murderer have been afraid that Jay might break down and give evidence to the police? Could Jay's stay in the jail have triggered this?

The chief swore again, this time to himself. Too many questions and too little evidence. He couldn't sort the good theories from the bad. He needed more information. He decided to take another look around Jay's house.

He wandered through the small house with Sims silently following along. His eyes cataloged the hunting magazines, the beer cans, and the clothes on the floor. He counted six mounted deer heads hanging on the various walls as well as at least ten deer racks. He noted the polished wood of Jay's gun cabinet and the spotless condition of the guns inside. A phone book lay beside the phone. The chief flipped through it. Nothing out of the ordinary. No names underlined. What did you expect? he asked himself disgustedly. A red line under a name with a note to the side that said it belonged to the killer? He set the book down and looked around the room.

"Chief, should they dust in here?" Sims asked, finally breaking the silence.

"They might as well," the chief said. "Maybe they'll come up with something. By the way, what are you doing here? I thought your shift ended already."

"I'm covering for Hayden," Sims said. "He's still out with his son. The little guy's not doing very well. Hayden said the doctors think it's viral pneumonia."

"Tell Hayden to take all the time he needs," the chief said. "But try to find someone else to cover for him."

"I don't mind," Sims said.

"I do," the chief said. "You're at the station all the time. If you keep it up, you'll be worn out when I actually need you." The chief smiled slightly. "Get a life, Sims."

Sims returned the smile hesitantly.

"In fact, I'm going to take my own advice," the chief said. "I need a break from this. I think I'll take Maggie out to eat tonight." He nodded firmly and walked out.

*

Bernard leaned back and stretched. A stack of papers lay before him, attesting to his long afternoon of phone calls and research. Although he didn't have packing slips, it had occurred to him that the checks from the Library Board would list each publisher's name. A quick call to the city offices and a longer wait, and he had a fairly complete list of whom the library had paid. He had called most of them and had gained more evidence for his embezzlement theory.

Now he was waiting for Lisa to return from Oklahoma City. He had started to call the chief but decided to wait and tell Lisa first. She would be here soon, and they would both go to the chief. It would give her a great story.

Bernard thought the murderer was Richard Storer. Or maybe someone who worked for him. As Bernard saw it, Agatha had finally decided she had enough money to buy back her family's home and live the good life for her remaining years. Of course, that would mean that the embezzlement would end. Richard still needed the money so he and Agatha had argued. He'd lost his head and killed Agatha.

Frowning, Bernard looked his theory over again. He didn't have any evidence. The whole basis for it was that Richard Storer owned a bookstore that would have allowed him to sell the books that he and Agatha had stolen. Perhaps if the police searched Storer's bookstore, they would find some evidence. Of course, Storer had already had a couple of weeks to dispose of anything that would link him to the murders, including any library books. Still, he shouldn't be given any more time to cover his tracks. Bernard reached for the phone. Millie rushed into his office.

"I've got to leave," she said excitedly. "My mama just called. She's coming to pick me up right now before someone kills me!"

"What?"

"I said my mama –"

Bernard cut her off. "I know what you said, but why would she think someone would want –"

"Because we're dropping like flies," Millie said.

"What are you talking about?"

"Haven't you heard?" Millie asked. "I guess you've been in here all afternoon, haven't you?"

"Heard what?" Lisa asked, coming up behind the excited day aide.

Millie yelped and whirled around. "Don't do that! You scared me."

Lisa looked at Bernard questioningly. He shrugged.

"Go on, Millie," Lisa said.

"Someone shot Jay today!" Millie said. "Shot him in the back right in front of his house. He's dead."

"Oh, no," Lisa said. She sat down on the couch. She looked at Bernard. "Why would Jay be killed?"

"Mama said a lot of people around town think that some crazy murderer – maybe a Satanist – is trying to kill everyone who works at the library," Millie said. "You know, maybe Mrs. Ryton-Storer was a Satanist, and they worshipped the devil right in this very room!" Millie shivered delightedly.

Deadpan, Lisa looked at Bernard. "The Cult of the Library Worshippers. Very ancient."

"Don't encourage her," Bernard said. "Millie, no one is worshipping the devil around here. I don't know why Jay was killed, but it doesn't have anything to do with the devil. And no one is targeting us. I think you're perfectly safe. If you'd like, I'll call your mother and tell her that."

"She said she was coming to pick me up," Millie said.

"Then I'll talk to her when she gets here," Bernard said. "Why don't you stay up front and tell me when she arrives."

"Well, okay," Millie said, her enthusiasm visibly wilting under the weight of Bernard's disbelief. "Can I use the phone? I left my cell at the house."

"No, I'm expecting an important call from the chief so the line has to stay open," Bernard said.

Lisa waited until Millie went back to the front desk, then asked, "What's the chief calling you about?"

"Actually, nothing. If she uses the phone though, she'll spread this Satanist story all over town," Bernard said. "I don't think we need that right now. But we will be calling the chief in a moment because" – he paused dramatically – "I know why Agatha was killed."

He told her his theory and what he'd found in his phone calls. Lisa sat silently for a moment when he finished.

"Could she have embezzled that much money?" Lisa asked.

"I think she started this almost as soon as she started working here," Bernard said. "If she saved her money and did some modest investing, I don't see why not."

Lisa rose and paced excitedly around the room. "Do you realize what a great story this is going to make?" She stopped. "There are only two questions left. Who was her partner? And who killed her?"

"Richard Storer," Bernard said.

"Why him?" Lisa asked. "No, I get it. Because he has a bookstore where he could sell the books, right?"

Bernard nodded. "I think Agatha finally decided that she had enough money to buy back the library and support herself for the rest of her life. Remember the appraisal she hired Neal Gibson to make? I think Richard lost his temper and killed her."

"No, I can't see him doing that," Lisa said.

"I didn't know you two were that close," Bernard said.

"Don't be snappy," Lisa said. "You could be right. But I went to his bookstore, and it didn't feel like that."

"Like what?"

"Like it was run by a murderer," Lisa said.

"When did you go to his bookstore?"

"This morning. I thought there'd be a new story angle in it. Richard wasn't in so I didn't get to talk to him. But as I was leaving, he pulled up, and guess who was with him."

"I have no idea," Bernard said.

"Evelyn Ryton," Lisa said. "Isn't that interesting?"

"You didn't tell me you were going to his bookstore," Bernard said. "I thought you went to Oklahoma City for a job interview."

"I also didn't tell you that I was going to the mall, but I did," Lisa said, annoyed.

"Lisa, you have someone trying to kill you," Bernard said. "And it's probably Storer. What if he had seen you? Did you tell the police you were going there?"

"He didn't see me," Lisa said. "And I did call the station."

"They should have sent an officer with you," Bernard said. "And you should have told me where you were going."

Lisa glared at him. "I'm not a child."

"I didn't say you were," Bernard said. "But I don't want

anything to happen to you." He took her hand. "You're too important to me, Lisa. I don't know what I would do without you. And I don't want to find out."

"I … I'll be more careful," Lisa said, her voice wavering for a moment.

Bernard nodded. "Thank you. What about his bookstore makes you think he's not a murderer?"

"It's a really good bookstore," Lisa said. "I've always found that people who have great bookstores are good people. When I was fourteen, we lived in Weatherford for a while. A lady by the name of Mabel ran the best bookstore there. Hooked On Books, it was called. And she was wonderful. I think bookstore owners absorb all the goodness of the books."

"Okay, I stand defeated by such logic," Bernard said, grinning as he slid his arms around her.

She put her arms around his neck. "Smart ass. You're cute but definitely a smart ass."

"As long as you think I'm cute, I can live with that." He began to kiss her, but she suddenly jumped.

"Oh, I forgot my great news," she said. "I got the job."

"That's great." Bernard moved away from her and sat on the couch. "When do you start?"

"June fifteenth. You don't sound like it's great," Lisa said.

"No, it's wonderful," he said. "I just hate that you'll have to move out of Ryton.

"Now, wait just a minute," Lisa said. "You told me that I should make my decisions based on what was good for me."

"Yeah, but that was before last night," Bernard said.

"Bernard, I nearly shot you last night," Lisa said. "We didn't get married. Besides, I've been hired to be a roving reporter for the Dispatch. I'll cover stories all over this area. I won't have to move."

"Why didn't you say so? That's great!"

"Oh, now it's great."

"Don't get mad because I don't want you to move away. I like having you around."

"I'm not mad," she said. "But I've worked hard the past few years, and working for the Dispatch will be quite a step up for me. I'd like you to be pleased about my accomplishments no matter what."

"I am. I'm sorry. I didn't mean to sound like I didn't."

"Forget it," Lisa said, looking out the window. "Well, hadn't you better call the chief?"

Glad to change the subject, Bernard reached for the phone, but the chief wasn't at the station. Neither was Sims. He called the chief's home number next. The chief answered.

"Hello, Chief. This is Bernard. I think I've discovered why Agatha was murdered."

"What? Tell me. No, wait, the missus and I are coming into town to go to dinner," the chief said. "Why don't you meet us at The Señor in about ten minutes?"

"Lisa's with me. We'll be there."

Bernard hung up the phone. "We're going to meet him."

Lisa nodded, still not looking at him.

"I really didn't mean it to sound that way," he said. "You'll do great for the Dispatch. I'm proud of you."

"I know," she said. "It's okay."

But Bernard knew that was a lie.

*

Over tacos, enchiladas, chips, and hot buttered corn tortillas, Lisa, Bernard, Maggie, and the chief discussed what Bernard had found. The chief was as excited as Lisa had ever seen him. He wanted to leave immediately and start making calls, but Maggie insisted he finish dinner first.

"It's waited all this time," Maggie said. "It can wait a little longer." She leaned toward Lisa. "Although really I shouldn't even let him eat Mexican food because of his ulcer, but he loves it so much. And you know how boys are."

Lisa smiled and watched as the older woman fussed over the chief. She wondered if she would ever be that close to anyone. Bernard's attitude toward her new job deeply disturbed her. She thought it was selfish. Ordinarily she might have brought it up, tried to talk it out, even argued about it, but at the moment, it made her feel tired, made her feel that his affection for her wasn't as deep as hers was for him. She found herself wondering again if he had just been on the rebound when they met. Or maybe the emotional impact of the murders had created a false bond between them. She realized that everyone at the table was looking at her. Apparently she had been asked a question.

"I'm sorry. I drifted off. What did you say?" she asked, wrenching her mind back to the conversation.

"I asked if you could hold off on writing a story about this until we can search Storer's bookstore," the chief said.

"As long as you don't talk to anyone else first," Lisa said. She was aware that Bernard was watching her, but she didn't meet his eyes. She didn't feel like reassuring him.

"All right," the chief answered.

"Lisa's been hired full-time by the Dispatch," Bernard said.

Maggie and the chief congratulated Lisa.

She thanked them, sending a mental dagger at Bernard. Now he's proud, she thought. To change the subject, she asked, "Chief, do you think Storer committed the murders?"

The chief shrugged. "At the moment, with no evidence, who can say? I'd really like to find out if he owns a rifle and if it was the one that shot Jay. That would wind things up. Do you think he could be the one who attacked you?"

Lisa thought about it. "I don't know. I've only seen him a couple of times. He doesn't seem big enough, though."

"The attack happened fast, Lisa," Bernard said. "Remember I saw the attacker, too. And I think it could have been Storer."

Lisa shook her head.

"And he is close to the same body type and height of your attacker," Bernard pointed out.

"This isn't a debate," Lisa snapped, irritated by Bernard's insistence. "You have your opinion; I have mine. And I don't think he did it."

Her sharpness silenced the conversation for a moment, the chief looking away, Bernard looking at her, and Maggie looking at both of them.

"Is there any way to identify the books?" the chief asked.

Bernard frowned. "I don't know. Agatha certainly wouldn't have stamped any of them. I was thinking he might have kept a record of them. Or maybe we can locate books that he doesn't have any documentation for. I've had most of the publishers send us duplicates of our orders. If enough books in his shop match up with what we've ordered, I think we have him."

"But he could have ordered those books, also," the chief said.

"He has a lot of second-hand books, too," Lisa said. "Most of them he probably got in trade. I doubt he would have any type of records about them."

"It would be new books we were looking for, right?" the chief asked Bernard.

"That's where the money is, but Lisa's right. Proving any of those books came from the library is going to be tough."

"This whole case has been one big pain in the ass," the chief said. "I wouldn't expect it to be any other way."

"He's also had a long time to cover his tracks," Bernard said.

"All the more reason we shouldn't give him any more," the chief said, looking at Maggie.

"Oh, all right, if Bernard and Lisa could give me a ride home, you can get started," Maggie said.

"Bernard, you'll need to come with me," the chief said, rising. "We'll take your statement and get it on record before I call some people in the city."

"I'll drive Maggie home," Lisa said. "And pick you up later."

Bernard gave her the keys and looked at her for a long moment. "I really am sorry," he said softly. "I mean it."

"It's okay," Lisa said. "Really." She managed a smile. He kissed her quickly and left with the chief.

"He seems like a nice young man," Maggie said. "How serious are you? Any wedding bells in the future?" She sipped her tea.

Flustered, Lisa laughed. Maggie joined in.

"There, that's better," Maggie said. "Whatever he did, it's not worth ruining your whole night. Forgive him or forget him. Now, tell me about this new job of yours." The two women talked all the way home, and as Lisa drove back into Ryton, she felt better and had decided she was being unfair to Bernard. She wouldn't be pleased if he had to move away from her – although she would definitely be more excited for him than he was for her.

Lisa glanced at the library as she drove past it. She slammed on the brakes. A light had briefly gleamed from Agatha's office. She watched the now dark window. It looked like a flashlight, she thought.

She checked the parking lot. No cars were in it. Could the chief have dropped Bernard off at the library? But why would Bernard be using a flashlight? A truck was coming up behind her so she pulled into the entrance of the library parking lot and parked. The shrubs that lined the front of the library's lawn partially screened the car. What should I do? she wondered. If I leave, whoever is in there – if anyone – will get away.

From her location she could see both the front and side entrances to the library. She decided it wouldn't hurt to wait for a few minutes and see if there were any more strange lights. After all, it could have been headlight reflections on the windows, she reasoned. That's probably what it was.

Just to be on the safe side, she locked all the doors. When she remembered that Jay had been shot from a distance, she nearly drove away. Instead, she crouched down in the seat as far as she could and still see the entrances. With the street lights the way they are, I don't think anyone could see in here, she thought. If he wanted to take a shot at me, he'd expect me to be on the driver's side. She slid over to the passenger's side and carefully peered at the library.

It stared blankly back at her. With no windows on the top floors, it looked like a man with no eyes, she thought shivering. Now, that's a cheery thought.

As she studied the library front, something began to bother her about it. She groped for her purse, opened it and dug out the Ryton family file that Veit had given her. She thumbed through the stories until she found the one about the founding of the library. The light from the street wasn't bright enough for her to see it well. She opened her purse and took out her pocket flashlight. She placed the file on the seat and bent over it, studying the photo.

The library hasn't changed much, she thought. Other than a few more bushes and the windows ... the windows. She looked up at the library. It had two large windows that flanked the door and went from the first floor to the second. One smaller frosted window that let light into the women's restroom was on the far left. On the right were the windows of the tower room, Agatha's office. But above the smaller windows, there were only blank walls. The second floor didn't have windows now.

An idea was on the tip of her mind. And she knew it had to do with the windows. She leaned over to look at the photo again.

The back window exploded as bullets hurled glass throughout the car.

*

"Well, that gets things started," the chief said as he hung up the phone and glanced over at Bernard who was sipping some coffee provided by one of the night officers. The coffee's sharp bittersweet aroma made the chief's mouth water. Of all things he missed most since he got an ulcer, coffee rated right up there. He was tempted to pour himself a cup. But I'm probably going to be up half the night already suffering from those tacos, the chief thought, reflexively reaching for his antacids.

"Actually, I'm surprised at how much you got accomplished," Bernard said.

"Why? Did you think the city shut down at five-thirty like Ryton does?" The chief chuckled. "In the city, the police are just as busy at night as they are in the day. They'll have that search warrant by nine in the morning if I don't miss my guess. I'll have to drive up there tomorrow so that I can participate. I think you'd better come along if you can. You have more of an idea of what we're looking for."

"I don't think that will be a problem – if Millie shows up, that is," Bernard amended. "Her mom got the idea that a madman was stalking the library employees. Millie decided that maybe it was a Satanist."

The chief laughed. "So she quit?"

"No, when Mrs. Sader came to pick Millie up, I talked to her for a moment and got her calmed down. At least I think I did."

"I have to say that you discovering this embezzlement has made me feel a lot better," the chief said. "I thought this old country boy was going down for the count, but things are moving again."

"I would have never figured it out if Millie hadn't told me about how a lost twin showed up on one of her TV shows," Bernard said. "That made me think of duplicates. Chief, I'm probably borrowing trouble, but what if we don't find anything? What if Storer didn't have anything at all to do with it?"

"Good question. Sure wish I had a good answer." The chief regarded Bernard soberly. "Our murderer has had a while to clean things up. Still, he did kill Jay so that tells me that he doesn't feel safe. And no cover-up is perfect. If this turns up nothing, we keep trying and hope for some luck."

Bernard nodded. He looked down at his coffee cup and took a swallow. "This is good coffee."

The chief grunted and decided to shoot anyone who drank coffee in front of him again. An officer walked past the chief's open door. "Sims, is that you?"

"Uh, yes, chief." Sims sheepishly stuck his head around the doorjamb.

"I don't think you're working tonight, are you?" the chief asked, looking pointedly at the duty roster posted on the wall across from his desk.

"Oh, I'm not. I went to see that new science fiction movie. It's good," Sims said, attempting to walk away.

"So what are you doing here?" The chief leaned back, folded his arms, and waited for an answer. It was extremely slow in coming.

"Well, I thought I'd check in and see how things were going," Sims said, looking trapped.

"They're fine," the chief said firmly. "See you tomorrow."

"Oh. Okay, well, good night." Sims nodded to Bernard and started to walk down the hall.

"The exit is the other way," the chief pointed out.

"I'm just going to say hi to Julie." Sims escaped up the hall.

The chief shook his head wryly. "You know, if I had twenty like Sims, we'd have to import criminals into Ryton. All the local ones would be locked away. But he needs to spend more time away from here." He glanced at his watch. "Speaking of time, I would have thought Lisa would be back now."

Bernard checked his watch. "I would have, too. If you have to go, I don't mind waiting by myself."

"Well, let me call home and see if Maggie is there yet," the chief said. "If Lisa hasn't left yet, I'll drop you at home, and she can come by there. They probably got to talking and forgot the time."

But Maggie said Lisa had left about two hours ago. "Is there something wrong, dear?"

"Probably not," the chief told his wife. It took about twenty minutes to drive to his house. And there were several houses along the way so even if she had had car trouble, she wouldn't have had to walk far to call for help. Surely she would have telephoned the station by this time.

"Will you be home soon?" Maggie asked.

"Probably about an hour still," the chief answered.

"I'll see you then," she said.

The chief hung up the phone with a pit in his stomach and looked at Bernard. "Did she have anywhere else to go?"

"Not that I know of. Maybe she stopped by her house," Bernard said. "Let me call." He dialed the number, waited a couple of minutes, and hung up. "I'm getting worried."

"Probably no reason to," the chief said. "Does she have a cell phone?"

"No," Bernard said. "But I'm going to get her one tomorrow. And get me one, too."

"Maggie has one, but we never use it," the chief said. "Let's give Lisa a few more minutes before we go look for her 'cause as sure as shooting, the minute we pulled away, she'd show up. That's how it always goes."

Bernard nodded.

"Still, I think I'll tell Julie to have the guys to keep an eye out for her," the chief said. "Don't worry. It's probably nothing." But the chief didn't know if he was trying to convince Bernard or himself.

*

Lisa screamed. Another shot sounded. The bullet buried in the dash, throwing out particles of plastic. Frantically she tried to squeeze herself into the floor. A shot smashed the wheel. Her horn sounded and continued to wail. More shots screamed into the car. She had to get out before the ricochets killed her.

She grabbed the door handle and flung herself out, rolling and scrambling as she ran for the bushes and trees. She felt something hot sting her back, and she stumbled to her knees. She pulled herself up and threw herself behind a tree. Oh, please, God, help me.

Two more shots sounded. The horn stopped blowing. In the silence, she could hear her heartbeat. She made herself as small as she could, trying to ignore the pain in her back. She reached back and felt for the wound. A wave of nausea and pain swamped her as she touched it. Her hand came back bloody. She felt faint. Gulping huge amounts of the cool night air, she tried to collect her thoughts. I've got to think or I'm dead.

Someone has to have heard those shots and called the police, she thought. Please, someone call the police. He won't hang around. He can't. Too much chance of being caught. Where are the police?

She looked one way and then the next. She could see up and down the deserted street. One car was parked a block down in front of the flower shop, but the shop was dark. In the other directions were more closed shops and offices. No houses with people who would hear and call the police. But Ryton's not that big, she thought. There are houses not more than three blocks from here. Surely someone will hear. The lights of a car startled her. She pulled back. It drove past.

I should have stopped them, but what if he was driving? Slowly she caught her breath. The pain in her back was lessening. She hoped that was a good sign. The silence continued. Is he still out there? Is he waiting for me?

Suddenly she heard a sharp ping as something metal hit the pavement. Something like a shell! She bolted to the side, weaving in and out of the bushes. Someone crashed through the underbrush behind her. She darted onto the street, running down the sidewalk a few feet and then plunging back into the greenery.

She crouched down and clapped her hand over her mouth to

muffle her gasps. She could hear someone coming closer. Closer. Quietly she pulled herself into a ball. Through the leaves, she could barely see someone walk closer. And then stop. Directly in front of where she was hiding. She leaned back. A sharp stick dug into her wounded back. She bit her lips to keep from crying out.

Suddenly a rifle barrel plunged into the brush straight at her.

*

Bernard put the phone down and shook his head at the chief. "She's not home. Or she's not answering. I'd like to go look for her."

The chief nodded. "Let me tell Julie where we're going so that if Lisa shows up, she'll know to wait."

"Don't have her wait," Bernard said. "Have Julie tell her to go on home, and you'll drop me there if that's okay."

"Okay by me," the chief said. He disappeared down the hall and came back accompanied by Sims. "Sims is going to help us look. If he's going to be here, I might as well get some work out of him."

"It's not like I'm not doing anything else right now," Sims pointed out.

"You know, some people sleep at night," the chief said. "Anyway, I thought Bernard and I would drive toward my place. Why don't you check toward Lisa's house?"

"I'll check Rochelle's, too," Sims said. "She could have stopped for a drink."

"I doubt that," Bernard said sharply. "She doesn't drink much."

Sims looked surprised. "I didn't mean she did, but she used to hang out there –"

"Yeah. Whatever." Bernard looked at the chief. "Let's go."

The chief raised his eyebrows. "Okay. Let's go."

Bernard followed him out.

*

The rifle barrel moved back and forth. Lisa was paralyzed, hypnotized by its movement. She could smell the cordite; a mouthful of its smell nearly gagged her. The barrel withdrew. It plunged into brush again but a couple of feet to Lisa's left. He was using the rifle to try to flush her out. He doesn't know where I am! He doesn't know where I am! She could hear the leaves rustle as he moved farther away from her down the street.

She became conscious of the stick stabbing into her back. Carefully she reached back to move it to the side. As she did, it broke, the crack filling the night like thunder. She froze. The sounds of him searching ceased. She heard him walk closer, heard a sharp metallic snap, then a gunshot.

A bullet whined through the brush to her left. She pulled her knees to her chest and clutched herself tight. A sharp snap, the shot, and another bullet tore through the leaves and branches, closer to where she hid. He was methodically shooting the brush, either hoping to scare her out or shoot her. She knew if she ran, he would have her. Her only hope was to stay absolutely still.

Another snap and shot. This bullet shredded a branch near her shoulder. She strangled a scream. If she didn't move when he shot her, if she didn't make a sound, he wouldn't know that he had hit her. People survive gunshot wounds, she told herself. So can I. But if he finds me, I'm dead.

The waiting seemed to go on forever, and then she heard that metallic snap, clear and crisp. It's the sound of death, she thought. It's the sound of death.

*

"I don't think Sims meant anything by what he said," the chief said, finally breaking the silence as he and Bernard drove slowly down Seventh Street.

"No, probably not," Bernard said, sighing. "I'm tired. Sometimes it seems like this thing will never be over." He rolled his window down. "I've been thinking I might leave Ryton. I don't want to be at the library when Evelyn takes over. She can't fire me, but she can make my life miserable. Worse than that, I can't see her doing any better job than Agatha. I'm not sure if it's worth it."

"What about Lisa?" the chief asked.

"Well, her job will let her live about anywhere in western Oklahoma," Bernard said. "I think she might like to live closer to the Dispatch. I could get a job in the city or in the suburbs so I could be close to her, but she might not want me to do so. We don't seem to be getting along very well."

The chief drove in silence for a moment. "Would you mind a little advice?"

"No, go ahead," Bernard said. "I need all the help I can get."

"You two haven't known each other very long," the chief said. "And a lot of excitement has happened in that time. It's not been easy on either of you, and people act funny under stress." He turned a corner. "What I am saying is that you both need more time to get to know each other. After this is all over and things calm down, I think things will work out okay. You've got to give it more time."

"Maybe so, but –"

"Wait." The chief stopped the car as they crossed Main. "I heard something."

He leaned his head out the window. There it was again!

"It's a gunshot! Hold on!" He turned onto Main and grabbed the radio mike. "Julie, I'm on Main, and I've heard shots, coming from the end of the street. Get me some backup." The chief drove down Main, scanning both sides of the street. They crossed Sixth, Fifth and Fourth streets.

"Wait!" Bernard yelled. "That's my car!" It was parked in the library driveway, one door hanging open. The back window was missing. "What's going on?!"

The chief slammed on the brakes. "Stay here and stay down!" He pulled out his gun, slid out of the police car, and ran over to Bernard's sedan. He knelt, checking all directions. All he could hear were the crickets and the wind in the trees.

He looked at Bernard's car. Someone had completely shot out its back window. The chief circled the car, going to the open door. He took a deep breath and looked inside, hoping he wouldn't find Lisa's dead body. He didn't, but the car's interior was bullet-riddled and covered by bits of plastic and glass. He looked for blood, but couldn't see any.

"Is Lisa –" Bernard asked from behind the chief.

"I told you to stay in the car," the chief snapped. He looked at Bernard's strained face and relented. "She's not in there."

"Thank God," Bernard breathed.

The chief looked around. "Let's get my flashlight." They

hurried back the chief's car. The chief took his flashlight and picked up the radio mike. "I'm at the library. Where's my backup?"

"They're on their way," the dispatcher replied.

"I can hear them," Bernard said.

The faint sound of a siren was getting closer. Probably Harris, he thought. Ryton wasn't large, but only two cars patrolled at night, Harris on the south side of town and Edwards on the north. Usually that was enough. He told the dispatcher, "Julie, call my wife and tell her that I'm going to be later than I thought." He tossed the microphone into the car.

Harris pulled up, his lights flashing. Another car pulled up and out jumped Sims, gun in one hand and flashlight in the other. The chief was glad to see him.

"Harris, stay here with Bernard," the chief ordered. "Call in everyone we can and search the area. Do it in pairs. Someone's out here with a gun so check in every five minutes. We're looking for Lisa Trent. She may be shot. Now, move!"

"Chief, I want to –" Bernard began.

"No, you're going to get in the car and stay there," the chief cut him off. "Sims, come with me. It looks like someone went through this brush. Let's see where."

Sims nodded and took the lead. The chief didn't mind; the lieutenant was a faster and better shot. He hoped Sims's skills would be unnecessary. They moved cautiously forward, checking all directions.

"Chief, look." Sims focused his light on the ground where several small dark spots glistened. "Blood. Someone's been shot."

The chief nodded grimly and motioned Sims to lead on. Carefully they threaded their way through the brush.

A voice sounded weakly from behind them. "Chief ..."

They whirled around, Sims raising his gun.

Lisa stood there, leaning against a tree, her face pale and frightened.

"Chief, I've been shot," she said faintly.

The chief caught her as she fell.

CHAPTER NINE

L isa wondered why hospital rooms were always white. Because it looks clean, she decided. Although white is probably not any cleaner than blue or green. I think I would decorate it in teal or maybe sea green. Or is that too dark?

"Lisa, how do you feel?"

Lisa turned her head so she could see the chief. She tried to answer and found her mouth was so dry that her tongue stuck to the roof of it. She tried again. "I'd like a drink. My mouth ..."

"That's the pain-killer, dear," a nurse said, busying herself at the bedside table. "It gives you cotton-mouth." She helped Lisa up.

Lisa sipped the water and carefully leaned back. Her back was still numb from the shots the doctor had given her. It had needed a couple of stitches from where a bullet had creased it when she ran from Bernard's car. The doctor wanted to keep her overnight. She wondered if the Dispatch's health insurance would cover her even though she hadn't started work yet. Looking up, she realized the chief was still waiting for an answer.

"I guess I'm okay. Did you catch him?" she asked hopefully. From his face she read the answer she dreaded.

The chief shook his head. "He was gone by the time we got there. Did you see him?"

Lisa closed her eyes to keep tears from escaping. "N-no, I never saw him. Just glimpses through the bushes. Oh, no ..." She turned her face away from the chief.

He waited for a few moments before asking, "Do you feel up to telling me what happened?"

"Yes." Lisa started to wipe her eyes with her hand and gratefully accepted a tissue from the nurse. She took a moment to order her thoughts, then told her story as completely as she could. When she reached the point when the rifle was pointed at her, she had to pause for a few moments before she could continue. "But he didn't shoot again," she said. "I guess he heard you coming because I heard him running away. I hid for a while longer before I started walking to the car. You found me then."

The chief looked at her intently. "Lisa, I'm sorry this has happened. Officer Jacobs is outside the door. We're not going to let anything else happen to you. I promise."

"Not your fault," Lisa said. "It was dumb of me to stop. Chief, what about the library? What was he doing in there?"

"We're checking it out now," he said. "You get some sleep. Bernard will be in to see you soon." He patted her hand and left. She could hear him talking softly outside.

The nurse straightened the bedclothes. "If you need anything, dear, the call button is on the rail beside your right hand. The bed controls are on the other side. There may be some pain later tonight or in the morning. Just let me know, and we'll give you something for it."

Bernard came in, looking drawn and tired. She tried to smile at him. He pulled up a chair and took her hand.

"I seem to remember that we've done this before," he said quietly. "I'd prefer we didn't do it again."

"I was thinking that maybe we're in a rut," she said. "But I'm afraid I'm getting good at this."

"You're going to have to pick up another hobby," Bernard said, gently hugging her. "I'm so glad you're not hurt."

She reached up with her free hand and placed it on his cheek. He kissed her palm. She smiled.

"She really should get some sleep," the nurse said.

"I'd like him to stay for a while," Lisa said.

The nurse looked doubtful.

"I can't stay long," Bernard said. "The chief is waiting to drive me to the library. We're going to meet Sims there."

The nurse nodded and left the room, leaving the door ajar. Lisa could see the blue-sleeved arm of a policeman – apparently Jacobs whom she had never met. If this keeps up, I'm going to know everyone on the force, she thought.

"Can I get anything for you?" Bernard asked, rubbing her hand gently.

She shook her head. "I just want you here." She shifted in the bed to bring herself closer to him. "Bernard, I was right next to him tonight. I could have touched him. And I never saw him. I never saw him." She shivered.

"You're safe now," he said, holding her.

"I know," Lisa said. "But I keep thinking about that old saying about third time being the charm. He's tried twice. I don't want him to have another chance."

"Maybe tomorrow it will all be over," he said. "If Storer has the gun that shot at you, that will be even better than finding some books that we can identify."

"And if he didn't do it, or if you don't find anything? Then what will we do?"

"We'll do something else," he said. He searched her face. "I've been thinking maybe we should move. We could get away from all this, get you away from him."

"I'm not going to leave until he's caught," Lisa said. "I'm not going to feel safe until I know he's behind bars."

"We can talk about it later," Bernard said.

"I'm not going to leave."

Bernard shook his head. "We'll hash it out later. It's nothing to get upset about. It's just a thought. Right now, all you need to do is get some rest."

She nodded but thought, it's amazing how awake I am. Her eyes were tired, though. She closed them to let them rest. Bernard's hand started to slip away, and she tightened her grip. "Don't go yet."

"All right, I'll stay a bit longer."

She fell asleep as he talked.

*

Standing outside the library with the chief, Bernard took off his glasses and rubbed his eyes. On the way over, he had asked the chief to stop by his apartment so that he could take out his contacts. His eyes felt tired and grainy. Which, he thought, is how I feel, too.

"Chief," Sims called from the library door. "It's clear. But someone tore Bimmer's office up good."

The chief glanced at Bernard. Bernard shrugged. He was too tired to care right now. He silently followed the chief into the brightly-lit building. He stopped inside the entrance and looked around the lobby, noting automatically the large stack of returned books on the circulation desk. It looked like the night aide was slacking off again. At the moment, he couldn't remember which one of them it was.

His gaze traveled across the black and white marble floor that was only becoming more beautiful after thirty years of wear, traced the ornate carvings on the wall pillars that collected dust and were practically impossible to clean, and followed the wide staircase with its railing set too low for most people but the right height for short Eliah Ryton, and he realized with an odd and almost painful clarity that he loved the old place. It was drafty, expensive to cool and heat, and in desperate need of remodeling, and he would miss it.

The chief waved for Bernard to come join him at the door of Bernard's office. Bernard went over slowly, reluctant to see the damage. While he didn't care for his office as much as Agatha had cared for hers, he was still attached to it. He looked inside and sighed. His books and papers lay scattered across the room, the desk on its back with the drawers and their contents in a huge pile, and the seats and backs of his chairs slashed.

"Whoever it was trashed the lounge and the closet, too," Sims said. "And it looks like he started on the shelves upstairs. A bunch of books are on the floor."

Bernard nodded wearily. "What could he be looking for?"

"I don't know," the chief said. "But I don't think he found it. I'd guess that it was something that linked him either to the murders or to the embezzlement."

"Maybe a record book of some sort," Sims suggested.

"Good idea, Sims," the chief said. "But whatever it is, he's still looking for it." The chief smiled grimly. "And that means we have a good chance of catching him."

"How do you figure?" Bernard asked.

"Because he's gonna keep searching for it, and it's in Ryton somewhere." The chief leaned against the circulation desk. "I don't think he'll let it rest now. He's gone to a lot of trouble to try to find it. Breaking in here –"

"No one broke in, Chief," Sims said. "There are no signs of forced entry or picklocks."

The chief looked puzzled for a moment, then he slammed his fist against the counter. "I am so slow. Bernard, were Agatha's keys ever found?"

"No," Bernard said. "I forgot about them."

"So did I." The chief turned to Sims. "Have someone stay here tonight. First thing in the morning, get a locksmith to change all these locks."

"It's almost morning now," Sims said, checking his watch.

His mornings must start a lot earlier than mine, Bernard thought. Another reason to not be a policeman.

"What time is it?" the chief asked.

"Nearly four."

"Have them dust Bernard's office for prints and anywhere else that seems likely," the chief said. "We might come up with something. I'm going to go home and catch an hour or two of sleep before I head to the city. I'll drop you off, Bernard."

"Chief, what about my car?" Bernard asked.

"Let them dig the bullets out of it, and you can pick it up tomorrow, I mean, today after we get back from Oklahoma City," the chief said.

"I can't wait to tell my insurance agent about this." Bernard rubbed his forehead.

"I think they file the claim under vandalism," the chief said. "I had it happen once before."

"Oh, I still need to call Millie to see if she's coming in if I'm going with you," Bernard said.

"Bimmer, we need the library closed today," Sims said with a look at the chief.

"Oh, okay." Bernard frowned. "I'm sorry. I'm not thinking. I guess I'll call Millie and tell her we're closed today."

"Let me take you home," the chief said.

In the car, Bernard asked, "Chief, why is he trying so hard to kill Lisa? He has to know by now that she can't identify him. It doesn't make sense. What kind of nut are we dealing with?"

"I was thinking about that," the chief said. "Perhaps he spotted Lisa and took a chance. He can't be sure that she might not see him on the street someday and suddenly recognize him. No one wants to live in fear." The chief turned a corner. "Or maybe he thought she saw him in the library or that she was waiting for him. There's no way to know until we catch him and wring some answers out of his sorry hide."

"How did he get out of the library without her seeing him?"

"It was dark," the chief said. "If he came out the side door and if Lisa looked away for a few moments, he could be in the trees before she saw him."

"The security light makes the side lot pretty bright, but I guess if she looked away, that wouldn't matter," Bernard said. "What I don't get is why no one called the police. My car had to be shot at least six or seven times, and counting the times he shot in the bushes, it must have sounded like a war zone."

"There aren't any houses within a couple of blocks of here, and the businesses are all closed around it," the chief said. "And I'm afraid that Ryton has people who don't want to get involved. That's not just a big city problem. It's easy to think that someone else will call the police. People don't want to take responsibility." He stopped the car in front of Bernard's apartment. "I'll pick you up at eight."

Bernard halfheartedly nodded and made his way up to his apartment. He stumbled to bed, barely remembering to set his alarm for seven-thirty. Seemingly five minutes later, his phone woke him. He moaned and answered it.

"Do you have it?" a muffled voice asked.

"What?" Bernard asked dully.

"Do you have it? I'm ready to deal if you do."

It was *him*, Bernard realized, a jolt of adrenaline bringing him wide awake, his heart pounding.

"Yes, I have it," Bernard said.

"Prove it," the voice said. "What are we talking about?"

Bernard frantically tried to figure out what to say.

"You don't have it." The voice sounded pleased.

"Yes, I do," Bernard said.

"No, you don't," the man said. "Listen to me. I can kill you or that girl any time I choose. Back off or you'll both be dead."

The man hung up.

Bernard looked at the caller ID. It showed that the call had been made by a pay phone. He placed the receiver in the cradle. Was it his imagination or had that voice sounded familiar? Who could it be? A loud buzz cut through the air. Bernard jumped, then leaned over, and shut off his alarm.

*

The night nurse woke Lisa up at seven to take her temperature, and the day nurse woke her up at eight to take it again. At nine, a volunteer woke her up for a breakfast of soggy oatmeal and warm orange juice, which she declined. Lisa woke up around ten herself, her back sore and her temper not much better. She buzzed the nurse.

"I'd like some painkillers and my clothes," Lisa said. "And I'd like both *now*."

"Your clothes are in the closet, and I'll bring you back something," the nurse said with a stiff smile.

"I'd also like to check out."

"Doctor Osborne will be in a few minutes."

An hour later, Lisa was still waiting and fuming. When Osborne finally arrived, she had already composed the outline and the first paragraph of a vicious medical expose. He gave her a brief examination and said she could check out.

"Call me if you have any problems," he said.

Lisa nodded but thought, I'd be dead by the time you showed up. An officer stood in the doorway. She looked up.

"Miss Trent, I'm Officer Harris," the officer said, looking nervous. "I've been assigned for your protection."

Hmm, this will be a new experience, she thought. "Call me Lisa. Well, I guess I'm ready to leave."

"I'll drive you home."

The bright sun welcomed Lisa as she stepped outside the hospital. The lawn was freshly mowed, and she took a deep breath, enjoying the strong grass odor.

"You know, I've never liked hospitals," Harris said as they walked to his black-and-white.

"Me, neither." She closed the door and was silent on the trip home. At her house, Harris killed the car and followed her up the walk.

"I'll be okay," Lisa said.

"I'd like to check the house out," he said, politely but firmly.

She started to protest but decided that it was better to be safe. "I'm sorry the house is such a mess," she called after him.

"It looks fine," he said from upstairs. "If my house ever looked this nice, my wife would sell it."

He must live in the town dump, she thought, surveying the cluttered living room and noticing at least two pizza boxes that needed to be thrown out before they showed any more signs of life. A black blur bounded for the open door. "Obsidian!" She lunged for the door, but the cat made it outside, neatly evading Lisa's hands.

"I've got to catch my cat," she yelled upstairs and hurried out. The last time Obsidian had made it out, he had been hit by a car. Lisa looked around. There he was, disappearing under the hedge that separated her house from the one next door.

"Come here, Obsidian, come to mama."

She stepped around the hedge. Obsidian sat there calmly, licking his paw. He looked at Lisa from a mental distance approximately equivalent to that of Jupiter.

"Bad kitty," she gently scolded. She leaned over, wincing a bit as her back reminded her that it was injured, and scooped the cat up. He purred as if that had been his idea all the time.

"Have I been neglecting you, baby?" she cooed.

"I thought that was you," a woman's voice said harshly from behind her.

Lisa whirled around, nearly falling. Sherry Hyatt stood by the hedge with her hands on her hips, her eyes glinting angrily.

"You startled me," Lisa said.

"I'm so sorry," Sherry said with a smirk.

Obsidian squirmed in Lisa's arms. She cradled him carefully but retained a firm grip.

"Were you coming to see me?" Lisa asked.

"What if I was?" Sherry asked, challenge in her voice.

Lisa looked skyward and shook her head. "This is unbelievable. What is this? Prehistoric Action Theater and we're two cavewomen about to fight it out over a man?"

Sherry looked taken aback. Her face hardened. "You think you're so smart," Sherry hissed. "But it doesn't impress anyone. We all know who you really are." Her voice sharpened. "And everyone knows what your father was."

"I think you'd better leave," Lisa said, her voice rising.

"Why? Don't like hearing the truth?" Sherry pointed her finger at Lisa. "As soon as Bernard figures out what you are and what you're after, he'll leave you."

"And if he does, what business is it of yours?" Lisa dropped Obsidian who hissed and stayed by her legs. "It's over between you two." She stepped toward Sherry. "He's not your property. Or anyone else's, for that matter. What is your problem? Did the spoiled little girl lose her boy toy?" Looking at Sherry's face, Lisa felt a flash of insight. "That's it, isn't it? You wanted him to wait for you, and he didn't do it. Your ego got stomped on. Well, that's too bad. Why don't you grow up?" Lisa met Sherry's eyes squarely. "And if you talk about my father *ever* again to anyone, you're going to regret it."

The front door opened, and Harris stepped out, looking around. He spotted Lisa and headed toward the two women.

Sherry glanced at Harris and leaned close to Lisa. "It's really terrible what happened to you last night. It's such a shame that no one is safe in Ryton these days. My daddy says we need a new police chief."

Sudden fear poured through Lisa. "How did you know what happened last night?"

Sherry smiled with cold malice. "Oh, I guess someone told me. Your name seems to come up a lot around town. I'd be more careful if I were you." She nodded to the approaching Harris. "Hello, Jimmy. It's good to see you. Take care, Lisa." She smiled again.

Lisa watched her walk down the street and get into her car.

"Is something wrong?" Harris asked.

Lisa took a deep breath. "No."

"Sherry sure is a nice girl," Harris said.

"Yes, isn't she." Lisa leaned down and picked up Obsidian again. She looked at Harris, suddenly grateful for the protection he represented. She looked back down the street and caught Sherry staring at her. Sherry looked away and drove off, her tires squealing.

Obsidian laid his ears back and hissed.

"My thoughts exactly," Lisa said and walked back to her house, followed by the puzzled Harris.

*

"Find something?"

Bernard looked up from where he was kneeling and guiltily re-shelved the book he had been reading. "Uh, no. It was a book on hang-gliding. I've always wanted to try it," he finished lamely.

The chief nodded, looked around The Bookworm, and knelt beside him. "Neither have we," the chief said in a low tone. "Newbold just told me that the search team finished at Storer's house. No gun of any type. No invoices, either. Storer is threatening us with every lawsuit in the whole world."

Bernard could hear a snatch of loud voices from up front where Storer and apparently his lawyer were arguing with Detective Newbold of the city police. He wearily rubbed his face. They had been in The Bookworm for over three hours and found nothing that would link Storer to the library or the murders.

"Where did he say he was last night?" Bernard asked.

"At home. Said he was reading a book," the chief answered.

"Can he prove it?" Bernard asked.

"No, but then he doesn't have to, you know," the chief said. "Innocent until proved guilty." He gestured at the surrounding shelves. "You haven't been able to identify any of these?"

"Sorry, Chief," Bernard said. "The used books could have come from anywhere, and there's no way to tell on the new ones. I really wish there was."

He looked at all the shelves of used hardcovers. No wonder Lisa liked this place, he thought. I could spend a couple of days here myself. Although it's unlikely that I'd be welcome now.

Newbold was walking back to them, his face set. Both the chief and Bernard straightened.

"Anything?" Newbold asked.

The chief shook his head.

"I think we're finished here," Newbold said.

"Thanks for the try," the chief said.

"No problem. Sure wish we'd found something, though. Every time we come up empty makes it that much harder to get a search warrant next time." Newbold looked meaningfully at the chief. "But I guess you know that."

"Yes, I do," the chief said shortly.

Newbold nodded to Bernard and left, gathering together his men as he went. Bernard could hear him thanking Storer for his "cooperation."

"I guess we'd better get out of here, too," the chief said.

Bernard silently followed the chief to the front part of The Bookworm. Someone grabbed his arm. Startled, Bernard turned to see Evelyn Ryton, her face red with anger.

"I should have known," Evelyn snapped. "You're going to pay for this, Worthington!"

"I don't know what you're talking about," Bernard said, pulling his arm away from her surprisingly strong grip. She must have arrived when the chief and I were in the back because he looks as startled to see her as I am, he thought.

"You did this to get back at me!" Evelyn said. "This is revenge pure and simple because I'm going to take your job."

"Miss Ryton," the chief cut in, "Bernard came along at my invitation. I don't think there's any need for this."

"Oh, do you not?!" Evelyn rounded on him.

"Sweetheart, calm down," Storer said as he came over by her. "We'll let the court deal with them." He protectively slid his arm around her shoulders. His action flabbergasted Bernard.

"Gentlemen, I think it's time you left," Storer's lawyer said. "You're about to cross the line into harassment."

The chief cocked his head and looked at the attorney reflectively. "You know, that's the second time this week I've been accused of that. Makes me wonder if you guys all read the same magazines or somethin'."

Bernard held the door open for the chief.

Out on the sidewalk, the chief chuckled. "Well, aren't they a pair of strange lovebirds."

"Lisa said she saw them together," Bernard said, "but I didn't think they were a couple. Didn't you say they were married once?"

"Yeah," the chief opened his car door. "It strikes me as awfully convenient that they should get back together now."

"Do you think they're up to something?" Bernard asked.

"Who knows?" the chief said. "I'm probably grabbing at straws." He got into the car.

Bernard slid in and buckled his seatbelt. "So what do we do now?"

"It's like I told Lisa, I don't know," the chief said. "I've done just about everything I can think to do. The only thing we've got going for us right now is that there's still something hidden somewhere, and our murderer wants it. That phone call of yours this morning proves that." He pulled out into traffic. "Oh, Sims called. The murderer used a pay phone out at the truck stop. No one saw anyone who used it. We dusted for prints, but I don't expect our killer to have left any."

"So basically we have to wait for him to make another move," Bernard said.

"Yeah, and the problem with that is that every time he does, someone pays the price. I don't like it. Not one bit."

Discouraged and depressed, Bernard watched the passing buildings and streets. He had hoped that the search would prove Storer was the murderer; not that he had anything against the man, he just wanted it to be over. And they hadn't even put Storer out of the running. Despite finding nothing, he could still be the murderer. Practically anyone could be. Bernard sighed. There was always a chance that the murders would never be solved. Bernard remembered reading about the Tixon murders in the southern Oklahoma town of Darkness. Those had happened over twenty years ago, and they were still unsolved.

Still, murders were also solved every day. And it wasn't true that anyone could have done the murders; it had to be someone with a motive. A motive that would justify three deaths.

Motive. Now, who could have a motive to kill Agatha? he wondered. Let's assume that the motive was that Agatha wanted to end the fraud and her partner – or partners – didn't. Bernard couldn't see how that was helpful as it still didn't point a finger at anyone.

Okay, he thought, let's make some assumptions. First, the murderer is not a stranger off the street. It's one of the people who have been involved in this.

Bernard made a mental list of all the people involved: Richard Storer, who did have a ready-made way to sell the books and had stayed in touch with Agatha. Evelyn Ryton, who might have hated her sister enough to kill. Of course, she would have to have a partner since a man attacked Lisa. Jay Jones, who could have committed the first murder, which would require a third person being involved. Bernard thought for a moment and added Mayor Brunson to the list. Brunson did, after all, make out the checks, and it might be interesting to find out how he had financed his political campaigns. And why not Harold Hastings? Although Bernard couldn't see a motive for the attorney, he threw him in on general principle. And if I'm going to add him, Bernard thought, I might as well put Neal Gibson, Millie, the chief, Sims, Lisa, and myself while I'm at it.

What about Michael Hyatt? As Bernard thought back on his move to Ryton, he realized that Michael had been a strong force in the decision. Could his motive in helping Bernard get a job have been that he wanted his son-in-law in the library? Or was it simply that he wanted his daughter to stay in town?

Let's be paranoid, Bernard thought. What if the only reason Sherry dated me was to get me to move here? Let's say her father had been Agatha's partner for years. Agatha was getting older, so Michael brought me in as her replacement. Michael has plenty of contacts from his real estate and accounting businesses, one of whom might own a bookstore. Michael might even own one somewhere.

Bernard turned the theory around in his mind. Besides being ridiculous, it also had one huge hole in it. If Michael and Sherry had been involved, why did Sherry break up with Bernard?

Maybe she had a change of heart. Maybe she broke the engagement off so that Bernard wouldn't be involved. Bernard shook his head in disgust. Maybe I've gone completely bonkers.

"Something wrong?" the chief asked.

"I think this is driving me crazy, Chief," Bernard said. "I've been sitting here trying to figure it out, and the only people I haven't accused have been you, Lisa, and me."

"You're just catching up with me," the chief said. "Except I'm worse off than you 'cause the one person I haven't accused is my wife Maggie." Deadpan, he looked at Bernard. "And lately I've been wondering if she has an alibi."

Bernard laughed. The rest of the trip passed in companionable silence.

*

Having Harris follow her around wasn't too bad, Lisa decided. He opened doors for her, drove her around, was generally solicitous of her welfare and proved to be a good conversationalist during lunch. But Lisa could still see how it could get old quickly. For instance, he didn't want her standing at her windows; he constantly scanned the surroundings to the point that he was making her nervous; and when she was shaving her legs and apparently being too quiet, he had knocked on the bathroom door twice to ask her if she was okay.

He was watching television in the living room as Lisa worked on a story covering the events of the last few days. She had called Veit at the Dispatch a couple of hours ago. After he had expressed his concern for her, he asked her to send a story as soon as possible.

"I think this should go on the front page," Veit had said. "It's big enough. Try to keep it as objective as possible. I know that will be hard since you're involved, but give it your best shot. I'd also like a sidebar with your reaction to this. And I'm going to send a photographer down there. I want a shot of the car and the library and anything else you can think of."

Lisa made a couple corrections and pulled the paper out of her typewriter. She had finished editing the factual story, but she didn't have a clue about how to write the sidebar.

"I'm going to have to call him back and get more direction," she said, thinking aloud. "And I don't think I can get it done today." She hated to disappoint him, but she had been through the wringer, and he would have to understand. She leaned down and stroked Obsidian who was curled around her feet. He arched his back and purred. She looked at her watch as she roughed up the cat's fur.

"Oh, no," she exclaimed. She was supposed to meet the photographer at the police station at four, and she was already late. She carefully slid the story into a file and the file into her purse. She ran down the stairs. Harris met her at the bottom, looking tense. She noticed his holster was unsnapped and felt a brief flare of irritation. If he didn't lighten up a bit, she was going to become as nervous as he was and start jumping at everything that moved or made a sound.

She explained her errand, and he drove her quickly down to the station. She briefly toyed with the idea of asking him to use the siren so that they could speed, but decided against it as he would probably refuse anyhow.

The photographer had already introduced himself to Sims and taken pictures of Bernard's car. Sims said that the chief and Bernard had returned from the city and hadn't found anything. Lisa, who had already decided Storer wasn't her attacker, wasn't too disappointed, although it would have been nice to have things wrapped up and feel safe again. The chief had gone home to rest and was going to drop Bernard off at his apartment.

Lisa and Harris then followed the photographer to the library after a quick stop at the office supply so she could fax the story to the Dispatch. She had the photographer take a few pictures outside of the library, but they couldn't get inside because it was locked. She wrote a short note to Veit about the sidebar and sent it back to the city with the photographer. She was looking forward to having the laptop so that she'd have access to email.

"I need to get back to the station," Harris said. "It's about time for the shift change."

Lisa smiled. "You know what? That just reminded me of that old cartoon where the sheepdog and the wolf beat up on each other until their shift ends, then they shake hands, punch out and go home." A cold chill ran down her back. "But I guess the murderer doesn't do that. He doesn't punch out and go home, does he?" She looked at Harris.

The policeman shook his head.

"Well, let's go," Lisa said. "On the way, could you drop me off at Bernard's? You can tell your replacement where I am. Who will that be, anyhow?"

"Probably Hayden if his son is doing better," Harris said, opening the door of the car for her. "If not, I think Sims is subbing."

Lisa nodded. This is so weird, she thought. Someone is trying to kill me. I have a police guard. How long can this go on?

Harris walked her to Bernard's door and waited until Bernard let her in before he left.

"How are you today?" Bernard asked, taking off his glasses and rubbing his eyes. His hair was mussed, apparently from sleep. Lisa thought he looked like a little boy.

Lisa dropped gratefully on the couch. "Doing okay, I guess. My back hurts a little, but nothing the painkillers can't handle. It may just be the drugs, but I'm ready for bed." At Bernard's raised eyebrows, she added, "For sleep, that is."

"I'm ready, too. For sleep, that is," Bernard said, sitting by her. "I took a nap, but all I think it did was make me realize how much sleep I need." He took her hand. "I can't tell you how glad I am that you weren't hurt bad."

"I have to say that I'm glad I wasn't, too," Lisa said.

"Smart aleck," Bernard said gently. He leaned over and kissed her. He pulled back. "I can't believe it."

"Believe what?" Lisa asked.

"Even my lips are tired."

"Poor baby," Lisa cooed. "Now what would make them feel better?" She leaned close to him.

"Well, I think ... I think that the best thing for them ... would be ..."

"Yes?" Lisa asked.

"I think it ... would be ... SLEEP!"

"You –!" She started tickling him. He escaped off the couch. She followed him, tickling his ribs. Finally he pinned her hands.

"Okay, enough," he said, trying to catch his breath. "I surrender. What do you want?"

"Well, I think that I would like ..." she breathed. "I mean, I would really, really like ..." She paused, licking her lips slowly. "To ... go to dinner!"

Bernard laughed and pulled her into a hug. "You're on. Let me wash my face and put in my contacts."

"Comb your hair, too." Lisa ran her hand through it.

Bernard went into his bedroom. Lisa walked around the living room. Idly she ran her hand along the window sill. No dust, she wryly noted.

"Is The Señor fine?" Bernard called out.

"Yes," Lisa said. "You know, eventually they're going to name a table after us. Not that there's that many places to eat here, anyhow."

"True, but we could go to the Steakhorn."

"No. The Señor's fine," Lisa said. "Oh, before I forget, where's your phone book?"

"It sounds like you already forgot."

"Are you going to be this funny all night?"

"Only if you're lucky. And it's by the phone."

It would be, she thought.

"Who are you going to call?"

"I need to let my 'guard' know where to meet us."

"Great, a chaperone."

"I wouldn't think that would bother you since you're so tired," said Lisa as she dialed the police station.

"But food and sparkling conversation could revive me."

"Could it now? We truly live in an age of miracles."

The dispatcher answered. Lisa asked for Sims, and when he got on the line, told him their plans for the evening. "Who is my guard tonight?"

"Hayden will take the first shift, and Edwards will relieve him later," Sims said. "You be careful. Don't make their jobs any harder."

"And here I was, intending to walk in the woods by myself later," she said tartly.

"You know what I mean."

"Don't worry. I'll be a good girl." Lisa sighed as she hung up. This is going to drive me crazy, she thought.

"Lisa, there's a file on my desk. I think it's yours," Bernard called from the bedroom. "It was on the front seat of my car."

She went over and picked it up. It was the Ryton family file that Veit had given her. I forgot about it, she realized. She also remembered what she had been looking at before the gunfire started.

"Bernard, I want to stop by the library after we eat."

"Okay, but why?"

"I'll tell you about it when we get there. And I thought of something else."

"What?" he said, coming into the living room with a fresh shirt on and his hair combed.

"What are we going to drive?" she asked. "Your car is shot up, and mine is at my apartment."

"Sims let me borrow his car," Bernard said. "Apparently he likes to drive around in his patrol car." He opened the front door. "That guy really needs to get a life."

*

"Chuck, do you want to get up and eat dinner?" Maggie gently shook the chief awake. "You should probably get up so that you can sleep tonight."

The chief opened his eyes, yawned twice, and smiled at her. "You know, I'm sure not as young as I used to be," he said. "A few years ago, I could stay up three nights in a row, and it didn't affect me. Look at me now. Taking a nap in the middle of the day." He scooted over so she could sit down. He smiled at her. "How come I keep getting older while you get younger?" He patted her hip.

"You're a lucky man," Maggie said, smiling.

"I haven't been lately."

"You've worked very hard on this case," Maggie said. "No one can fault you on that. Not even that half-wit Brunson."

Sighing, the chief placed his hands behind his head. "You know, the murderer has to be the luckiest guy in the world. He's committed three murders, two of them in broad daylight, and attempted to kill Lisa twice, once shooting a rifle repeatedly right smack in the middle of downtown Ryton. How is it possible that no one saw him doing any of it?"

"Maybe they did, and they don't realize it," Maggie said. "Maybe he's someone that you don't pay attention to. You know, like a street worker, for instance."

"Good idea," the chief said thoughtfully. "I'll have Sims start re-questioning people tomorrow."

"You'll catch him. You always do." Maggie dropped a kiss on his forehead. "Now, get on up and come on downstairs. Dinner will be ready in a few minutes. I'd like some company while I cook."

The chief nodded and yawned again. "I'll be there in a minute."

Maggie walked out of the bedroom. The chief watched her walk down the stairs. A fine woman, he thought. I've done some dumb things in my life, but marrying her must make me a genius.

Downstairs, Maggie had cooked a dinner of breaded pork chops, baked potatoes, and corn on the cob. She was tossing a spinach salad as she cradled the phone on her shoulder.

He inhaled the delicious aromas. "That smells wonderful."

"Make us some tea, would you," she said. She hung up the phone and concentrated on the salad.

The phone caught the chief's eye. It looked like the one at Jay's house. He resolutely pushed Jay's death out of his mind.

Maggie deserved his total attention tonight. She got it too rarely as it was. As he dropped the heaping spoonfuls of instant tea in a pitcher, he asked, "Who were you talking to?"

"No one," she said, placing the salad on the table. "I've been trying to call AnnaMay Watts, but she's not home. Her daughter's son is bad sick, and I wanted to see how he was doing. You know Tina, don't you?"

"Tina Watts?" The chief tried to place her.

"No, she's married now. Tina Hayden," Maggie said. She sat down at the table. The chief sat down beside her.

"That's right. Rick's wife. How's the boy doing?"

"Well, he had seemed a little better yesterday," Maggie said. "Pneumonia is so tough on children. He's not more than nine, I think."

"You'd think with all those miracle drugs that they could fix him right up," the chief said.

For the rest of the meal, the chief listened contentedly as Maggie caught him up on all the current gossip. Over the years, he had come to respect her ability to pick out the truth from the lies. She had given him more than one insight into a crime.

"Well, that was good if I do say so myself," Maggie said. "Let's leave the dishes and take our tea in the living room."

"I think I'll cut us some carrot cake," the chief said.

"That sounds good," Maggie said. "I think I'll try to call AnnaMay again." She picked up the phone, punched a button, and listened. "Now, it's busy." The chief stared at her. "What? Is there something wrong?"

"What did you do?" the chief asked.

"What?" She looked at the chief.

He grabbed his startled wife and kissed her. "Call the station. Have them call Sims and tell him to meet me at Jay Jones's house." He was out the door, leaving her staring after him from the porch.

CHAPTER TEN

"Here we are," Bernard said as he swung open the doors to the library and flipped on the lights. "You realize that if the chief knew your bodyguard wasn't with us, he'd have our heads."

"We can call the station and tell them Hayden had to go," Lisa said, stepping into the lobby and glancing around. "I sure hope everything goes okay for his boy."

Bernard nodded. Hayden had joined them at The Señor as they were finishing their meal. The officer had received a call on his cell phone, then rushed over to them and said his son was being air-lifted to Baptist Medical in the city. Hayden left immediately.

"Besides, I thought you wanted me alone," Lisa continued.

"So true, my lady," Bernard said with a mock flourish. "But in more congenial and less public surroundings than this. What did you want to come here for?"

Lisa opened her purse and took out a file folder. She walked over to the circulation desk and spread out the folder's contents. She held out a photocopy of a newspaper clipping. "Look at this."

Bernard walked over and took it from her. The clipping concerned the founding of the library and showed a picture of the mansion. He carefully read through the story, but couldn't figure out what Lisa thought was so important about it. He looked up at her. "I don't understand what I'm looking for."

"Look at the picture," Lisa said.

Bernard did. It showed the Ryton mansion in all its dubious glory. "You know, I think it was even uglier then than now."

"Me, too," Lisa said. "And I didn't think that was possible, but that's not I wanted you to see."

"How about a hint?"

"The windows on the second floor," Lisa said.

Bernard studied the photo intently and then looked at Lisa, puzzled. "There are windows all across the front."

"So what happened to them?" Lisa said.

"Obviously, they were bricked up," Bernard said.

"I know that," Lisa said, slightly exasperated. "But what about the rooms behind them?"

"Oh. Good question." Bernard looked up and at the left wall. "I know that over the restrooms and the workroom is where they have the air conditioning and heating units and the elevator equipment. The air conditioning has had to be worked on several times since I've been here. You have to crawl though a small opening above the elevator to get back there. Not much fun."

"What's over there?" Lisa pointed at the blank wall above the lounge and Agatha's and Bernard's offices.

"I don't know," Bernard said. "But there couldn't be ..." His voice trailed off as he remembered the hidden safe. The library might contain more secrets that anyone knew.

"You know, that would be quite a large room up there," Lisa said, staring intently at the upper wall.

"And if there was a room up there, that would explain why the murderer was taking her body upstairs," Bernard said slowly. "He was going to hide it."

For a long moment, they looked at each other.

Bernard broke the silence. "Let's see what we can find."

Bernard led the way up the stairs and across the room to stand in front of the Civil War wall display case. "I've never had a key for this case. Agatha never wanted us to touch it. Those precious Civil War mementos." He leaned over and looked at the lock and then at Lisa's purse. "I don't suppose you have a screwdriver in there, do you?"

"Flathead or Phillips?" Lisa asked as she rummaged in her purse.

"Flathead would be fine," Bernard said.

She handed one to him. "I've also got a pair of pliers if that would help."

"No, I think I can get it," Bernard said as he pushed the blade into the space between the frame and the lock. He tried to push the bolt up. "It doesn't want to move." He inserted the screwdriver from above and pulled down. "I think it's giving –"

The glass in the cabinet cracked. Bernard jumped back, nearly losing his balance on the slick marble floor. Lisa reached out and steadied him. The glass fell in two large pieces, shattering into hundreds of smaller ones as they hit the floor with a crash that echoed throughout the library.

Bernard looked at Lisa. She looked as shocked as he was.

"I must have twisted the frame when I was prying on it."

The Civil War diary plopped onto the floor, making both of them jump. They laughed nervously. Lisa leaned down and picked the thick book up, brushing shards of glass off it. She looked around, apparently for a place to sit it, then resignedly stuffed it into her purse.

"How much can one purse hold?" Bernard asked in mock amazement.

"Don't be funny."

"Just trying to find out if you were violating the laws of physics."

She sighed.

Grinning, Bernard knelt and examined the lock. "It looks like there's a latch here," he said, probing around with the screwdriver. "I think if I ..."

He hammered on the end of the screwdriver with his hand and pushed down on the tool.

A sharp click sounded. The whole wall opened inward a couple of inches. Lisa gasped. Bernard stepped back.

"Well, well, well," Bernard said. "I wonder what we have in here." He looked at Lisa. "Only one way to find out."

She nodded, her face alight with excitement.

He pushed on the wall and it swung back, opening into darkness. He peered in but couldn't make out anything in the gloom.

"Our eyes will have to adjust –"

"I've got a flashlight," Lisa said, digging it out of her purse and handing it to him.

"I should have known." He took the light, clicked it on, and slowly entered the hidden room, Lisa close behind him.

"Look, a light switch," Bernard said. He flipped it up. A small chandelier, recessed in the ceiling and dusty with cobwebs, illuminated the long room. Strips of wallpaper hung off the walls and crunched under foot. A faded sofa that had collapsed under the weight of years leaned against the left wall, and several boxes sporting the names of publishing companies were stacked beside it. A few piles of books lay on an old dining table in the middle of the room.

Bernard went to the table and rapidly scanned the titles in the first pile of books. "This is the missing shipment of books," he said, looking at Lisa.

Lisa was peering into the boxes and moving them. Apparently they were empty from her ease in doing so.

Bernard turned back to the books and examined the second pile. The books in it already carried their Dewey Decimal number along with a small 'a' at either the top or the bottom. "I get it," Bernard thought aloud. "That's how they told them apart."

"What?" Lisa asked, coming up behind him.

"The 'a' on these books," Bernard said, handing one to her. "A lot of the books on the shelves have one, too. It must have been how they marked the ones that they had already stolen the duplicates of." Bernard paused. "I realized something else. Agatha really had a passion for replacing books that were damaged. I bet that when one came in without the 'a', she'd order a new one, place the 'a' on the old one and put it back on the shelves and sell the new one." He shook his head. "No wonder our books are falling apart."

"Bernard, look," Lisa said, running her hand up and down the wall. "There's a seam here. I think there's another door here."

Bernard went over to it. "You're right." He inspected the outline. He placed his hands against it and pushed. It didn't budge. "There must be a latch somewhere around here." Both of them ran their hands across the wall but only found dust.

"Let's see," Lisa went back to the secret door and counted her steps. "That wall is right over the far wall of your office downstairs. The room in there must be over Agatha's office." She paused.

"Yes?" Bernard asked after a moment.

Lisa shook her head. "You know, this is too weird. You don't think there's a cult of library worshipers behind there, do you?"

"I'd be afraid to say right now," Bernard said. "How does this open?" He pounded on the wall in various places, dislodging chips of plaster from the ceiling that settled on his hair and shoulders.

Lisa walked back to the open secret door and examined the latch from their side. "I want to know is why no one knew about this."

"Who would imagine it?" Bernard asked. "It's pretty crazy. You don't expect to find a secret room in a library. And with Agatha as the Head Librarian, I bet she saw to it that no one got the chance to look very close."

"I wonder why it was built in the first place." Lisa rummaged in her purse and pulled out a pocketknife. She started digging along the corner of the room.

"Secret rooms were popular among the rich during old Eliah's day," Bernard said. "Maybe he hid money in here. Did you find something?"

"There's a cord here. I wonder ..." Lisa pushed the secret door shut. "Now try it."

Bernard shoved against the wall. A section of the wall swung in so suddenly he couldn't stop himself from falling in.

"Are you okay?" Lisa asked.

"Yes, just surprised," Bernard said.

"I guess the second door can't be opened until the first one is closed," Lisa said. "That cord must connect the two."

Bernard stood and dusted off his pants. Lisa shone the flashlight into the room. It was empty. One corner was curved, following the outline of the tower. The bricked-up windows were obvious.

"Bernard, over there." The flashlight beam showed a rectangular hole in the floor to the right of them and next to the inside wall. The top of a metal ladder showed from it.

"That's got to go to Agatha's office," Lisa said.

"Yeah, but why?" Bernard said. They walked over to it. Lisa directed the flashlight beam down it.

"I always wondered why the walls of her office were so thick," Bernard said.

"Look at the grooves on the sides of the hole," Lisa said. "This must have been a dumbwaiter."

"I'm going to climb down it," Bernard decided. He swung out on the ladder and quickly climbed down the hole. At the bottom, he discovered a latch on the wall. He flipped it and then pushed. A section of the wall moved out about an inch but would go no further.

"What did you find?"

"Another secret door," Bernard called. "But it's stuck."

"Wouldn't that be about where we pushed Agatha's desk?" Lisa asked.

"I bet that's it," Bernard answered. "The desk is blocking it." He noticed a light switch on the wall. He flipped it on. The hole remained dark. "Lisa, did the lights come on up there?"

"No," Lisa said. "In fact, there isn't a light fixture. There's a place for one, though. Why?"

"There's a light switch down here." He flipped it a couple more times, puzzling over its purpose. Could it turn something on in Agatha's office? He thought back to the night that he thought he had seen a light in her office. "That's it!"

"What?" Lisa asked.

He quickly climbed back up. "I bet that switch turns on the light in Agatha's office. It must be a two-way switch. That night that I called the police to come here, Sims tested the light switch in there to see if it had a short. He flipped it up to turn it off. I noticed, but I didn't really pay attention. The next day, when we were in there, I turned the light off by flipping it down." He smiled with vindication. "Someone was in there that night. And when I came in, he hid in the hole and turned the light out from there."

"Why have a light switch in there?" Lisa asked.

Bernard shrugged. "Who knows? Why have the ladder in there?"

Lisa paced the floor, raising small clouds of dust. "Let's think. Maybe they had the ladder in there so that Agatha's accomplice could hide up here if someone like you or Jay Jones came in at night. Agatha could always claim that she had work to do" – Bernard snorted at that – "but he couldn't."

"And the light switch could have been a precaution of some sort," Bernard said. "In case, he didn't have time to reach the light switch by the office door."

"That makes sense to me," Lisa said, shining the light around the room. "But what doesn't make sense is this room. I can buy the first secret room being hidden, but these windows were bricked up. Someone had to know a room was here."

"I don't understand it, either," Bernard said. "I'd like to know who did the construction."

"At least we know why the murderer was bringing her body up here," Lisa said. "He was going to hide it, probably so that he would have more time to search for whatever he's looking for before any fuss was raised."

"That's why her office was locked," Bernard said, snapping his fingers. "He didn't want anyone to know she had been killed. He could have typed a note from her saying that she was sick and wouldn't be in, and I wouldn't have thought a thing about it, other than being relieved that she was gone."

"And he carried her up the stairs or the elevator because that was easier than trying to pull her up the hole," Lisa said. "The only trouble was you came to work early."

Bernard nodded, then frowned. "We have the answers to a lot of questions," he said. "But not the important one: who is the murderer?"

Lisa shook her head.

"I'm going to call the chief," Bernard said.

"I'm going to climb down and look around," Lisa said. "Move the desk, would you?"

Bernard nodded and tripped the latch on the second secret door. He walked out on the second floor of the library, avoiding the shattered glass, puzzling over what they had found. A strange smell assaulted his nostrils as he reached the stairs.

"What's th –" he started to ask. A crushing blow landed on the back of his head. The world roared, then sound disappeared. He toppled, barely conscious of hitting the hard marble floor. Everything blurred and faded.

*

Sims was waiting for the chief when he arrived at Jay Jones's house. The chief barely spared him a nod before rushing to the front door, which was, of course, locked. He waited impatiently as Sims brought out the keys and opened the door.

The chief flipped on the light and went straight to the phone. He picked it up.

"Look," the chief said, holding the phone out to Sims. Sims looked at it, then at the chief, apparently baffled.

"I've been thinking about Jay's death," the chief said. "He left his house with a handgun. Why? He was a hunter, more comfortable with a rifle or shotgun. I think he took that gun for protection. He was going to meet someone he thought was dangerous." The chief paused. "I have a hunch that Jay talked to the murderer before he left the house, and they set up a meeting. And that's why Jay was carrying a gun. Because he was afraid of becoming a victim."

Sims looked baffled. "Can the phone company trace the call?"

"Maybe, if it was long distance," the chief said. "I should have already thought about asking for his phone records, and we'll do that first thing tomorrow if this doesn't pan out."

"If what doesn't pan out?" Sims asked

"We've got a phone like this at my house," the chief said. "It has a redial button. Maggie used the one on our phone tonight. If Jay used this phone to call our murderer …"

Comprehension dawned on Sims. "We'll have him!"

"If we're lucky and that's who he called and not a pizza parlor," the chief said. He took a deep breath and pushed the redial button. He turned the phone out so that Sims could also hear. There was a series of beeps, a brief pause, then the loud buzz of a busy signal.

"I can't believe it!" the chief exclaimed. He was tempted to hurl the phone against the wall but instead carefully hung up.

"They'll have to hang up sometime," Sims said.

The chief nodded. His stomach churned. Please let this be the break we need, he thought. Whoever you are, get off the phone!

*

"Bernard," Lisa called. She pounded on the wall inside the hole again and climbed back up the ladder, wondering what could be taking him so long to call the chief. She had waited at least ten minutes – more than enough time for her to see that there was only dust in the hole – and he never moved the desk so that she could open the secret door into Agatha's office.

She thumbed open the second secret door and was halfway

across the room when something stopped her. She looked around the room, her heart pounding. She felt something was wrong. She hurried to the first secret door, swearing to herself that if this was Bernard's idea of joke, she'd chop him off at the knees.

She pulled on the door, but it wouldn't open!

Terror choked her for a moment. Then she remembered the first secret door had to be closed before the second one would open. Perhaps it worked both ways. She closed the second door and pushed on the first, breathing a sigh of relief when it swung back.

It opened on a darkened library. The lights had been turned off. Lisa froze in the doorway. What was going on? She could smell something. Something chemical – gasoline! She gasped and ran for the stairs. She fell over someone, her flashlight skidding across the floor and sliding around so that it shone in her eyes.

She yelled and threw herself back before her eyes registered that the person on the floor was Bernard. "Bernard!" She felt his neck. His skin was cold, and she couldn't locate a pulse. She could feel a scream building in the back of her throat. She put her head down on his chest. She couldn't hear a heartbeat. "Oh, no –"

He moaned then. The blood rushed to her head, and she felt woozy for a moment. He raised a hand to his head.

"Bernard!" She carefully touched his head, sliding her hand around to the back. She felt moisture. Her hand was covered in blood.

"Lisa …" Bernard's eyes fluttered open. "What happen –"

Lisa clapped her hand over his mouth.

Footsteps echoed from the lobby. Someone was downstairs. She looked around frantically. There was nowhere to run. Unless they went back to the secret room. But they'd be trapped. Maybe both of us can open the door into Agatha's office, she thought frantically.

"Bernard, come on," she whispered, helping him sit up. "We've got to get back in the room."

He tried to rise and slumped back. He reached up and touched the back of his head. "I'm bleeding."

"Yes, you are," Lisa whispered, pulling on him. Someone was running up the stairs!

"Come on!" she gasped. "Come on!" She pulled him up and half-dragged him through the open door. She slammed it shut. He dropped to his knees. She ran and opened the second door. The first door shook as someone outside the room hit it.

Bernard looked dully around. "What is going on?"

Suddenly a bullet exploded through the wall, close to his head.

Lisa screamed and scrambled to help him, pulling him into the front room. More bullets whined past them.

The two landed in a heap on the floor near the hole.

"Down the hole!" Lisa said. "While he's still up here!"

Bernard nodded and led the way down, getting steadier as he went. When he reached the bottom, he moved over as far as he could and helped her down. He put his shoulder against the wall and pushed. Lisa braced herself and added her strength. The wall opened so suddenly that they had to scramble to keep on their feet. The room had been drenched in gasoline, the harsh smell gagging them. Lisa started toward the door, but Bernard grabbed her arm.

"He'll have a clear shot at us," Bernard said, looking around. "Out the window!"

They rushed to the window. He jerked it open and shoved the screen out. He helped her up on the sill.

"No!" a hard voice said from the doorway. "If you move another inch out that window, I'll shoot you!"

Lisa froze, with one leg out the window. Bernard moved between her and the door.

"Come back in now! Or he dies!"

"Go, Lisa –"

"SHUT UP!" the voice ordered. "Get back in here. Now!"

Lisa slid back in. She slowly turned and looked in the face of the murderer.

*

The chief hung up the phone, cutting the answering machine's reply off. It didn't matter; he had already heard it twice. He looked at the puzzled Sims.

"Why would Jay be calling him?" Sims asked, echoing the chief's thoughts exactly.

"I don't know," the chief said slowly, trying to make this new piece of the puzzle fit. "Who owns this house?"

"I think Jay did," Sims said.

"I can't make this fit exactly," the chief said as he started to pace the floor. "Maybe it means nothing."

"Maybe," Sims said.

"Still, it wouldn't hurt to go and talk to him," the chief decided. "Get on the radio and call the station and get his address. And tell them to come here and make a recording of who this phone calls just in case it's important."

In his car, Sims radioed the station while the chief paced around the lawn in front of Jay's house. The chief felt restless; he had hoped the phone would call someone clear-cut, maybe even Richard Storer. Instead, all it had done was muddy the water even more.

"Chief, Julie said Hayden's boy had to be rushed to the city," Sims said, sticking his head out the car window. "His lungs collapsed."

"Poor kid." The chief shook his head. "Did she say how the boy was doing?"

"She hasn't heard yet," Sims said. "Hayden was watching Lisa tonight, but Julie said he called in before he left. He said he left Lisa with Bernard at The Señor. And Edwards called in sick."

"Great," the chief said, mentally reviewing the shift schedule.

"Want me to call in Jacobs?" Sims asked.

"No, I can't afford to pay any more overtime this month. Brunson offered extra money, but I don't want to take him up on it if I can help it." The chief thought for a moment. "Tell Julie to call Lisa and have her stay with a friend tonight. Get the address and have McGraw drive by it a few times tonight. Oh, tell her to stay with someone at all times. I don't want her alone."

Sims picked up the radio, but the chief put out his hand.

"Wait," the chief said. "Let's stop by the station, and I'll tell her myself. Then we'll go and see why Jay Jones was calling Neal Gibson."

*

Neal Gibson stood in the doorway of the office, holding a pistol. In torn and crumpled clothes, he looked frightened and desperate.

"No one's going anywhere," Gibson rasped. "Don't move."

Lisa felt frozen. This was what she'd been afraid of? A middle-aged real estate agent? This was the man who had tormented her dreams? She wanted to scream, but she stayed still. She recognized him now as her attacker. She had nearly recognized him in his office, she realized. No wonder he had ran from Bernard; Bernard could beat him to a pulp. If he hadn't surprised her, she could have.

"I should have known it was you," Bernard said slowly. "The day after the murder, I caught you looking in this office. Until now I had forgotten that I had locked the doors of the library. You used Agatha's keys to get in."

"You couldn't leave me alone, could you?" Gibson said. "You just had to keep digging, didn't you? Why? She was dead. No one loved her. No one missed her. You got her job. Why couldn't you let it go? Why?"

"Because you kept trying to kill Lisa," Bernard said.

"I found out she didn't know anything," Gibson said. "If you two had left it alone, she would have been safe. This is all your fault."

"You tried to kill me last night," Lisa said, willing her voice to be calm, to not waver with rage.

"Because you saw me here!" Gibson yelled. "I had to kill you. And you got away again!"

Lisa shook her head. "I didn't see anything. It was too dark. I couldn't see anything at all."

"Liar!" Gibson's hand tightened on his gun. "I hid all night. All night I waited for them to come for me. All night I've been afraid. I was going to kill myself, but then it came to me. Without the book, no one can prove anything." Gibson looked wildly around the room. "I know it's here. She hid it somewhere in this library. I know she did. I have to destroy it. I'll be safe then."

"The book?" Bernard asked.

"No, you don't know about the book, do you?" Gibson sneered. "Not as smart as you think you are, are you?" He looked at them and sighed. "Still, you don't deserve this. But I don't have any choice. Just like with Agatha. She didn't give me any choice."

"She wanted out, didn't she?" Bernard asked.

"She'd always wanted to buy this place back," Gibson said dully. "It was going to be her revenge on old man Ryton. I did the appraisal to humor her. I didn't know she wanted to stop now. I couldn't let her stop now. Not yet."

"Why not?" Lisa asked.

Gibson's gaze darted to her.

"I have – debts," Gibson said. "My divorce took almost everything. I don't want to lose what's left. I tried to explain it to Agatha. I tried to make her understand. She wouldn't listen. She called me names. I grabbed her, and she slapped me." He closed his eyes but too briefly for Lisa or Bernard to make a move. "We'd been opening book boxes. The knife was right there. I didn't mean to ..."

"And Leonard was an accident, too?" Lisa snapped before she could stop herself. Horrified by her words, she waited for his reaction. He smiled sadly.

"See, you don't understand," Gibson said. He held out his hand almost as if he was pleading with her. "I have a daughter. You know her. She's bright and ... and beautiful. This would ruin her life. I couldn't let that happen. And Brewer had seen me. I helped him fix a flat that night because he was blocking the entrance. I had to kill him, but I couldn't get the knife out of his chest." He looked baffled. "I didn't know it could get stuck."

"And Jay Jones?" Bernard asked softly.

"He tried to be smart, but he was so dumb," Gibson said. "He was going to blackmail me. I didn't have the money to pay him. If I'd had money, none of this would have happened. He actually called me from his house. His name was on my caller ID. He tried to bluff me, tried to tell me that he had left a letter, but I knew he was lying. He wasn't smart enough to do that. So I took a chance. When the police didn't come for me, it was a sign that I was doing the right thing."

"By killing three people?" Bernard asked, his voice hard.

"Shut up! SHUT UP!" Gibson motioned violently with the gun. "I'm just protecting my little girl. But you don't understand." He took a deep breath. "I'm sorry about this, really I am. But I can't put my baby through this. I have to take care of her." He brought the gun up and grasped it with both hands.

"Wait!" Bernard said.

"I'm going to have to burn the library so that I can be sure that the book is destroyed," Storer said. "This is less painful than being burned to death. I don't have any choice."

"You do," Bernard said urgently. "You don't have to kill us. Let me in on it."

"What?" Gibson looked puzzled.

"You don't want to kill us. I know you don't want to," Bernard said, stepping forward. "Nobody has to die today."

"I'm not going to jail," Gibson said.

"You don't have to," Bernard said. "What do I care about Agatha or Leonard or Jay? I didn't know Leonard, and I didn't like Agatha or Jay." He took another step toward Gibson, his hands spread wide. "We can work this out. I'm going to be the new Head Librarian. We could go on like you did before. You still need the money, don't you? We can be partners, and no one else has to die."

"She'll tell," Gibson said, indicating Lisa with his gun.

"No, she wouldn't," Bernard said. "She needs money, too. She could split my half."

"I wouldn't tell," Lisa said, licking dry lips. "It's like he said. I can use the money."

Bernard stretched out his hand. "Come on. We can be partners. We can make a lot of money together."

Gibson looked at Bernard's hand. Lisa held her breath.

"No," Gibson said. "You're lying. You're LYING!"

Bernard lunged forward.

Gibson shot him twice.

Everything went in slow motion for Lisa. She watched Bernard stumble back, his hands clutching his stomach. Bernard fell forward. Lisa moved toward Bernard. She could hear shouting, but the words didn't make sense.

Gibson raised his gun. She screamed, but the sound was lost in the thunder.

Gibson moved his mouth, but no words came out, only a soft sigh. He dropped his gun and crumpled. Lisa watched him fall. She looked up to see Sims standing in the lobby, his gun outstretched.

Lisa wanted to sink to the floor, but she forced her legs to walk to Bernard. She knelt beside him. From a distance, she heard the chief tell Sims to call an ambulance. She carefully turned Bernard over and held his head in her lap until they took him away.

*

"With information in the book, the Library Board has sorted out what money belonged to the library and what belonged to Agatha," the chief said. "You know, it's ironic. Gibson passed that display every time he came in and out of the secret rooms. I guess he never thought of looking inside the Civil War diary."

"I only opened it because I stuck it in my purse when the display broke," Lisa said, not looking at him. "I was looking for something to read, and I remembered it. I thought it might be interesting to read how the Civil War was viewed by someone who was in it."

But inside the diary covers, Lisa had found a notebook listing all of the books that Agatha and Gibson had stolen and what they had received from the sale of them. A careful record that mentioned Gibson's name more than once and had given the real estate agent his motive for most of what had happened.

"Anyway," the chief went on, "it now looks like the rest of the money in her estate may not have belonged to her, either."

Lisa turned to look at him. The past two weeks had been hard on her, and it showed in dark circles around her eyes and a slight tremble in her hands at odd times. But the chief could see that she was getting better every day. He believed she would be okay.

"Where did she steal that money from?" she asked.

"Remember the Ryton jewels?" the chief asked. "Gibson and Agatha stole them."

"You're kidding!" Lisa exclaimed.

The chief shook his head. "No. In fact, I think the remaining jewels were in the library safe. We found some jewelry at Gibson's house that Evelyn identified as her mother's. Apparently Agatha talked Gibson into stealing them so that she could frame her sister. Evelyn thinks she did it for revenge; Agatha never blamed her husband for what happened, just her sister. She held onto the jewels, and over the years had been slowly selling them for quite a profit."

"How did you find out?" Lisa asked, sounding interested.

She is doing better, the chief thought. She's beginning to act like a reporter again. "Gibson's ex-wife told us," he said. "Gibson told her a couple of years ago before they divorced. She swears that she knew nothing about the fraud. I don't really believe her, but it's not worth pursuing." The chief also had the idea that she might have blackmailed Gibson with the information. It would explain why the woman had come off so well in the divorce.

"Do you think Agatha and Gibson were lovers?" Lisa asked.

The chief shrugged. "Could be. It's hard to say now. We certainly didn't find anything in either of their houses to suggest that."

"It would be more romantic if they had been, don't you think?" Lisa asked.

"If you think murder is a prelude to romance, sure," Bernard said from the hospital bed. Two weeks after his emergency surgery, he still looked weak and tired, but the doctors said that he was on the road to recovery.

"I'll be glad to show you what I consider a prelude as soon as you're up and around," Lisa said, smiling.

"I'm checking out today," Bernard said, pretending to rise.

She gently pushed him back and took his hand in hers.

The chief chuckled. "So when will you get to leave here?"

"The doctor said if he continues to improve, it shouldn't be more than another week or so," Lisa said. "He was lucky that Gibson didn't take the time to aim better."

The thought sobered the chief. He remembered a brief flash of that night: Gibson's still body, the blood on the carpet, the strange and unnerving calmness of Lisa and her tears later. When he and Sims had got the call about shots at the library, they had only been a couple of blocks away. The chief had known immediately that Lisa and Bernard were involved.

"Chief, what was Gibson doing with the books?" Bernard asked.

"Oh, I'm sorry. I keep forgetting that you were out of it while we were putting all the pieces together," the chief said. "Gibson owned several businesses before his divorce. After it, he only owned three: Skyways Real Estate here in Ryton, and a computer assembly plant and a bookstore in Oklahoma City. The ex Mrs. Gibson remembered that he really wanted the bookstore in the divorce." Although the chief saw no reason to tell Bernard and Lisa since they had never known about it, Gibson had also been behind the offer to purchase the library, apparently another attempt to hide his tracks.

"Look at this, Bernard," Lisa said, pulling out a file folder and opening it to a clipping. "I meant to show this to you earlier. See this picture? Remember we were so interested in the windows? We should have looked on the ground." She placed her finger on the picture. "Look at this sign."

Bernard peered at it. "I can't make it out."

"Actually, I couldn't either," Lisa admitted. "But after the chief checked the construction records, I realized that it was a Gibson Builders sign. Neal's dad owned the company that did the original remodeling on the library. I'd bet Neal was one of the workers."

"Why didn't the city know about the secret rooms?" Bernard asked. "Didn't they have to approve the plans?"

"No," the chief said. "The remodeling was specified in the will, and it was contracted by the executor. The city didn't take possession until the remodeling was finished." The chief smiled. He had quizzed Harold Hastings at great length about the lawyer's father's role as executor. Hastings swore his father knew nothing about the secret rooms, and since the senior Hastings had passed away years ago, the chief let it go. But he had enjoyed rattling the lawyer's cage.

As for the mayor, when the chief had questioned him about his strange reaction, Brunson had been baffled.

"I must have been tired that day, Chuck," Brunson had said. "Sorry if it offended you." The chief believed him. What he had found unbelievable was the news that he had originally intended to deliver to Lisa and Bernard before Bernard had started questioning him.

"I almost forgot what I came over here to tell you," the chief said. "You'll never guess who's getting married – again."

"Evelyn Ryton and Richard Storer," Lisa said smugly.

The chief blinked.

"She called the wedding announcement into the Dispatch," Lisa said. "The lifestyles editor told me about it. And that is romantic."

"Well, Miss Smarty, did you know she called the mayor and turned down the job of Head Librarian?" the chief asked. "She's going to help Storer run his bookstore. That means Bernard has the job."

"Bernard, that's great!" Lisa exclaimed.

Bernard smiled and laid back. Lisa looked at him with concern.

"Are you okay?" she asked.

"A little tired," he said. "Which is funny, considering I haven't done anything all day except lie here."

The chief studied the two of them together and smiled. "Well, I'd better get going," he said. "Maggie wanted me to tell you that if you needed anything, give her a call. Bernard, you get better now.' He looked at Lisa. "You take care of him – and yourself, too."

"I will," Lisa said. "Chief, how is Sims? I know he was upset, but if he hadn't stopped Gibson, we wouldn't be here."

The chief paused. "He's doing better, I think. It's not easy killing a man even when it was justified. He decided to take some vacation time. He'll be okay. He's a good man and a good policeman. Him being gone is going to allow Hayden to make up some hours now that his little boy is doing better."

"Tell Sims to come by when he gets back," Bernard said. "I'd like to thank him."

"I will," the chief said. He tipped his hat and left. Outside, he took a deep breath of air. He had to stop by the orchard to meet with the county agent, then he was going home. It was early afternoon, but the chief had decided that he deserved a little more time with Maggie.

He wondered what the tests of the trees had revealed. The county agent sounded ominous on the phone, but the chief was feeling too good to worry about it. And his mood was only a little dampened when he drove into his driveway.

Maggie came outside. "Why are you home early?"

"I thought I'd spend the afternoon with you," the chief said, kissing her cheek.

"I thought it might have something to do with Jerry Wilson," Maggie said, pulling away. "He called a few minutes ago and said that he ordered the fungicide for you. It should be here the day after tomorrow. Why are you ordering fungicide?" She crossed her arms and stared at him.

The chief sighed and decided to get it over with. "Well, it turns out that our trees have some sort of fungus. It's attacking the fruit. Jerry says the orchard is going to have to be quarantined until we get it cleared up. That means we're going to lose this crop."

Maggie pursed her lips and looked out across the lawn.

The chief considered her, took a deep breath, and threw caution to the winds. "But I've been thinking this may have been a bad idea in the first place. Raising peaches in western Oklahoma, I mean. Maybe this place is all wrong for them."

Maggie didn't say anything, just peered at him suspiciously.

"In fact, I was talking to Jerry about putting in some apples," the chief said.

Maggie looked shocked, her eyebrows traveling up.

"I think about a hundred trees to start," the chief said, mentall counting down.

Her face turned red.

"And then add a hundred next year and the year after that. Of course, we're going to have to dip into our retirement savings again."

That did it.

"I told you when you bought that money pit that you'd be sorry," Maggie said. "Did you listen? No, you didn't! And now you want to put even more money in it? No, sir! I'm not going to be spending my last years in the poor house."

The chief settled down in the porch swing.

"We're not going to do it," Maggie said, firmly. "We're already stuck with an orchard that we can't even sell the fruit from – are you smiling?"

"No, dear," the chief said.

"Because this isn't funny and I'm not smiling, I tell you," Maggie said. "And another thing, how do we know that Jerry Wilson knows what he's doing? Just 'cause he's a county agent doesn't mean he knows anything about farming. He's been helping you from the start, hasn't he? And what has it got us?"

The chief relaxed and enjoyed the scolding, the afternoon, and the thought of delicious Winesaps and juicy McIntoshes.

THE END

Bernard, Lisa, and the chief will return in
Murder by the Acre
Coming Soon

Stephen B. Bagley wrote the full-length plays *Murder at the Witch's Cottage* and *Two Writers in the Hands of an Angry God* and co-wrote *Turnabout*. His poetry has been published in Byline Magazine, Prairie Songs, Free Star, and other publications. He coauthored two one-act plays ("Hogwild" and "There's A Body In The Closet") that were published by Dramatic Publishing Company. Articles he wrote have been published in Nautilus Magazine, OKMagazine, Pontotoc County Chronicles, Country Music Magazine, various newspapers, and other publications. He graduated from Oklahoma State University and still lives in Oklahoma where he is busy with his job and writing five or six books and two or three plays, depending on what day it is. For the latest news and information about the *Measurements of Murder*™ series and his other books, plays, essays, chapbooks, and publications, visit 51313 Harbor Street at *www.51313.blogspot.com*. *Measurements of Murder*™ merchandise is currently available exclusively online at *www.cafepress.com/harborstreet*.

Printed in the United States
107429LV00006B/2/A